Downpour
Christopher Hawkins

Coronis Publishing

Published by Coronis Publishing.

www.coronispublishing.com
www.christopher-hawkins.com

Horror/Fiction, Thrillers/Fiction

Print ISBN: 978-1-937346-14-0
Ebook ISBN: 978-1-937346-15-7

Praise for Downpour

"This weatherman is forecasting nightmares coming in from the North. Not since Stephen King's "*The Mist*" has a shift in meteorology felt this terrifying, but it's the human drama playing out under these cosmic storm conditions that truly elevates Christopher Hawkins' novel."

Clay McLeod Chapman, author of *Ghost Eaters*

"Seamlessly blending horror, speculative fiction, and urgent domestic drama, *Downpour* offers a fast-paced thriller fueled by themes of family discourse, childhood traumas, and a gripping and original environmental danger worthy of *The Birds*... This is a propulsive horror story, suspenseful throughout, and readers who enjoy genre-blending thrillers will tear through the pages."

Booklife (Editor's Pick)

"This book hits like a summer squall and never lets up, a real-time, one-location doom machine that earns its place beside *The Mist*."

Daniel Kraus, author of *Whalefall*

"Dread descends in unrelenting sheets throughout Downpour. The moment you think the skies will clear, a roar of thunder cracks the walls of reality, and you fall into darkness."

Alan Lastufka, author of *Face the Night*

"Christopher Hawkins's DOWNPOUR delivers tension and dread with excellent prose, but it's the complex dynamics of modern family structures that will ultimately haunt the reader.

"Like much of the best speculative fiction, Christopher Hawkins's DOWNPOUR transmutes social and cultural anxieties into a compellingly-visceral conflict with forces that defy understanding."

IndieReader (Starred Review)

"*Downpour* is a frickin' beautiful, gorgeous little novel. Love seeps out of every page just as the 'relentless and unnatural' rain seeps into the lives of the characters."

HorrorTree

"Downpour hammers out a harrowing, heart-wrenching tale of loss of control. A stellar setup that absolutely delivers when the violence and chaos come to collect. A thrilling ride from start to finish."

Lauren Bolger, author of *Kill Radio*

"Gripping... Riveting... As the tension and violence effectively build, readers will keep anticipating how events are going to play out."

Kirkus Reviews

Also by Christopher Hawkins

Suburban Monsters

for Tim and Ben

1

They knelt together, father and daughter, and looked down at the dead thing in its box. Tallie had found it next to the washing machine, a little gray mouse caught in the trap that her mother had set for it. She'd brought him over to the tiny body, little hands pulling at his calloused fingers, and told him she wanted to give it a funeral. He might have said no, but she'd come to him about it first, before her mother, and that made him want to do whatever she asked. So he'd dug through the drawers of the old roll-top desk, found a little box, and dumped out the checks that were inside. He dropped the mouse in and before long he had a hole scooped out of the earth next to the porch that was big enough for the box to fit inside.

Tallie had the mouse laid out in front of her and was pulling tissues out of a box at her side. She stacked them and laid them out carefully to cover the little furry body like a blanket, like she was tucking it into bed.

"Careful you don't touch it, Pumpkin," he said. "Mice can be dirty."

"She's not *dirty*," Tallie said with a roll of her eyes, and in that moment her face was so much like her mother's that it made him frown. "She's a nice mouse and her name is Daisy."

Daisy the mouse stared up at him, black-marble eyes unblinking, its neck not just broken but creased, like a dog-eared page in a book.

"Just be careful," he said. Something about the sight of the mouse, its head sticking out from under the tissues, struck a perverse chord in his brain, and he added, "You don't want to wake her up."

"Daddy, she's dead." She gave another roll of her eyes, a Dana roll. "You can't wake up from dead."

He had no answer for that. Tallie didn't seem to need one. She only waved goodbye to Daisy the mouse and pressed the top of the box down over it as gently as any four-year-old could. As they scooped the dirt over it with their hands, he thought of what else they might find if he told her where to dig. A guinea pig in a shoebox. A garter snake. A dried-out toad. A half-starved stray dog that he'd never had the chance to give a name.

"Scott, it needs to be deeper or else the dog's going to dig it up." Dana's shadow at his back, her arms folded. He tensed a little at the sound of her voice, and didn't want it to show.

"Wilbur wouldn't do that," Tallie said. "Wilbur's nice."

"Wilbur's very nice, Sweetie," Dana said, talking over Scott's head. "But dogs don't always know when they're doing something wrong, do they?"

Wilbur watched them, panting contentedly at the edge of the yard beneath the shade of the willow tree. His ears were pricked. He'd heard his name, even over the sound of the wind through the branches, and was waiting to see what it might mean.

"It'll be fine," Scott said, instantly regretting the harsh note that had crept into his voice. "Besides, Wilbur can't get all the way over here. And even if he did, you're right. He's a very good dog."

Tallie smiled at this and patted down the dirt. Scott joined in, making handprints and rubbing at her wrists with his thumbs until she started to giggle. Then they stood, and Tallie slapped what was left of the dirt from her hands before she turned and bounded toward the house, Daisy the mouse disappeared and forgotten.

"Make sure to wash your hands," Dana called after her, but Tallie was already stomping up the creaky wooden steps to the big wraparound porch. Dana took a step to follow her, but reconsidered. She hugged her arms across her chest.

Wilbur watched Tallie go, his mouth open, his tongue lolling. He slapped his tail against the ground, ground that might be right on top of that other dog's grave, the bones dead so long that they no longer held the scent of anything more than dirt. Wilbur nosed his water dish, yawned, then stretched. The long leash that held him to the tree dragged in the dust.

"I wish you wouldn't leave him chained up like that," Scott said.

"If we don't, he's going to end up in the road," Dana said. "A mouse is bad enough. I don't think you want to be the one to tell Tallie why we have to do this all over again."

He looked down the dirt and gravel road that ran along the edge of the soybean fields. Out in the distance a pickup truck was kicking up dust, probably going too fast. She was right, of course. That only made it worse.

The morning air was hot and getting hotter, but Dana rubbed at her arms like she was bracing against a chill breeze. "I'm sorry," she said. "Look, could we just—"

"It's fine," Scott said, and wiped his hands against his jeans. The road stretched away in both directions, rising and falling with the curve of the land, everywhere in the whole world starting at one end of that road or the other. He watched the wind ripple through the rows of green soybean plants on land that once belonged to his father, and *his* father before that. The crops crowded the road, thriving now that they were beyond the old man's reach. The little patch of land where the house stood felt smaller than ever.

Dana unfolded her arms and stepped in close to him, hesitating, waiting to see if she would let him. Her hands brushed his waist and he flinched away. He regretted it instantly, but he didn't turn back to face her. He didn't want to have to see the look in her eyes.

"It's fine," he said again, not meaning it, not meaning it at all. He followed after Tallie, taking the steps two at a time, hearing the boards creak and groan beneath his weight. He told himself for maybe the hundredth time that he should fix them, that he *could* fix them, and at least that would be something.

He climbed the wide staircase to the second floor, gripping the railing a little too tight. The wood beneath his fingers was worn, and he could feel the places where the varnish gave way to bare wood that had grown cracked and gray with age. His hand slipped and caught. The wood bit into his palm. He flinched and a piece of it came away with a snap.

He looked down at the inch-long sliver of wood that rose at an angle out of his skin. He barely felt it, but he still swore under his breath, suddenly angry at himself for not having done something about that railing before now. It could have just as easily had been Jacob or even Tallie getting hurt in his place, and for what? A little wood putty, a little varnish and the space of a few hours? *Lazy*, said the voice in his head that sounded so much like his father. *Lazy and stupid.*

He pulled the splinter out. Another half inch of the thing had stuck deep in the meat of his palm. The point came out red and it tented the skin as it slid free. Blood welled up from the wound and he made a fist to stop it.

All at once he took in the threadbare state of the carpet, the wallpaper corners that were peeling up behind the old framed photos. The photos hadn't been changed in at least twenty years. There were pictures of himself from when he was barely more than five, smiling easy, in a way he'd long since forgotten. There were pictures of his grandparents, long dead and barely remembered. There was his father, impossibly young, solemn and sober, leaning against an old powder-blue Chevy. There were no pictures of his mother, here in the stairwell where the pictures had always hung. There were no pictures of Dana, or of Jacob, or of Tallie either. Not one.

He knocked on the door of the old bedroom and gave himself a slow count of five before he turned the knob. Jacob was sitting with his back to the door and his headphones on. On the computer screen, a man with a sword was swinging at a winged creature ten times his size, and Scott couldn't tell who was winning. He waited in the doorway for the fight to be over, knowing his son had already sensed him there, knowing that he'd only have to wait a moment, knowing because they'd already done this dance a hundred times before.

"Yeah, dad? What's up?"

Scott stood staring at his son's face, at the expectant look that was gathering there, and realized then that he had no idea why he had come. His feet had been on autopilot, his mind elsewhere, and they had brought him to this place, this little room that used to be his own. A memory nagged at the back of his mind, but he could not chase it down.

"I, um... I was just thinking about going out to see if I could get that mower running. Thought I'd see if you wanted to lend a hand."

"Does it have to be right now?" Jacob asked. Scott could see the answer he was hoping for written across his face. He was still just a kid, even at sixteen, and didn't have much practice at hiding what was on his mind. Still, Scott knew that Jacob would shut the game down if he asked him to. He wouldn't be thrilled about it, but he'd do it anyway. He was a good kid. Everyone said so, and Scott knew they were right.

"Nah," Scott said. "I'll probably be out there for a while anyway, so if you're looking for something to do, just come on out."

Scott didn't think he would, and maybe that was okay. Jacob nodded anyway and snapped the headphones back on as he turned around. Scott looked over the piles of clothes on the floor, the unmade bed in a different corner than the one where his own had once been. He thought about saying something about the mess, but didn't. There was no sense adding one more thing to the unease that was hardening in his gut. He was glad that the kid had his headphones, that he probably hadn't heard any of the things that were said last night. He was glad too that the bed was in a different corner. It helped him pretend that it wasn't the same room at all.

"I'll be out in the shed," he said as he closed the door. *I love you*, was what he wanted to say, but he knew the boy wouldn't hear him either way.

He passed the big bedroom and paused in the doorway, staring at the unmade bed, at the way the blankets had bunched up in the middle of the thing, two empty spots in the vague shape of people on either side. He'd wanted to sleep on the couch last night, but decided not to just on principle. If anyone should have slept on the couch it was Dana, though it never would have occurred to him to ask her to. She wouldn't have asked him to either, and he supposed that was at least something, that she didn't expect to chase him out of his own bed.

No, not *his* bed. The mattress was newer but the frame was old, with the same heavy oak headboard that had probably stood witness to his own conception, this bed in this room he'd never been allowed to enter as a child, now his for no other reason than that he was the last one left to claim it. But it was never his, not really. Nothing in this place was.

So he and Dana had slept back-to-back, the little window air conditioner rattling away, doing nothing to cool the thick summer air. He'd kicked off his blankets and let them pile at his back, all the while listening to the irregular sound of his wife's breathing, knowing that she wasn't sleeping either. There was a part of him that had taken satisfaction in that, in knowing that she had been just as restless as he was. But that was last night, and seemed like an eternity ago. Now he was just tired.

He felt her come up behind him as he stood in the doorway, felt her hesitate before she snaked her arms around his body and pressed herself in close against his back. He tensed, not wanting her to touch him, not wanting anything but for her to touch him. Her hands moved up to his chest, rising and falling with him as he breathed.

"It's okay," she said, her words tickling soft against his neck. "It's going to... It's okay."

He turned around in her arms, his wounded hand still clenched into a fist. She moved against his body, her legs warm, squeezing his thigh between them. He felt his cheeks go hot, felt the unwelcome stirring against the zipper of his jeans. He saw the way her mouth was parted, waiting for his to do the same. But he wasn't ready for that, not yet.

"I'm sorry," she said. "I'm just... Please. I'm sorry."

He looked at her, this woman, his wife. Her eyes were wide, almost pleading, and he knew her well enough to know that she was waiting for him to close the distance between them. And yet, it was as if those eyes, that mouth, had become so unfamiliar that they were almost repulsive now. He wanted to find that familiar place again as much as she did, wanted to see her with the same eyes he'd had only a day ago, but he couldn't.

The pleading faded into disappointment, maybe even a little shame, and all at once, the moment was gone.

She stepped back, fingers trailing down his arms, feeling for his hands. She found them balled at his sides but still she took hold of them and brought them up to her chest.

"Oh, you're bleeding," she said, her stance suddenly shifting into one of concern.

"No, it's fine," he said. "It's just a splinter."

"Let me take a look," she said, and pried his fingers open. A streak of reddish-brown had dried against his palm and made little branching tracks through the creases in his fingers. The wound was a black line near the hinge of his thumb. It was smaller than he'd thought, but it still hurt when he moved it.

"It's pretty bad," she said. "We should clean it up so it doesn't get infected."

She brought his hand to her mouth and kissed his bloody fingers. The pleading was back in her eyes, and he shut his own because he still could not bring himself to look at her. He felt her lips, soft against his bony knuckles. He thought of the red trails that had dried there, and for a moment he imagined that she might put her lips to the wound and suck the blood from it like a vampire.

"It's all right," she said, and brought his other hand to her breast. He squeezed, and felt her mouth slip around the tip of his finger. Her breath quickened as he found her nipple through the fabric of her shirt. The heat rose, shameful and insistent, as his pulse beat tight against the sides of his skull. He tried to pull away but she held his hand tight. He winced as her thumb grazed the hole the splinter had made. At once he remembered the dead mouse, it's neck pressed flat, the little marbles of its eyes staring up at him, judging him.

He pulled away, quicker than he'd meant to. Her face fell, confused, and all at once the distance was back between them.

"I should get out there before the sun gets too high," he said, ducking around her toward the stairs. She opened her mouth to say something, then pressed her lips together in a tight little line. Her eyes were shining, threatening to spill over. He didn't want to be there when they did, so he took the stairs at a trot and didn't look back until he was out the front door.

Outside, the sun blared so bright that he had to squint against it. The sky stretched out, clear and blue over the flat expanse of what had once been his father's land. Jet contrails criss-crossed the sky, and there was only a single patch of dark cloud to mar the blue, so distant and small that it might as well not have been there at all.

2

Apart from the house, the only things left of his father's farm were a storm cellar—its door little more than a rusted patch angled into the weedy earth—and the old shed. It sat at the edge of the new property line, thriving crops lined up tauntingly close as it leaned like a drunkard, belligerent and sullen. It was only appropriate, he supposed. It was where his old man had always retreated when he sponged himself up off the kitchen table, after mother, after selling off the land. Scott had retreated here too, more than once, in those darker times when the bottle seemed better than facing the stack of unpaid bills. Better than admitting to his family that he'd failed them.

Still, there were good memories here, beneath the cobwebs and the dust. Scott could remember watching his father as he stood at the workbench he had made with his own hands, looking up at the old man as he hammered metal and cut wood for reasons his younger self hadn't understood, to run the farm, to fix the house. All those improvements were long-since lost to time and debt and peeling paint. Now the shed was little more than a storage space, one that Scott suspected was only held up by the strength of the old junk packed up to its rafters.

The old riding mower squatted just behind the double doors on flattened tires. The rusted cowling was off the engine, propped against one of the wheels. He had taken it off at the end of last summer when he'd grown tired of fighting with Jacob to get him to tend to the yard with the push-mower. Scott wasn't good with engines, and held no real hope of getting the thing started now. He didn't really care if he ever got it started. He only needed a place to be for a little while, a place that wasn't the house with its dead mice behind the washing machine and its sheets piled up in the middle of the bed.

He pulled the lead off of a spark plug and stared into it, careful not to get any of the grime on the hole in his palm. The blood had dried solid, and he had the distant thought that he should wash it. But that could wait. The air in the shed was warm and, despite the heaviness of the air, he breathed it in and let it fill him with calm. A beam of light filtered in through a grimy window and the dust was dancing in it. The old workbench was still where it had always been. It was covered over with boxes now, but he could still just about picture his father standing there, looking down at him. He had more and more trouble picturing the old man's face these days. He considered that a mercy.

Scott barely remembered his mother either. He supposed that was a mercy, too. He had a dim recollection of a slender woman in heavy shoes that echoed against the hardwood floor of the hallway, and then nothing. How old had he been when she left? Four? Five? Too young to have any sense of time, one day there, the next day gone. Too young to understand that she wasn't coming back.

He remembered hearing shouting in the night when they'd thought he was sleeping, raised voices behind the door of the big bedroom. He'd been afraid of the old man, even then. Had he been afraid of her, too? He supposed that he must have been. There were nights, after the voices had gone quiet, when she'd come to him. He'd pretended to sleep while she sat at the edge of his bed and smoothed back his hair. On those nights she'd sat there like that until he fell asleep for real.

He couldn't remember her face—there were no pictures left of her in the house, not anymore—but when he tried to conjure an image of her in his mind, he imagined her sitting on the sofa in the front room, her hair pulled back in a long ponytail, a plastic tumbler dangling from thin fingers. He hadn't been there to see her leave, but still he imagined a tiny version of himself clinging to her leg as she walked out the door.

Only, she'd never given him that chance. She'd left them both in the middle of the night, leaving everything behind except two suitcases packed full of her best clothes. She hadn't even told him goodbye, at least not so he'd remember it. What he did remember was his father sitting him down at the kitchen table some days after and telling him that she'd gone. He remembered listening from the top of the stairs, his body pressed flat against the floor, his father at the kitchen table, talking to aunts, now long gone, talking to cousins. He remembered the awful things his father had said about his mother. He hadn't understood what the words meant, not until he'd grown older, but he remembered them. Every word.

Had she paused on her way out, long enough to whisper in his ear and lay a little kiss on his sleeping cheek? He didn't think she had. He had no way of knowing, because they'd never seen her again. He never knew why. *That's the way it was sometimes,* his father had told him. *Sometimes they don't come back and they never say why.*

His father would have been able to fix the mower, that much Scott was sure of. He would have fixed it before the grass got so high that the push mower bogged down and died every few feet. It's what his father would have done sober, at least. If he'd been in the bottle he might have left it alone, pushed it to the back of the shed with everything else that was unwanted and unfinished. Maybe he would have just sat at that kitchen table, like he had so many nights in those last few years, staring into the bottom of an empty glass. Scott had no way of knowing that, either.

He thought that he should probably pull the spark plug loose. There was a tool for it on a pegboard somewhere behind all the sagging boxes, but he wasn't about to go searching for it. He thought about putting the cowling back on top of the engine, but that felt too much like giving up. He thought about taking the rusty axe from its spot by the door and chopping the whole shed down. He thought of his wife, then, of her arms surrounding him, of her lips soft against his. He closed his eyes to push the image away, but all he could see was his hand on her breast, and then not his own hand but some other hand, tanned, maybe calloused, maybe larger than his own.

He curled his hands into fists and felt the sting of the wound in his palm. He squeezed down harder and let the pain drive the image from his mind. A bit of the wood had stayed behind and he felt the insistent stab of it just beneath his skin. He breathed through the pain until it didn't hurt anymore.

He left the cable hanging loose, left the cowling on the ground next to the useless flat tire. When he came back outside, squinting against the sun, he pushed hard against the shed door, trying to get it to close all the way.

He couldn't seem to manage that either.

3

Wilbur's head was up, his ears pricked, as he stared out at the gravel road. Scott followed his gaze to the black pickup truck, fresh-washed and gleaming in the sunlight, a cloud of dust trailing off behind it as it trundled its way toward the house. There was no mistaking that it was Ned Colby's truck, brand-new, with pop-country guitar on the stereo turned up so loud that he could hear it a quarter mile away.

Ned Colby was the last person Scott wanted to talk to right now, but he still held up a hand in greeting and walked out to meet the truck as it turned into the driveway. Wilbur rose with mild interest and padded out to test the limit of his chain before he thought better of it and retreated back into the shade.

"Hey, Ned," Scott said as the pickup door opened. "Look, now's not really a great time."

Ned heard him. Scott was sure that Ned heard him, but he was pretending not to. The big man levered himself out of the driver's seat, leading with his belly. His boots sent up a little puff of dust as they hit the ground, boots that looked fresh enough that they might have been bought yesterday.

"Heya Scott," he said, swinging the door closed like a punctuation mark. "Sorry for dropping in like this. I tried calling, but you didn't pick up your phone."

Scott knew that if he checked his phone he wouldn't find any new calls from Ned Colby, and knew that it wouldn't make one bit of difference if he brought it up. Ned scuffed at the dirt, pulled his cowboy hat off by the crown, and wiped an arm across his hairless forehead. "Hoo," he said, squinting into the sun. "Shapin' up to be a hot one today."

Scott shaded his eyes with his hand, following Ned's gaze out over the endless fields of soybeans. They were Ned's fields now, and from the way the big man's gaze lingered on them, there was no doubt that he wanted to make sure Scott knew it.

"Yeah. Look, Ned—"

"Looks like your lawn could use some doin'," Ned said, pointing with his hat toward the shin-high tufts of grass that peppered the yard. "I've got a guy, I'll get you his number. Guatemalan fella'. Got all his own equipment. Mows, fertilizes. Does a hell of a job, too. I promise you, in two months you won't even recognize the place."

A note of doubt crept into his voice at the end as he surveyed the porch with its peeling paint, the bits of lattice cracked away near the ground. He knew well enough that Scott couldn't afford a lawn service any more than he could hire someone to paint the house. Scott suspected that, if he didn't already know all that, he wouldn't be here at all.

"Course, with the weather bein' what it is, it's all apt to break off at the roots and blow away, lest we get some moisture into this soil. I've had the irrigation rigs running twenty-four-seven, or at least it seems pretty close to it. Just about cost me my left nut when the water bill come due, but needs must, like they say. Needs must."

The rows of soybeans just beyond the shed were a sea of lush, green leaves stretching out as far as he could see. Scott had been watching them shoot up all spring, and it would be a good harvest, he could tell. Even with the added expense, Ned's operation was set to turn a decent profit. Scott felt the heat of the sun on his skin and imagined the whole crop wilting and drying beneath it. Without Ned's money, there'd be nothing to stop it, nothing but that distant tuft of dark cloud, almost a perfect circle, hovering against the bright blue sky.

"Yeah. Ned. Look, I don't mean to be rude or anything, but it's a Sunday and I've got a lot of things that need doing before I get myself back to work tomorrow. You know how it is."

Ned dismissed him with a wave of his hat before he set it back onto his head. "Say no more, Scotty. I won't be but a minute." He settled back against the side of his truck, getting comfortable. "This lot we're sittin' on here. What would you call it? Eight? Nine acres?"

"Twelve-point-six."

Ned nodded, calculating. "Twelve-point-six. Gotcha." He made a show of looking out over the place, pretending to make up his mind. "What do you say you let me take it off your hands?"

Scott shook his head, but Ned put up his hands before he could get a word out. "Now, I know what you're gonna say, but just hear me out, all right?"

He waited long enough to know for sure that Scott wasn't going to shut him down or run him off. He wanted to do both, but he knew that Ned would find a way to have his say one way or another, so he might as well let him say it.

"Now, way I see it, you're not gettin' all that much use out of the place. You ain't put a crop down in, what? Eight years? Ten? And if you had it in mind to start one tomorrow, I know you don't have the equipment anymore to get 'er goin'."

Ned knew because Scott had sold him most of the equipment his father had left, along with most of what was left of the land. There'd been a broken-down barn to hold it all too, but Ned had torn that the rest of the way down more than a decade ago. Scott could still picture it sometimes, if he stared long enough at the spot where it had stood.

"And that's all good," Ned said, "'cause a crop this small wouldn't be worth losing time on, even if you could make 'er work. And not everybody *could* make 'er work. Ain't no shame in it, but not everybody's got it in 'em to be a farmer."

His new boots scuffed up a tuft of grass from the dry ground. He kicked it away.

"And I get that this was your daddy's land. You got history here. I can respect that. But I look around this place and I have to wonder what the hell you're still doin' here. It's twenty miles to get to any place worth gettin' to. Cell reception sucks. Internet's worse. Never see a snow plow in the wintertime. And if you ain't workin' the land, there ain't a damn thing to recommend it."

Ned was right. Scott knew he was right. He looked back out over the patchy grass to the rusty storm cellar doors, to the once-white house now gone over to the dull gray of weathered wood. He thought about what it might be like to not live in this place anymore. He thought of the people inside and for a moment he wondered what it would be like to live without any of it, without any of them.

"I guess what I'm tryin' to say is, you've got nothin' left to tie you to this place, so why let it keep hold of you?"

The screen door banged and Tallie ran out onto the porch in her bare feet. Dana followed after her, bent over with her hands outstretched, in the middle of some game. She stopped as soon as she saw the two men standing near the pickup truck and straightened, suddenly self-conscious in her faded t-shirt and yoga pants. A guilty heat rose in Scott's cheeks.

Ned doffed his hat and held it to his chest like he was singing the national anthem at a baseball game. "Well, hey there, Mrs. Baker."

"Hey there yourself, Ned." Dana's eyes were wary, darting from Ned to Scott and back again. "What brings you out this way so early?"

Ned chuckled. If he'd heard the note of reproach in Dana's voice, he wasn't letting on. "Nothin' special," he said. "Just thought I'd drop by and see how you're faring in this heat. When are you and the mister here gonna come out for a visit? Angie's been asking after ya. Wants an excuse to bring out the good china."

Dana smiled at this. Ned's eyes dropped to look her over, just for an instant, but Scott caught it all the same. Before he could stop himself, he was imagining Ned's meaty hand closing over her breast, his finger in her mouth the way his own had been in her mouth not long ago. It hadn't been Ned. He knew that. But it had been someone.

Again, Scott thought that maybe he could just go. Maybe they wouldn't miss him one bit.

"Well, that sounds great to me," Dana said with a smile that only Scott would see was forced. "Just say the word and we'll be there."

"I most surely will," Ned said.

Scott knew that he wouldn't, that the offer was as much a put-on as his folksy, downstate drawl. He couldn't fault Ned for it, though. Even if the offer had been sincere, there was no way Scott could have brought himself to go to the man's house, to see the life that his own father's land had helped buy for him. On some level, Ned probably knew that, and kept his distance on purpose.

Tallie was at the railing, wedging her foot between the cracked and paint-bare slats, trying to pull herself up, chinning the handrail. "Dana, could you get Tallie?"

"She's just fine," Dana said, still watching their visitor.

"I'm fine, Daddy," Tallie echoed.

"I don't want her to get a splinter." The words came out harsher than he'd meant them, and he saw the way they made his wife's face harden. She recovered her smile quickly and scooped Tallie up to perch on her hip. Tallie squirmed a bit before she hugged on tight, like a koala on a tree branch.

"Now, if you ladies will excuse us," Ned said, "I've just got a little bit more to talk over with your fella here and I don't want to keep him from you any longer than I have to." He pressed his hat down tight onto his head. Another punctuation mark, this one a full-stop period.

Dana turned and took hold of the door handle. "Don't keep him too long, now."

Ned gave a tip of his hat as the screen door closed behind her. "No ma'am. I most surely won't."

Ned took hold of Scott's shoulder then, turning him around, walking him toward the back of the truck. "Scott, I've known you since the second grade, and you know what? I always figgered you'd be one of the first ones to get out of this place."

Out past the rows of soybeans, Scott watched the single dark cloud hovering in the distance. It seemed larger now, or maybe it was only closer, a rough disc the color of cigarette ash. He could see the soft shadow of rain falling beneath it, too distant to offer any respite from the heat.

"I always thought you'd go off and be an architect or a lawyer or somethin', not wastin' your life pullin' cable for ComEd. This life is fine for a guy like me, barely made it through high school, but you? This could be a fresh start. For you. For Dana. For all of you."

There was something about the cloud that Scott couldn't put his finger on, some nagging detail that couldn't quite find its way to the front of his mind. He watched it hang in the sky, watched the faint sheen of the rain sheeting down underneath it, drifting with the wind.

"I'll tell you what," Ned said. "Think it over, and I mean *really* think it over. Then name your price. And don't be afraid to go high, neither."

Scott shook his head, but didn't take his eyes off that darkened patch of sky. "I ain't looking for charity, Ned."

"Ain't hardly charity. That land you sold me backawhen been real good to me, better than I had a right to by a long ways. Way I see it, you gave me one hell of a bargain and ever since I've been feelin' like I took advantage. You'd be doin' my conscience a courtesy, that's for—"

"Hey, Ned?"

Ned got quiet, but his eyes stayed eager.

"What do you make of that cloud?"

The big man squinted, considering, before a smile crept its way across his face.

"Well," he said. "I'd say it looks like we're finally gonna get some rain. Not a moment too soon, neither. Been a long time comin'."

"Yeah, but nothing about it strikes you... I don't know? Weird?"

Ned tilted his head, let the hat shade his eyes. At once Scott knew what had bothered him about the cloud. The wind was taking the rain that fell from it, drawing it out. The rain should have been taking the cloud with it, but the cloud wasn't moving at all.

Ned thought about it for a moment and shrugged. "Looks angry. I'll give you that. Little fella, though. Unless it finds a bigger brother, I doubt it's gonna amount to much. Shame too. We need every drop we can get." He stepped in front of Scott, his big hat eclipsing the cloud entirely.

"Look," he said. "All I'm askin' is that you take a couple days, think it over. You do that and, come next weekend, you want to tell me to shut my mouth and mind my business, then that's exactly what I'll do. But if you *do* think about it, and what I'm saying starts to make sense—and it does make sense, Scott. It makes all the sense in the world—well, you call me, all right? You call me any time."

He patted Scott on the shoulder, a final punctuation mark before he heaved himself back into his truck and drove away.

Scott didn't turn to see him go. He only watched the cloud, a dark blot in an otherwise perfect sky. The longer he looked, the more he was sure that it was growing.

4

"What was that all about?" Dana was at the kitchen counter with a butter knife in her hand, chopping grapes in half for Tallie. Scott didn't look at her as he passed, but went straight for the laundry room and opened the tap in the wash basin.

"Nothing," he said. He stuck his hand beneath the cold water, and watched the dirt and the blood swirl down the drain. The drain was slow, and as the water began to pool it turned an ashy gray, like gathering clouds.

Behind him, the sounds of chopping stopped. "It didn't look like nothing," Dana said. Tallie was sitting at the kitchen table, kicking her feet as she munched thoughtfully on a triangle of sandwich. Probably Nutella. Tallie loved Nutella. She smiled as she tore off another bite, her head rocking to some music that only she could hear. Nutella was expensive, which made it only a sometimes food. It meant that Dana was feeling guilty. Scott watched her, watched the both of them. He tried to picture them all together in another kitchen, in another place, and found that it wasn't all that hard.

"Nah, it's nothing," he said, scrubbing his hands. "Ned was just saying hi. Just like he said."

He leaned his elbows on the basin and rubbed his thumb against the rip in his palm. There was something still in there. He could feel it moving but couldn't tell if he was working it out or pushing it in deeper. Behind him he could hear the knife again, rising and falling, rising and falling. Looking out

the window, the sky seemed darker. Or maybe it was just a trick
of the light.

"You know, maybe we should invite them over sometime,"
Dana said. "Call their bluff and see what happens."

"I don't want to invite the Colbys over." Scott watched the
darkening sky outside the window, watched the water make a
lazy circle down the drain.

Dana pulled the knife between her fingers and sucked the
juice off of her thumb. "Well, I don't really want to invite them
over either, but it might be fun to watch them squirm a bit,
see what they say." She gave him a sly little half-wink as she set
the knife on the edge of the sink, inviting him into this tiny
conspiracy. "Besides, I don't think Angie'd let me set one foot
inside her house. She's hated me ever since junior prom, ever
since she—"

She stopped herself there, but Scott already knew what she
was about to say. She'd told him the story a hundred times
before, how Angie Colby—she'd been Angie Dern, then—had
found out that her boyfriend Robbie had given Dana a ride
to a party. Angie had made a big stink about it later at the
prom, accusing Dana and Robbie of cheating on her. It almost
ended with the two of them coming to blows right there on the
dance floor, and probably would have if their gym teacher—all
muscle in a red sequin dress—hadn't pulled them apart. It was
one of those stories that seemed to grow with every telling, and
Scott had always taken for granted that Dana's part in it had
been more or less exactly what she'd said it was. Now, he wasn't
so sure.

He dried his hands and came out of the laundry room with
Tallie still sitting at the table, kicking her feet, oblivious to
everything that wasn't her sandwich. Dana stood behind her,
anxious. Seeing her standing like that put Scott on edge. Had
she done that on purpose, putting Tallie between them, using
her like a shield? Acting like he was the one to blame, like he

was the one who had caused all this? Like she was afraid of him, even though he had never so much as raised a hand to her in all the seventeen years they'd been together. Not once.

Still there was something in Dana's eyes that made him stop right there and look at her. A hopeful glint, an invitation, if only he'd take it. He wanted to take it, but the wound was too fresh and he wasn't ready to. He wondered now if he ever would be.

The lights were off in the front room, but the windows were open, the curtains billowing with the morning breeze. Only, it didn't feel like morning. The sky outside was definitely darker, he was almost sure of it now. The angles of the shadows, once familiar, seemed wrong. There was something about the way the light fell across the worn old coffee table, across the threadbare cushions of the couch that had sat in that very same spot since he was a child. It nagged at his thoughts like a distant warning bell.

Tallie was looking up at him now, her little face smiling, smeared with chocolate. He tried to smile back at her, but felt like he'd forgotten how.

⁂

The cloud was *definitely* bigger now. Or was it only closer? Scott stood on the porch and shaded his eyes, trying to judge its proportions. It seemed flatter than it had before, like a squashed hat with a narrow brim, all of it that same, dull gray, set off against the clear blue sky. It had to be bigger, he thought, though he knew in his gut that it was impossible. If it was bigger, that meant that it hadn't moved at all.

Behind him, the screen door creaked, slow and tentative. Footsteps on the weathered wood that he would have recognized anywhere, soft sounds written deep into his heart.

"Come here and take a look at this," he said.

Dana stepped in next to him and put her arm around his waist. When he didn't shy away she rested her head on his shoulder. He moved to pull her close, moving out of habit, but he did not stop himself.

"What do you make of that cloud out there?"

"What?" she said softly, not wanting to spoil the moment. "It's a rain cloud."

"Yeah, but just..." He pulled her forward, held her just a little bit closer. "Just look at it for a second."

She did. The cloud had grown larger, even in the time since he'd come out onto the porch. Its edges seemed thicker now, and curled back on themselves like a pot of simmering water. The sky below it was dark with sheeting rain, but all around it was clear blue. Wisps of white drifted across the sky, contrails spreading out from a passing plane. He watched the wind take them, but the cloud did not budge.

"Okay," Dana said. "It's a *weird* cloud. But it's just rain, right? What else could it be?"

"I don't know, but when did you ever see a rain cloud that looked like that?"

Dana shrugged. Scott felt her body move against his, warm and familiar. "It's just rain, though. It'll pass. Right?"

"Maybe," Scott said.

He felt her body tense against his, holding her breath, gathering courage. After a moment she slipped out of his arm and turned around to face him. "Do you think we could just go inside for a minute? I just want to talk."

She stared at him, watching his eyes, waiting. The cloud hung behind her, framing her head like a crown of ash.

"Maybe *I* don't."

"Look." She rubbed at her arms, as if she'd been taken with a sudden chill. "I fucked up, okay. Is that what you want me to say? I fucked up. You don't think I know that? That I don't think about how stupid I was? Every single fucking day, I think about it, and I know that I…"

She pressed the heels of her hands against her eyes, so hard that it looked as if she was trying to blind herself to the whole world. The wind blew, and it stood up the hairs on his arms. He closed his fingers against his palm. The splinter was sharp, and the wound ached.

"Scott, please. I just want to… I can't take it back. I know I can't. But could we just… I don't know. Could we just talk about it? Could we just do that? Please?"

He watched her shuffle her bare feet against the paint-bare planks of the porch decking. He remembered his father standing almost in that very spot, a bottle in his hand, staring out over withering crops, watching for a wife who was never coming back. Scott stared out over that same land, barely any of it still unsold beyond the storm cellar and the willow tree. He stood wondering about the wife that was still here and already gone. He watched the cloud growing larger, growing so fast now that it was happening right before his eyes, and knew that the rain was inevitable.

The screen door banged behind them, hard enough to make Dana jump. Jacob burst through the door at a run and only stopped when he hit the railing. He stared up at the cloud, eyes wide and mouth open, and said, "Woah."

Dana went to him, the vulnerable woman of a moment ago hardening into motherly concern. "What? What is it?"

"That cloud," Jacob said. "I mean, it's really there. It's right there."

"What?" Scott stepped to the rail. The edge of the cloud was close enough now that he could see it roiling, turning in on itself. "What do you know about it?"

"It's all over the Internet," Jacob said. "Everyone's taking pictures, posting videos. It's super weird. Nikki made it a meme already. It's everywhere!"

"Does anyone know what it is?" Scott scratched at his neck. "What kind of cloud, I mean."

Jacob shrugged. "It's just rain." He said it dismissively, then he caught the frown on Scott's face. "I mean, I think someone was calling it a *mammoth cloud* or something like that. It looks really messed up, but they're saying it's not really anything to worry about."

"That's a relief," Dana said. "The way you came out here, I thought we were going to end up in the basement. Like last year? When the tornado touched down by Clarksdale. Remember that? We practically needed a forklift to get you out of bed." She reached up and tousled his hair. He pulled away, but smiled when he did it. Scott couldn't help but smile, too.

"Nah. Nothing like that." Jacob reached into his pocket, pulled out his phone. "There's a video. Here, let me find it."

The three of them crowded around the little screen while Jacob thumbed through a blur of images and mashed down on it like a brake pedal when he found the right one. Recorded with an unsteady hand, the video tilted and shook until it centered on a rain-slick street, split-level suburban houses crowded close to the sidewalks. The view panned up to a darkened sky, the sun blotted out by a cover of gray cloud.

"Wait," Jacob said as he brought the phone to his chest to fiddle with the side buttons. "You need the sound on."

When he held the phone out again, the speaker crackled with the heavy sound of the wind, of fingers rubbing against the microphone. "...looking at, I think, is a mammatus cloud." The voice was male, talking fast. "I don't know for sure. I had to look it up. I didn't spend a lot of time on it because I didn't want to miss this. If anyone knows for sure, let me know in the comments. But I mean... oh wow. Just look at it!"

The camera did a slow pan over the roiling mass of cloud. It seemed to seethe and writhe like a nest of rodents, with new protrusions blistering out, only to fall back again to make way for the new ones that bubbled up in their place. When the view reached the cloud's edge, the picture zoomed out to show the clear boundary between dark cloud and bright blue sky, a boundary that was spreading so fast that the camera had to move to keep up with it.

"Wow." The voice on the video was breathless, drawing out the words like a kid watching fireworks. "I have never seen... Just, wow."

The image shook again as a man's face took over the frame. He wore glasses and an orange knit beanie, his features mostly hidden by a thick, unruly beard. "So, this thing showed up over my house maybe half an hour ago. Just came out of nowhere. Keeps getting bigger, too. It looks really nasty, I mean, just... Wow. I don't think it's dangerous, though. There's not a lot of wind and so far, all it's done is rain. Otherwise I'd be inside. I'm not out here taking chances, you know? But if you want me to keep at it, be sure to hit that subscribe button."

Something wobbled through the background. A kid on his bicycle, drenched and moving slow, turned his head toward the camera before he drifted out of frame. The speaker didn't notice. His eyes were pointed skyward, the camera forgotten as he turned to take it all in. The wind blew across the microphone, the picture bobbing as he turned. Scott could see the man's front door behind him, painted blue, a concrete stoop with an aluminum awning over it. He raised his face as he took the steps down. Rain dripped from his glasses and soaked into his beard.

Something in his face changed then, his eyes narrowing from wonder into confusion. He licked his lips, tasting the rain. Then something out of frame caught his eye and his face lit up in recognition. He said something that Scott couldn't make out, something that sounded like, "oh hey!" The picture shook, swinging wildly. The video cut out, but not before it gave Scott one last glimpse of the roiling cloud. Something had lit it up from the inside like lightning, something tinged with green.

Jacob pulled the phone back and hid it away in his pocket, as if it were a sacred thing that had been gazed upon too long. "So yeah," he said. "There are other videos but that's the best one. The rest are kind of garbage, really. But it's just a raincloud, right? There's not going to be a tornado, is there?"

Dana had drifted away. She was standing at the railing, staring out at the darkening sky. The edge of the cloud was nearing the arc of the sun and was threatening to overtake it, like an eclipse. Scott watched her stare up at it, and thought that her face looked wistful, maybe even eager.

"No," he said. "No, there's not going to be a tornado."

Jacob nodded, and stood with them, watching the cloud for a moment before his face lit up. "Oh shit. I should be recording this." He pulled his phone back out and held it up, framing his shot.

"Language, young man," Dana said without turning away.

Jacob shrugged a little but his grip on the phone didn't waver. "Sorry, sorry," he said. "I have to show this to Deacon, though. His parents took him to Florida. He's going to be so pissed that he missed it."

"Language, son," Scott said. Jacob didn't say anything more. Scott could see the cloud in miniature on the phone's tiny screen, so small that it almost seemed manageable, a curiosity meant to be shared and forgotten. But the real thing was at the edge of the sun now, biting into that bright circle of light. Before long it would be covered completely.

5

Scott ran his hand under the bathroom tap, waiting for it to warm up, tweezers at the ready on the side of the sink. All that water swirling down the drain seemed like a waste. They might end up needing it later. He wondered how many water bottles they had in the basement. A days worth? Maybe two? He wondered if they had any jars or empty plastic milk bottles in the garbage, and wondered if he should start filling them now, just in case.

Once the water felt warm he dialed it back to just a trickle and set to work with the tweezers. Whatever piece of the handrail was still in there, it was in deep, deeper than it would have been if he'd just taken out when it had first happened. He probed at the wound with the metal pincers and winced as he imagined his father standing just over his shoulder, chiding him for leaving the railing like that for so long, telling him that if he wanted the splinter out he should have done it right the first time. The metal teased blood from the wound, but the splinter kept its secrets. No matter how much he prodded and pulled, he could not find it.

That cloud could end up being a tornado after all. He hadn't really considered that as a possibility until Jacob mentioned it, but now that he had, it was all he could think about. He'd told himself after the last one that he'd open up the storm cellar, get it in shape in case they needed it, but of course he hadn't. They could get to the basement quick enough, and there were a few old blankets and probably some canned goods down there if it came to that. There was gas in the shed for the generator if they needed it, which was fine because by the time they needed it the storm would have passed. Assuming it was a storm at all.

He thought of the video on Jacob's phone, that little tinge of green light inside the cloud at the end. Had he ever seen lightning like that? It had to be lighting, though. There was no other explanation for it. Some weird reflection? Or maybe even just a shitty, outdated camera? It was probably just his imagination getting ahead of him. It was a weird storm, but still just a storm. They happened sometimes, and in a few hours it would be gone, one way or another.

Only, his father's voice was still in his head, nagging from the back of his mind, telling him that there was something about that cloud that was wrong, maybe even very wrong. Maybe so wrong that there weren't even words for it yet. And the way the video had just cut out at the end? Something was wrong there too, but no matter how much he picked it over he couldn't quite get at it.

He focused again on the tweezers, but it was getting too dark to see. Outside the window, the sky was still blue, but it had taken on a brassy, twilight quality, as if the sun itself had dimmed. He recalled the edge of the cloud, the way it seemed to be racing after the light. He wondered if, now, the sun had been blotted out entirely.

The splinter was a lost cause, and he gave it up. He reached for the towel and caught movement out of the corner of his eye. It was low to the ground and sudden enough that it startled the tweezers out of his hand. They fell, and rattled around the porcelain bowl of the sink.

Tallie was there in the doorway, holding her little stuffed giraffe by the neck, her doe-brown eyes wide with concern.

"Did you hurt your hand, daddy?"

Scott forced a smile. "Nah," he said. "I mean, yeah, but just a little bit. It's okay, though. Daddy's gonna be fine."

Her expression didn't change, and he could see that she was deep in thought about something, grim wheels turning behind those shining eyes.

"Oh, what's wrong, Pumpkin?"

When she didn't answer he slid down to the floor with his back against the tub and opened his arms to her. She fell against him and pulled his arms around her like a blanket. He held her there, wondering how much longer he would have before she stopped coming to him like this, before she stopped laying claim to his affection because she knew it would never be denied. He'd had these moments with Jacob, so long ago that it felt like forever. One day they'd just withered away, and they never came back.

When at last she spoke, she said, "Is Daisy going to be okay?"

"Who's Daisy, Sweetie?"

"Mommy said Wilbur's going to dig her up. I don't want Wilbur to dig her up. If he digs he up, he's gonna eat her."

Daisy. The little dead mouse with the broken neck and the black marble eyes. "No, Pumpkin," he said. "Wilbur's not going to dig her up. Mommy just said that because she wanted to make sure is all."

"But Mommy said it's going to rain. Daisy's going to get all wet, and if she gets all wet, she's going to be sad."

He squeezed her to his chest and kissed the top of her head. "No, Sweetie. Daisy's safe underground. She won't get wet." He thought for a moment and tried to stop himself from saying the next bit, but it came out anyway. "Besides, Sweetie, Daisy's dead. She can't get sad anymore."

"But she'll get wet."

"She'll be okay," Scott said. "She's got her box and she's got lots of dirt on top of her to keep her dry."

They hadn't buried the thing very deep, and he didn't really think what he was telling his daughter was true. She seemed to accept it anyway. He hoped that the lie wasn't the kind that would last, the kind that would keep her from trusting him down the road, the kind that would lead to years of therapy. He wished for a moment that he'd dug the hole under the willow tree, made its grave alongside that old stray dog. But Wilbur would have definitely dug it up then, and maybe some of those long-dead bones and everything that had been buried with them.

Tallie pulled his injured hand into her lap and peeled his fingers back one by one. She stared down at the little smear of blood in his palm, at the black scab that was reforming at its center. "You have an owie on your hand," she said.

"Yes, Sweetie. I have an owie on my hand."

"Does it hurt?" she asked, prodding the wound with her finger.

He winced, but covered it with a smile. "Only a little," he said. "Daddy's going to be fine." That last bit, he thought, might be a therapy lie. A string of bad boyfriends and lingering trust issues lie.

"You should tell Mommy to give you a band-aid," Tallie said, turning to look up at him, her little face serious. "One time, I had an owie on my knee and Mommy kissed it to make it better and then she put a band-aid on it and the band-aid had Dora the Explorer on it and it made the owie all better." She brought up her own knee and motioned as if she was smoothing a band-aid down across it for emphasis.

"You're right. I should do that," he said.

"Mommy's good at fixing owies," she said, her look serious beyond her years. *Good at making them, too*, he thought, though he would never say that out loud, not to Tallie. Was that why Tallie had come to him? Had she seen the hurt on his face and known that it had been there long before he'd ever gotten the splinter? Had she sensed that there was a problem in the air that she didn't know how to fix, that none of them knew how to fix?

"You're right," he said. "Mommy's good at fixing owies."

There it was. The last lie, and definitely the biggest. Would that be the one that Tallie would remember when the two of them were standing on the crumbling porch, watching her mother drive away? Would it matter to her that it wasn't his fault? Would she find a way to blame him anyway? Or worse, would *he* find a way to blame *her*?

She pushed his arms away and only then did he realize how tight he was holding onto her. Without another word she scooped up her stuffed giraffe and bounded out the bathroom door. He sat and listened to her footsteps falling heavy on the stairs, listened until he could no longer hear her at all. From his spot on the floor he could see the copper pipes beneath the pedestal sink, their joints crusted over with verdegris. He could see the old cracks in the tile, the black mildew that gathered in the corners.

He remembered the tweezers then, but when he looked for them they weren't in the sink. He recalled the way they had rattled against the porcelain and reached a finger into the drain to try to snag them. They were too far down, but they were big enough that they wouldn't make it past the j-bend. That much he was sure of. Still, he'd have to take the drain apart if he wanted them them back, and he wasn't feeling much up to the task. There was already so much that needed fixing. The room was dark now, dark enough that it felt like night was falling early. He could hear a faint tapping against the window, and when he looked outside he saw that it was starting to rain.

6

The rain fell gently on the ground, on the roof, on the distant, leaning shed. Scott stood on the porch and listened to it, the sound almost a comfort, like the sound of seeds pouring out of a burlap sack, like the soft hiss of a librarian bringing quiet to a room. There were no storm winds, no hail, no stinging sheets. Just a gentle pitter-pat. Still, he watched it fall, and it worried him.

The cloud had overtaken the sun, but he could still see the distant arc of clear blue sky, a line of demarcation as plain as a shoreline, almost too perfect to be real. It was hard to tell from the ground, but the cloud still seemed to be holding its circular shape. The near edge of that circle had just passed over the house and he could see clear sky through the rain out over Ned Colby's soybean fields. The cloud roiled above him, and he could see the edge of it moving, spilling like lava across the blue.

He went through a mental inventory of windows that might still be open, of worn spots in the roof that would probably still hold, at least for the rest of the year. He couldn't remember the last time he had cleaned out the gutters but he remembered promising to himself after the last rain that he'd get it done. The water had already overtopped them and was spilling out in little rivulets that smacked against the wet ground. The cloud seemed to pulse and fall back again, great puffs of it inflating and deflating like balloons. For an instant, he saw a burst of lightning flicker across it, illuminating it from the inside, and the lighting was tinged with green.

That flash in the video hadn't been his imagination. Nor was the cameraman's voice at the end, the voice that said something that sounded like "Oh, hey" before the view started shaking and the camera shut off. But there was something more, something that had wormed into his mind and stuck at the back where he couldn't quite reach it. It wasn't anything about the cameraman that was setting off the warning bells. No, it was something else.

Scott pulled out his phone and texted Jacob, asking for a link to the video. He stared at the screen, waiting for the notice that the text had been read, but it didn't come.

"Oh, it's beautiful!"

Dana stepped in behind him, and moved right past him to the edge of the porch. She walked with her head thrown back, her mouth open as she stared up into the roiling gray mass, writhing and alive with its own seething energy. She was walking toward the steps, and Scott had the mad urge to reach out and stop her, but she stopped herself, just short of the line where the falling water had begun to darken the wood.

"The light!" she said, breathless. "Have you ever seen anything like it?" The sun was hidden behind the cloud, completely obscured by the crawling darkness, but the blue sky still held the promise of daylight, as if the cloud was just a passing shadow and nothing more. Scott could see that light shining against Dana's face as she raised her arm, saw it glint in her eyes as she held her hand beneath the rain. The warning bells sounded again in his mind, more distant now, and more easily dismissed.

The rain glistened against her skin, running down her bare arm, tracing paths like pale veins, merging with new droplets until her whole arm shined with it. "It's warm," she said, sounding a little amazed. She turned her hand over, admiring the back of it like she was showing off a ring.

"You probably shouldn't do that," Scott said. He had to fight the urge to pull her back, to grab her by the waist and haul her inside if he had to. She must have seen it in his face because she smiled at him then, smiled with a little bit of the old Dana, the Dana who used to steal little kisses against his neck when he was driving in his old Dodge Challenger, the Dana who would slide her feet beneath his thigh when they were reading together on the couch. When was the last time he had seen that Dana? It had been years; that much was certain. Maybe even before Tallie was born.

"It's fine," she said, and that smile made his heart break a little.

"There might be chemicals," he said, though he knew that wasn't what was setting him on edge. "That cloud. It could be—I don't know—polluted or something."

She regarded him from the corner of her eye, telling him to not be silly without ever saying a word. She ran a hand over her wet arm, sending little sprays of water out over the steps, rubbing the rest of it into her skin the way she might if she was in the shower. "So," she said, "are we going to talk about this, or are you just going to keep avoiding me all day?"

She didn't look at him as she said it, but she had to have noticed the way he bristled at this new candidness in her voice, this confidence that held so little of her earlier timidity. She had to have noticed, because her thin-set lips softened into the barest hint of a smile. This, too, was the old Dana, and maybe something new as well.

"I don't know that there's all that much to talk about," he said.

"Of course there is." She pulled her arm back out of the rain and rubbed it dry against her shirt. She turned to face him then, the soft rush of falling water whispering behind her, like it was telling secrets. Suddenly it was just the two of them, alone on that porch that seemed to be the entire world. They weren't mother and father. They weren't wife and husband. They were only Dana and Scott, the way they had started, the way they always had been.

"I hurt you," she said, rubbing at her arms. "I know that. I was stupid and I was selfish and I made a terrible mistake. But If we don't talk about it, we can't fix it."

She stood there, watching him expectantly, like she wanted him to come closer. He could see it in her face, in the way she hugged her arms to her body, that little tilt to her head that meant that she wanted him to hold her, that had always meant that she wanted him to hold her, ever since those early days, when everything between them had been new, when this farm still had a chance at being a farm. But he couldn't even fix the mower in the shed. How could he ever hope to fix this?

She lowered her eyes, the invitation lost. "Assuming you *want* to fix it," she said.

The screen door creaked. Jacob pushed the door aside. He paused in the doorway, eyes darting, widening with the understanding that he had just stepped into a situation he'd do better to avoid. Tallie followed behind him and peeked out from behind his leg.

"Go back in the house," Scott said. At once he regretted the edge in his voice, the knee-jerk speed with which his anxiousness came boiling to the surface. He closed his eyes and listened to the patter of the falling rain. He took a deep breath before he spoke again. "It's not safe out here. You guys should go back inside."

"Why?" Dana asked. "It's just a little rain." She turned back to watch the sky, the tension between them forgotten, everything forgotten except for the rain and the little cascades of water overtopping the gutters.

Scott nodded at Jacob, and Jacob closed the front door behind him, taking it slow, as if he knew not to let it creak, not to let it break whatever awkward spell had come over the two adults on the porch. Dana leaned against a post and stared up at that dark and undulating cloud. The distance between them had returned, and a part of him welcomed it. He hadn't been the one who'd broken things between them. He didn't see why she thought that he should be the one to have to fix them.

He looked out at the willow tree, its branches sagging now with the weight of the water. Wilbur's lead lay coiled at the base of the tree, the end of it lost in the depths of the doghouse. "Crap," Scott said. "We forgot about the dog."

Dana shrugged. "He'll be fine. You worry too much." That last bit, the way she said it, felt like a jab. The words had barbs in them, and they made him wonder if they had been meant to lay their problems at his feet, to suggest that all of it was his fault after all. He wanted to ask her what she meant by it, but by the time he had his thoughts in a place where he could do something about them, the screen door had banged once more and she was gone.

Beneath the willow tree, the ground that Wilbur had worn bare was now turning to mud. He wished that Dana hadn't made him chain up the dog, that he could just whistle for Wilbur to come inside. Maybe he *was* worrying too much.

Hesitating, he raised his hand and let the rain wash the dried blood from his palm. It was warm, so warm that he could barely feel the temperature change on his skin. He rubbed his fingers together and was surprised to find that it didn't feel like water at all. It was slippery, like soapy dishwater. He wiped it off on his jeans, but even after his hand was dry, he could still feel it clinging there.

7

It took Scott a while to find Jacob. He'd gone upstairs first, expecting his son to be in the old bedroom, but all that was there was an unmade bed and a computer that hadn't been turned off. The light was still on, too, despite all his mother's reminders, both patient and otherwise. Scott flipped the switch, remembering when he was young and had to be told the same. His father's reminders were rarely patient and never had to be given twice.

When Scott did finally find his son, he was standing at the kitchen door, watching through the screen as the rain fell on the roof of the little Kia hatchback at the end of the driveway. That was Dana's car. He'd sold his Challenger almost a year ago when the early winter cold snap turned the heating bill into a little bomb that laid waste to their meager savings. They'd gotten enough for it to get by, but not anywhere near as much as it was worth. He'd been bumming rides from Dana ever since, taking her ten miles out of her way to drop him off at his job before she went on to hers. He kept telling himself that he'd pick up something else, some used car that they could pay cash for and own free and clear, but they always managed to find some new bill to put it off.

Jacob didn't hear him come into the kitchen. He was almost as tall as his dad now, sixteen years old and already a man. Scott could still remember when he'd been small enough to fit in the crook of his arm when they'd fallen asleep together in his father's old armchair, baby Jacob tiny and perfect, snoring softly on his chest. They still had most of his father's land, then. The old man hadn't lived to see his grandson, but Scott supposed that was just as well. He might have lived a few more years, the way he was at the end, but they would have inherited his debt all the same.

"Don't get too close," Scott said to his son. "I don't want you to get wet."

"It's fine," Jacob said. "The wind's taking it in the other direction anyway."

Only, there was no wind. Not much of it, anyway. Outside the window screen, the sky was still mostly blue, but Scott could see the dark edge of the cloud casting its long shadow out over the soybean fields. Jacob stood with his arm up, leaning against the door jamb. It was a pose he'd seen his father take so many times, a pose he'd imitated so many times himself. But this time there was an odd tension in it, and Scott could see that his son was gathering himself ahead of something.

"Hey," Jacob said after a moment, "do you think once the rain stops I could take the car for a while?"

"What for?"

Jacob shrugged. "There's a thing at the mall. No big deal. I just want to go."

Twenty miles each way to get to the mall on a quarter tank of gas, Scott thought, and a near-guarantee that he wasn't going to fill it up before he brought it back. Assuming that the mall was really where he was going.

"The lawn still needs mowing," Scott said.

"Yeah, but the ground's all wet now."

"I still needed you to do it. I've been telling you about it all week."

Jacob frowned, and Scott could see in his face a hint of the way he used to pout when he was child. "Maybe if I had the riding mower, I could have gotten it done by now."

"Well, maybe if you'd get off your computer for a few minutes, we could have had it fixed up by now."

He still was a child. Scott forgot that sometimes. He remembered it now as he saw the flash of hurt in his son's eyes, so quickly hidden that it could only have come with practice. He took a deep breath, searching for a way to take his words back, or at least pour water on the rising flames. Jacob turned back to the door, to the darkening sky just beyond the window.

"It doesn't look like it's going to stop anytime soon," Scott said.

"Yeah, I guess not." Jacob made a quick turn to leave, sliding past Scott like a batter dodging an inside pitch. Scott caught him by the arm. He'd meant it as an affectionate thing, but he did it wrong and it ruined the last chance he had at salvaging the moment. Jacob pulled back, startled, and shrank away. In that instant his eyes were wide, as if he were expecting violence. Scott's hand sprang open. He tried to adjust, to put his hand on his son's shoulder, but it was a weak effort, a mere brush against his shirt before the boy was gone.

Scott stood in the doorway, unconsciously assuming the same position that Jacob had held just a moment before. He watched the rain move out over the soybean fields and thought about Ned Colby and his money. *Don't be afraid to go high*, the man had said. Land prices were good right now, and if he could take Ned at his word, they'd be even better. Enough to start over, at any rate. Enough to get his old Challenger back, maybe even enough to give Jacob a shot at college. He thought about that until his phone buzzed in his pocket. He pulled it out and saw that it was a text from Jacob. No words, just a link to the video. Exactly what he'd asked for, and no more.

Scott slid into a seat at the kitchen table, holding his phone in both hands, bracing his elbows so the screen wouldn't shake. The timestamp on the video said that it had been live less than an hour ago, but it already had more than twenty thousand views. The sky above that suburban street looked much like the sky above his own house right now, that curving border of blue against the relentless gray, the light brassy, like sunset on some other world.

"Okay," the voice on the screen said. "Hopefully this is all coming through. The camera on this phone is for shit. But, you know, if you like this video and subscribe to my channel, maybe you can help me get a better one. I don't know."

He was breathless, talking a mile a minute, as if he'd just run a race, as if he knew he didn't have much time to get the words out. "So yeah, I hope you can see this. What we're looking at, I think, is a mammatus cloud. I don't know for sure. I had to look it up. I didn't spend a lot of time on it because I didn't want to miss this. If anyone knows for sure, let me know in the comments. But I mean... Oh wow. Just look at it!"

Now that Scott had seen them up close, the rolling blisters of gray cloud in the video seemed so much more sinister. The way that they pulsed made him think of the way a fetus stretched the skin of its mother's belly as it moved, like there was something terrible up there just waiting to be born.

"Wow," the voice said. "I have never seen... Just, wow."

Here the camera turned around, and Scott brought the phone closer to his face. The cameraman with his bushy beard came into frame, but it was the background that Scott wanted to see. The rows of houses were out of focus, mailboxes and trash cans blurred and pixelated. The kid rode by on his bicycle. "So, this thing showed up over my house maybe half an hour ago," the bearded man in the orange beanie said. "Just came out of nowhere. Keeps getting bigger, too."

Scott backed the video up and played that part again. It was too dark to make out much beyond the fronts of the houses, too shaky to see much detail. The kid rode by on his bike again. Scott hit the pause icon. The kid's face was pale, shining in the odd half-light from the still-blue part of the sky. His features were fuzzy, hard to make out from a single frame, but Scott could still see he was looking right at the camera.

He rewound again and let it play this time, squinting to get a good look at the kid as he passed. The moving video revealed so much more than a single image ever could. The kid's head was definitely turned toward the camera. Scott could make out the dark recesses of his eyes, the narrow gash of his mouth. The rain had plastered his clothes to his skin, but he didn't seem to be in any hurry to get out of it. He rode slow, his bike wobbling, struggling to stay upright.

"Just came out of nowhere," the voice said. "Keeps getting bigger, too."

Scott rewound again, and this time he saw that the kid was holding something across the handlebars, something long and thin that glinted in the weird light. A metal pipe, or maybe a golf club. It was too blurry to say for sure. But the face was clear, or at least clear enough to be troubling. It seemed to be staring straight at him through the screen, the mouth slack and scowling.

Scott backed the video up again, but this time let it play through to the end. The kid wobbled out of frame, scowling at the camera—or was it at the cameraman?—holding the length of metal across the handlebars like a tightrope walker. The bike wobbled again as he left the frame, lurching sideways before it was gone from view. The movement seemed deliberate, the kid's head tracking with the camera before it disappeared.

It looked like he was turning around.

"It looks really nasty, I mean, just... Wow. I don't think it's dangerous, though. There's not a lot of wind and so far, all it's done is rain. Otherwise I'd be inside. I'm not out here taking chances, you know? But if you want me to keep at it, be sure to hit that subscribe button."

The picture spun, panning across the sky to fall on the concrete steps and the dripping aluminum awning. The man with the beard walked down the steps, and something in his look changed. Scott had taken it as recognition earlier, but now he could see that it was surprise. "Oh hey!" the man with the beard said, but his words were cut off as the camera began to spin. What he had taken for sounds made by wind blowing across the microphone were now clearly the sounds of struggle. He backed up the video again, and as the camera swung he heard the high, hollow sound of ringing metal. Striking concrete, maybe. Maybe striking something else. In the blur, Scott could see—just for a few frames—the pale moon of the kid's face, his eyes dark and hollow.

Just came out of nowhere, Scott thought.

He backed up the video again, just to make sure he was really seeing what he thought he saw. Now that he knew what to look for, it was obvious what had happened. The kid on the bike had circled back for the cameraman. He had circled back and used that metal pipe that was slung across his handlebars. Unless Scott missed his guess, he had brought it down right on top of the orange beanie on the guy's head.

The timestamp said that the livestream had ended 43 minutes ago. Scott tried to think back to how big the cloud had been then. He had first seen it in the east, and if he could judge how fast it was growing he might know which police department to report the video to. It was a silly thought. One of the neighbors would have reported it already. Or maybe the guy with the beard had already reported it himself, assuming that the scuffle wasn't as bad as it looked, assuming it wasn't as bad as Scott was telling himself it was.

He clicked on the guy's profile, a little cartoon caricature of the face he had seen in the video, this one with sunglasses and making the Star Trek "Live Long and Prosper" sign with one hand above the name KING_CAESAR91. A list of videos came up. There was only a handful of them—a couple of movie reviews, some toy monster being unboxed, and an instructional video on how to grow magic mushrooms (For Educational Purposes ONLY!) At the top of the list was a flashing icon with the words NOW LIVE.

So, not dead at least, Scott thought. He clicked on the link.

The screen was so dark at first that he wasn't sure if the video had started, but as he watched he began to pick out little details. The edge of a couch. A table leg. A stack of magazines. The phone had fallen sideways, or else KING_CAESAR91 had put it down in the middle of recording. Scott waited a minute for him to come back. When he didn't, Scott turned up the volume and held the speaker close to his ear.

He listened for voices, for some indication that KING_CAESAR91 was about to pick up the phone again, maybe even explain what had happened in the other video. All he could hear was a distant grumbling, like an old man trying to clear his throat, like a dog worrying a bone. There was a steady hiss in the background. He didn't need to guess at what that sound was. He was hearing it all around him. It was the steady drum of falling rain.

He listened, holding his breath lest it obscure some detail, some clue that might make all of it make sense. The sound of the rain outside his window mingled with the sound of the rain through the little speaker. He couldn't be sure, but the rain on the other end of the video sounded heavier, less a gentle fall than a full-on storm. He listened to the weird grunting, heard what could be the shuffle of feet somewhere off camera. There was something sinister in the sound, something that tightened his stomach and tensed his muscles. Whatever was happening there, right now as he watched, it wasn't anything good.

Something went bang, a wood-on-wood sound, like something being dropped on a table, like the slamming of a door. The suddenness of it made him jump, and by the time he got the phone under control the view had changed. The picture had gotten brighter, as if someone had turned on a light in another room. He could see the edge of the couch more clearly now, and the wooden leg that was now obviously part of a coffee table.

Between them was a set of feet.

They stood, unmoving, a ratty pair of sneakers with the frayed hem of blue jeans draped over them, so still that it might have been a single image except for the fact that Scott could make out the little drips of water that fell from the jeans to the carpet. The grumbling was louder now, a frantic muttering that he could almost decipher but for the way the words tumbled and blurred into each other. There was something else too, a coughing sound, closer to the microphone, but hoarse and wheezing.

The feet stepped closer to the screen, and at once the coughing became a cry. The phone spun, and when it stopped, all Scott could see was the edge of a tarnished brass chandelier throwing pale light against a water-stained ceiling. Something went thump. The phone bounced, the chandelier gone, the screen blank. The odd muttering got louder, the voice closer. The phone bounced again and something sent it spinning. When it came to rest, Scott could see the metal awning through the open doorway, the the dark sky churning above. The muttering was gone now, and so was the coughing. The only thing he could hear was the sound of the rain.

8

The pistol was his dad's too. Scott had watched him kill a stray dog with it once, when the old man was deep in the bottle and didn't know that Scott was still awake, hiding at the top of the stairs behind the rail, watching with wide eyes. He'd stood over the thing for a long time, gun in one hand, bottle in the other, like he was getting ready to shoot it again. But the second shot never came. Scott hadn't waited for him to come inside but instead sneaked back upstairs into bed and lay there, heart thumping, with the covers up to his nose until the sun came up in the morning. When he came back downstairs, the dog's body was gone, and there was a mound of fresh dirt beneath the willow tree.

Holding the gun now, it still felt like someone else's, one more thing that he'd inherited that didn't really belong to him. He'd never fired it, and only touched it once before when he'd found it, still loaded, while packing up his father's things to store them in the shed. He loaded it again now, thinking that it probably needed to be cleaned, thinking that it probably wouldn't even fire if he needed it to. He hoped that he wouldn't need it to. He hoped that the video had just spooked him, that he was wrong about the kid and the metal pipe, that he was wrong about it being more than an isolated thing that happened to get caught on camera. He hoped that he was wrong, but the more he listened to the steady tapping of rain, like long fingernails against the window, the more convinced he became that he wasn't.

He reached back and tucked the gun into the waistband of his jeans.

9

The television was on in the front room, blaring loud enough that the level drone of the newscaster carried all the way to the top of the staircase. Scott took the stairs slowly, his shirt untucked to hide the gun. He kept his hands in his pockets, not wanting to risk another splinter. He touched a finger to the wound in his palm, and felt it sting.

He found Tallie camped out at the foot of the screen, hugging her legs to her body, her chin resting on her knees. Dana was on the couch, half under a blanket. They both had the same blank look on their faces, staring at the TV like raccoons caught raiding a garbage can. They didn't even notice when he came in the room.

On the screen was a thin man in a brown sport coat. He stood sideways in front of a map, his hands outstretched to encompass a mass of cloud that was swirling through an animation cycle, expanding outward. Scott didn't need the state borders on the map to tell him what he was looking at. It was the same cloud that was above their heads right now.

"...really fascinating formation," the man on the screen was saying. He was balding and the sport coat seemed a size too large, a skinny kid playing dress-up in a fat man's clothes. His neck was long and his Adam's apple bobbed as he talked. "This circular pattern you're seeing is really unique. Usually this kind of isolated thunderstorm is the result of cold air at higher altitudes. Warm air rises up from the ground and when it hits that cold air, there's a lot of energy that causes this cycle of rising and falling, rising and falling until a storm cloud forms. But I've never seen one quite so neatly contained or so almost perfectly circular."

He pantomimed the words as he said them, raising his arms and then lowering them in dramatic fashion, encompassing the cloud like he was conjuring it up from the map. Dana watched from the couch as if in a trance, her hand at her mouth, her fingertips brushing her lips. She stared at the cloud growing and shrinking again on the screen, like there was nothing left in the world but the image and herself. Her hand brushed her cheek, slowly, almost in a caress, and something about the motion sent a little wobble of longing through his insides, a distant need to touch her just like that, to be touched again, just like that. The splinter in his palm ached.

"...problem with this system is that it's not following normal storm formation patterns, which makes it completely unpredictable." The man's throat bobbed as he talked, the tendons moving at the sides of his neck, his face drawn and skeletal. "We'll be monitoring this storm system as it develops, but if you're in this area it wouldn't hurt to stay inside. Conditions could change very quickly, resulting in sixty, eighty, perhaps even ninety mile an hour winds. Right now the National Weather Service has a severe storm watch posted for Fayette and Montgomery counties, but that could become a tornado watch or even a tornado warning at any time, so stay alert, have a plan for taking shelter, and keep it tuned right here to Channel Seven for all the latest news and updates. Sharon?"

The picture changed to a blonde woman in a blazer sitting behind a desk. Tallie rocked back and forth on the floor, watching with wide eyes. No screens before lunchtime was the rule on weekends, and she seemed excited enough with the transgression that she didn't care what she was looking at.

"You shouldn't let Tallie watch this," Scott said.

Dana turned to him then, as if she were surprised to see him standing there. "Scott, it's the *weather*." She brushed the hair back from her face, taking her time, trailing her fingers through it.

"I know. It's just..." The way she was looking at him, her jaw set, almost daring him to speak, made him suddenly feel small. "I don't want to scare her, is all."

"It's just a little rain."

"Now, yeah." He stepped in closer, not wanting to give any ground. "But all that talk about, you know..." He made a show of mouthing the word. *Tor-nay-does.*

Tallie was probably too young to remember the last one. Probably. They'd spent three hours hunkered in the basement, the wind whistling, the house creaking. The power had gone out and they'd all sat huddled together around the few candles they'd brought for light, wondering if there would be a house to come back to when it was all done. Tallie had sat in his lap, shivering, sucking her thumb the whole time. She still came running to their bedroom at night whenever there was thunder.

"There's not going to be a *tornado*," Dana said, leaning into the last word out of spite. "And I don't know what the weather guy's even talking about. There's barely even any wind at all. I kind of like it, actually. I think it's soothing."

She leaned forward, getting down to Tallie's level. "You're not afraid of a little rain, are you, sweetheart?"

Tallie had been watching their back-and-forth with her neck craned back. She shook her head slowly, all pride and bravery.

"See? She's perfectly fine." Dana stood up from the couch and held out her hand to her daughter. "Come on, baby. Do you want to go outside and play in the rain?"

Tallie nodded and shot to her feet. Scott stepped between them. "No!"

It came out harsher than he'd meant it, so harsh that it startled him a little. It startled Tallie, too. She froze, her little hand up in the air, watching her mother, unsure of what to do.

"I just don't think it's a good idea, is all," he said.

"Oh, it'll be fine." She scooped up Tallie, who flung her arms around her mother's neck. "We'll get you a bath after, make sure you stay nice and warm."

"I said no."

Dana stared at him with narrowed eyes. She bounced on the balls of her feet, the way she always had when she wanted to comfort Tallie, but now it seemed like she was trying to comfort herself. She ran a hand through her daughter's hair, taking her time, drawing out each strand. It was the same hand she had held out in the rain.

"Really, Scott?"

"Really," he said. "It's not safe out there."

"You're being silly."

"You're being selfish."

She gathered herself as if she was about to say something more, but she only turned away. He'd wounded her. He hadn't meant to. Or maybe he had. There was a part of him, a distant, nagging part of him, that was glad to have landed a blow. Tallie looked at her father, not knowing what was going on, only knowing that she was caught in the middle of it. Scott wanted to reach out and hold her, to hold them both, but he was afraid of what might happen if he tried.

When Dana spoke again, her voice was only a whisper and she did not look him in the eye. "You're right."

"Dana, I—"

"No, you're right." She wiped at her eye with the heel of her palm. "I was selfish."

She pulled Tallie close, her hand on the back of her neck.

"And I know I hurt you, Scott. I hurt everyone and I'm sorry."

Scott watched her arms tighten around her daughter. It made him think of the gun at his back, of his palm which had started to throb again.

"I don't even know why I did it. I didn't even really like the guy." She let out a little laugh. Tallie squirmed. "I didn't. He was just there and he was looking at me, and I knew it was going to be easy. Just so easy, and I just... did it. I don't know why."

Tallie squirmed again, pushing against her mother, going limp as she attempted to slide free.

"Maybe I was just sick of living out here in the middle of nowhere. Maybe I was just sick of living in this house. It's never been *my* house. Never. You never let me put one bit of myself into it. You never let me change one thing. Not one."

Tallie slid the rest of the way, landing on her feet and bounding out of the room. Scott felt his muscles unclench in relief. Dana didn't even seem to notice.

"Or maybe I just wanted to be someone else for a little while, you know? Someone who didn't have to drive a shitty car and pinch every penny until it screams and can't find a shirt to wear that doesn't have sticky little fingerprints all over it."

Now that Tallie was gone, her voice was louder, and she was shaking. She hugged herself, as if the room was getting cold, as if it was taking all her strength to hold herself in.

"And I'm sorry that I want to go out and play in the rain, just so I can... I don't know, feel something good again. What I did was bad. I know it was bad. But I still have a right to feel *good* sometimes."

Scott watched her hand—the rain hand—clench. Long nails dug into the bare skin of her arm, raking down, hard enough to scratch but not quite hard enough to break the skin.

"So yeah. I was selfish. One time. I was... lonely and I was stupid and I was selfish. Once. Once in seventeen years."

Her head was down, her hair hanging in her face. The hand squeezed down on her arm, making red divots in her pale skin. Scott held his breath. In the silence that surrounded them, there was only the sound of the rain.

"How long do I have to suffer for that, Scott?" She looked at him then, her eyes pleading, brimming with tears. "How long is enough?"

Something banged against the front door, something loud and heavy enough to shake the walls. Dana started as if she was coming out of a trance. Scott spun toward the sound. His heart was suddenly hammering, but a distant part of him was relieved at the interruption. The bang came again, louder this time. Something was on the other side of the door, and it was trying to get in.

Dana and Scott looked at each other, all their harsh words forgotten. The door banged once more, a heavy sound, as if something were being thrown against it. From where he was standing, Scott could see it shaking, straining against its frame.

He read the look on Dana's face, the fearful hint of confusion, the need to know where the kids were. This was his wife standing next to him, the woman he'd loved and still loved, right by his side. In that moment, it felt as if nothing had ever happened between them at all. In that moment, he felt as if he could forgive her anything.

The sound came again, softer this time and low to the ground, over and over, hollow scratching against the metal screen door. Scott's breath came out in a shudder. He saw Dana relax too. It was just Wilbur, begging to come in. Scott heard Tallie's eager footsteps as she ran to the door. Then he remembered the rain, the sunken look on the kid's pale face in the video. He called out to Tallie to wait, but she didn't hear him. She jumped at the latch and pushed the door wide open.

Wilbur padded inside, his fur sodden, his head hung low. Tallie bounced up and down when she saw him, but the dog paid her no mind. He moved right on past her toward the kitchen, in no particular hurry, dragging his leash behind him.

"Mommy, it's Wilbur!" Tallie said, as if she had just seen a magic trick. Dana ran to scoop her up and Scott followed just in time to see the dog disappear around the kitchen doorway, leaving a trail of muddy footprints across the wooden floor. The screen door swung, bent, in the breeze, and Scott did his best to try and close it. Despite the darkening sky, he could still see Wilbur's spot across the yard. The doghouse had been reduced to splinters, its pieces scattered beneath the willow tree. Wilbur's leash was in tatters. The end of it had been chewed right through.

10

S cott motioned for the girls to stay behind him as he crept
toward the kitchen doorway. When Tallie tried to climb
down to follow, Dana caught hold of her and held her tight to
her chest. Scott listened to the sound Wilbur's nails clicking
on the tile and the heavy thud of his body as he slumped down
on the kitchen floor. Dana wrestled with the squirming Tallie
and watched his movements, her eyes widening with concern.
"Scott, what—"

He silenced her with a wave and thought about pulling the
gun from his belt, but one look at the unfocused concern on
his daughter's face made him reconsider. He realized that he'd
been crouching, ready to run, ready for who knew what. He
straightened, and forced himself to relax, if only for Tallie's
sake.

"I just want to make sure Wilbur's okay," he said, certain
already that Wilbur was *not* okay, that nothing about the dog
or this rain or even his own wife was okay. He'd held his own
hand out in that rain. Jesus, what had he been thinking? That
had only been a few seconds, but it was still enough to set the
splinter in his hand throbbing. The dog had been out there for,
what? Almost an hour? He thought of the video, of the sound
of the metal bar ringing against the concrete steps, ringing
against the bearded man's head.

"Just... Just stay here a minute, okay?"

He slid forward, up on tiptoes, afraid to make a sound. He
could hear the dog just out of sight beyond the doorway, his

breath quick and rattling, like there was something caught in his throat. Scott thought about how long it would take him to get the gun out if he needed it, and how many seconds it would take him to sight it and pull the trigger. He heard the dog shift, a slight scrape of claws against tile, followed by a wheeze that trailed off into a whine.

Wilbur had found his usual spot underneath the kitchen table and lay there on his stomach with his head down over his paws. His sides were expanding and contracting like a bellows, his breath going a mile a minute. But he wasn't panting. Instead, his breath came out in a series of labored huffs, like the chugging of a train. His coat was streaked with dirt. The rain had plastered it down against his skin, turning his whole body a dingy, muddy gray. Water pooled beneath him, and Scott realized then that the dog hadn't tried to shake out his fur when he came in out of the rain.

The dog watched Scott step into the room, but his eyes were unfocused, almost disinterested. Scott watched him back, searching for some sign of recognition, some sign that the inner voice that was screaming at him to take out the gun was nothing more than a paranoid overreaction. The dog's tail flopped once—a lazy effort—then lay still.

At once Scott remembered that this was Wilbur, the same dog that had let Tallie pull his ears when she was a toddler, patiently enduring every indignity, licking her messy face after she'd eaten and curling around her when she fell asleep on the floor. *Wilbur's a good boy*, Tallie had said, and Tallie was right.

Damnit, Dana. Why did you have to tie him up outside?

In his head, a low voice answered. *Why didn't you think to bring him in?*

"Hey there, Wilbur," he said, fighting to keep his voice light. "You doing okay over there, buddy?"

Wilbur's tail gave a little flip in answer, but his eyes still had that dazed, faraway look, like he was looking right *at* Scott, but not actually seeing him. There were wide patches on his haunches and his back where his fur had fallen out. In its place were thick, scabby growths. They rose up in long trails across his skin like hardened lava. Some of them had cracked and were starting to ooze.

"What happened to you, boy?"

The dog's tail flipped as he let out a little whine. It sounded choked, like his throat was full of something thick that he couldn't get clear. Scott bent low to get closer, moving slow, watching those vacant eyes for any change. They seemed darker than they had been. Or was it only his imagination?

He reached out, taking care that the dog would see his hand coming, assuming he could still see at all. The tail flipped again, thumping once, then twice against the muddy tile floor. He touched a spot behind the dog's ear and found one of the growths. It felt hard and bumpy beneath his fingertips. Wilbur didn't move, didn't even seem to know that Scott was touching him. His eyes were unfocused, as if he'd been drugged, and Scott pulled his hand back when he saw that the dog's mouth had curled up just enough to bare his teeth.

"What is it? What's wrong with him?" Dana stood in the doorway, Tallie peeking out from behind her.

"Maybe he got into something?" Scott said. "I don't know." But he did know. He knew down deep in his bones. He just couldn't bring himself to say it out loud.

Dana crouched low to get a closer look. Tallie crouched behind her and did the same. "Did he get into a fight?" Dana asked. "Those raccoons got into the garbage last week. Maybe they came back."

Scott shook his head. "I don't think so. I think—"

Think what, Scott? That the rain did this to him? How do you tell them something like that and not sound like a lunatic?

"Daddy, is Wilbur sick?"

"Yeah, Sweetie," he said, not taking his eyes off the dog. "I think he might be."

"We should get him to the vet, then." Dana reached for her purse on the counter and started digging through it for the keys. "There's the place in Montgomery where we got him fixed. It's, like, forty minutes away though. Do you think you can carry him to the car?"

"No, we need to wait." Scott said. *Wait for the rain to stop,* was what he was thinking, but he stopped himself before he could say it out loud.

Dana stopped rummaging and looked at him like a kid who'd just had her ice cream taken away. "Wait? Why?"

"Well, he came in on his own." *Chewed right through the leash and took the whole doghouse down, too.* "He probably just needs a little time to dry off, get some rest. He'll be fine."

"He doesn't look fine. He looks hurt." Dana had her keys clenched in her fist. Her knuckles were white.

"Dana, it's not safe out there." Scott heard himself, then added, "The roads are probably starting to get bad."

"Well what if he's... I don't know? Bleeding internally or something?"

"Would you please stop scaring Tallie?"

"I'm just trying to be realistic," Dana said. "He could be hurt. Hell, for all we know, he could be dying."

Tallie looked stricken. "Is Wilbur going to die?"

Wilbur's tail thumped at the sound of his name, but his lips were pulled back in a snarl. A thin line of slobber dripped down onto his paws.

"No, Sweetie," Scott said. "Wilbur's only... Well, we don't know exactly what happened to him, but he's going to be just fine." He shot Dana a look, pleading with her to give him this one thing, this one lie to get Tallie out of the room, to get them all out of the room. Dana didn't notice. She was looking out the window at the rain.

"I'm going to draw Wilbur a picture to help him feel better," Tallie said, and set off at a run to look for crayons.

"I think Wilbur would like that, Honey," Dana called after her. When she turned back to Scott, her eyes were narrow and serious. "He needs a doctor."

He looked back at the dog. He couldn't argue. Wilbur was breathing hard, and the sound from his throat was wet and raspy. He stared back at Scott with those unblinking eyes, and it made him wonder if the dog still knew who he was, if he still knew who any of them were.

Heavy footsteps sounded on the stairs. Jacob appeared in the doorway, full of concern. "What happened? What's going on?"

"Wilbur's sick," Dana said offhandedly. "Your father doesn't want to take him to the vet."

"I can drive," Jacob said, a little too eager until he got a good look at the dog. "Oh wow. Did he get into a fight or something?"

"Just stay back, okay?" Scott said as his son inched closer. "He definitely seems hurt."

Dana folded her arms across her chest. "Which is exactly why he needs a doctor, Scott."

"I can get him to the car," Jacob said. "Do you think he'd let me carry him to the car."

"No," Scott said, loud enough to startle. "No one is going out in that rain, and that's final."

For a moment the only sounds in the kitchen were the harsh rattle of Wilbur's breathing and the steady patter of the rain outside.

"Fine," Dana said, and threw her keys back into her purse. She pushed past Jacob, who barely seemed to notice for the way he was looking at Wilbur, getting close, getting too close.

"Has he got, like... rabies? What's that stuff on his back?"

"I don't know," Scott said, thinking of the slippery feel of the rain between his fingers, of the way it shined on Dana's skin. "Let's just let him be for a while. Once the weather clears, we'll take him to the vet, okay?"

Outside the sky was dark, the last stretch of blue sky just visible at the horizon.

"Dad, what's going on?"

"It's probably nothing," Scott said, though he knew deep down that it was a long way from nothing. "Let's all just stay clear of Wilbur for a while. Let him get some rest while we figure out what to do for him. All right?"

Jacob nodded, but still looked doubtful as he backed away. Wilbur watched him go, staring with those unfocused eyes. His tail wagged once, then lay still.

11

Scott filled Wilbur's bowl with water and slid it beneath the table, close enough to the dog's muzzle that he wouldn't have to move much to take a drink. Now that the kitchen was mostly empty, the dog's eyes were closed. His mouth still kept that bare-toothed grimace, thick drool pooling with the water that dripped around his paws. Scott thought that there might be blood in it, but didn't want to get close enough to tell for sure.

Wilbur's breath seemed steadier now, though it still came quickly, inflating and deflating his sides like a great, shaggy balloon. There was a crack in one of the scabs on his flank, and it leaked a shiny yellow-brown. A little shudder went up the dog's hind leg, rippling beneath the fur, and the water beneath him rippled along with it. Scott thought about getting a towel to dry him off, but realized then that he was afraid to touch him again. He wondered what the rain had done to him, might still be doing to him. He didn't want to risk doing anything that might get himself wet.

Once he was sure Wilbur was sleeping, Scott leaned back against the counter and pulled out his phone. It was still open to KING_CAESAR91's profile. The icon next to the newest video still flashed LIVE NOW! though Scott was sure that, by now, the man with the bushy beard and the orange beanie was almost certainly dead. The thought sent a wave of unease through his gut. It meant that Scott had most likely been watching when the man died.

He refreshed the screen, but the icon was still there. Next to it, the thumbnail image showed the same view of the doorway, unchanged since he'd last seen it. He tapped it anyway. The sky on the screen was darker now, but the view was the same. The phone that was recording it hadn't moved from its spot on the floor, and that all but confirmed Scott's worst fears. The sky beyond the open doorway still churned and roiled. Water sluiced down the corners of the aluminum awning. The awning looked pitted now, as if it had suddenly gone to rust.

From somewhere out beyond the soybean fields came the distant sound of police sirens. The land was flat out here, and sounds could carry, sometimes for miles. He and Dana heard them sometimes in the middle of the night when the windows were open against the heat. He tried not to read too much into them now, but the sound still filled him with dread. It was the same dread that he'd felt at the ghostly wail of the tornado siren, the urge to run and take shelter. The urge to gather his family and hide.

Scott wondered if he should try to put the dog outside. The end of Wilbur's leash was still hooked to his collar, and there was enough length in it to let him get a grip but still keep his distance. If he could get the dog to wake up then maybe he could use it to lead him back out the front door. Not all the way into the yard, of course. He couldn't risk that. But at least onto the porch where Scott could close the door behind him. At least that would keep him away from everyone else, away from Tallie, until he could figure out what was going on with him.

He took up the leash and gave it a gentle tug, just enough to take up the slack. Wilbur didn't open his eyes. The rhythm of his labored breaths didn't change. Scott tugged again, a little harder this time. The dog didn't budge, but let out a pained, halfhearted growl that didn't trail away until after Scott let go of the leash.

At once he thought of the times that Wilbur had fallen asleep against his leg on the couch, of the way he would trip over his own legs at the thought of chasing a tennis ball that Scott had tried to hide in his hand. Was that dog even still in there anymore? He wanted to think so, but that persistent snarl on the beast's mouth told him otherwise.

He coiled up the lead and slid it under the table next to the water dish. A terrible thought came to him then—terrible because it came to him so quickly, so fully-formed and reasonable—that he should drag the dog out to the porch and shoot it. It had to be quicker than whatever it was that was eating at him. It would be a mercy, in fact. When the rain stopped, he could bury the body beneath the willow tree. The dog wouldn't be hurting anymore. He wouldn't be alone.

That old stray dog had let his father put the barrel of the gun right up to its head before he pulled the trigger, like it hadn't even known what a gun was. Or had it just been too tired to care? Its tail had been wagging and Scott had thought that maybe his father had given it some food to lure it close. Scott could still see the thing crumple, a live dog one instant and a dead thing the next, like the gunshot had just flipped a switch and turned it off for good. Now that same gun was tucked against his back. It would be a simple thing to press the barrel to the side of Wilbur's head. Wilbur would probably let him. If he timed it just right, waited for the sound of thunder, Tallie might not even hear the shot.

He looked at the screen again, at the image that seemed frozen there but for the swirling motion of the clouds and the water that poured off the metal awning in thick streams. There were more of those streams than there had been before. Before, there had just been one line of water coming down from the awning's corner. Now there were four of them that Scott could see, and one of them seemed to be coming from the middle of the awning, like the thing had sprung a leak.

Scott went for the front door, careful to step around Wilbur's muddy footprints. Through the screen door, he could see the remains of the doghouse strewn across the ground beneath the willow tree. He'd built that doghouse with his own hands, used weather-treated pine and galvanized nails. Now its splintered edges were pitted and sodden, like they'd gone to rot or been eaten through by termites. The rain was heavier now, but he could still see the distant shed through the storm. He couldn't be sure that it wasn't just his imagination, but it seemed to be leaning more than normal.

"Dad!"

It was Jacob, calling from upstairs, and there was an edge in his voice that got Scott moving. He took the stairs two at a time, forgetting about the broken railing but managing to avoid getting bitten by it again. He found his son sitting on his bed, phone in hand, staring at the screen as if he'd never yelled at all, and it made Scott wonder if he'd been hearing things.

"What is it? What's wrong?"

Jacob pointed at the ceiling. There, in the corner above his computer, was an irregular blot of darkened plaster. A taut bubble of water grew out from the middle of it. Scott watched it fall with a wet plop onto the carpet.

"Did it touch you?"

Jacob looked up at him, not comprehending. Scott wanted to shake him.

"Did it get you wet? Did it get on you at all?"

"No," Jacob said, drawing the word out, looking at his father with a doubtful eye. Scott went around the bed to look at the damage. Jacob had pulled the chair out of the way, but it was still dry. Another drop fell from the ceiling. The spot on the carpet where it landed was soaked through and starting to puddle.

"You're sure you didn't get any on you?" Scott asked in what he thought of as his Dad Voice. His not-fucking-around voice. "Absolutely sure?"

Jacob was looking at him like he was crazy. He didn't like that look. It reminded him of Dana.

"Yeah, I'm sure," Jacob said, a fearful edge creeping into his voice. "Why? What's wrong?"

All of it. All of it was wrong. The rain. That cloud. The dog. The kid in the video with the metal pipe. His own wife.

"It's just a leak, right?"

Scott took a deep breath. "Yeah," he said, trying to make himself believe it. "Just a leak."

He pulled the plastic wastebasket out from under the desk and dumped its contents out onto the floor. He placed it on top of the wet carpet just in time to catch the next drop. It made a hollow thump in the bottom of the basket, like someone tapping on a drum.

"How long has it been like this?"

"I don't know," Jacob said, casting a chagrined look at the little mound of candy wrappers and wadded-up tissues on the floor. "I must not have noticed it, but I called you as soon as I saw it."

Scott nodded. "Just keep away from it, okay? Actually, why don't you keep out of this room entirely, at least until the rain stops."

"Really?"

Yes, Jacob, really!" His fists clenched. He found the splinter still stuck in his palm and squeezed. "Would you please just do this one thing? Please."

Jacob stared at him, scared now. "Dad, what's going on?"

Scott looked down at his son. He'd made the boy afraid of him, and that was the one thing he'd promised himself he'd never do. He'd promised himself that ever since the day Jacob was born. He pictured himself sitting on that same bed, watching for his father's shadow at the crack beneath the door. He'd never wanted to scare the boy, never wanted him to feel that fear. But maybe this time was different. Maybe this time, afraid was right.

"I don't know," Scott said, still thinking of the bits of doghouse strewn across the yard, of the holes in the metal awning in the video. "But this storm... I don't know. There's something not right about it. Until it blows over, I think it's better if we all stay inside, okay?"

Jacob nodded, but the fear was still in his eyes. Scott heard heavy footsteps on the stairs and turned to find his wife in the doorway.

"What? What is it?"

"Just a leak," Scott said, wondering about the asphalt shingles on the roof, wondering if they'd fare any better than bare wood. "I'll have to get up there after the rain stops, see where it's coming from."

Dana looked up at the ceiling, frowning, wheels turning. Scott could see her calculating, figuring out how much it would cost to fix, deciding whether or not they could do it themselves to save money. Here was the old Dana again, the Dana from before the arguments, before the rain, with no sign of the tentative, shrinking creature that had haunted the house for the past few days. It was only in seeing her now that he realized how much he'd missed her.

"It figures," she said. "I just got the bill for the septic tank paid off."

"Probably just a few shingles need replacing," Scott said, ready to do anything, to say anything to make this Dana stay. "I'll take a look tomorrow when the weather's better."

She put a hand on his shoulder as he passed her. It was the hand she'd kept out of the rain. Just like that, they were a couple again, making plans for a future where the both of them were still together, a future where the sun was shining again.

The only problem was that he couldn't quite bring himself to believe in it. Even so, he put his hand over hers and held it there. He wanted to tell her—wanted to tell all of them—that he loved them. He wanted to forgive her, but he still hadn't quite figured out how.

12

The wind—what little there was of it—was coming from the other side of the house, and it had left the porch mostly dry. Scott decided it was worth taking a chance, and stepped out the door, careful to keep close to the side of the house in case the rain decided to angle in towards him.

The smart thing would have been to wait until the sun came back out. Even if this had been a regular rainstorm, that would have been the right call. But this was no regular rainstorm. He was more sure of that with every passing moment. It had almost killed his dog. Maybe it still would. He had to find out what it was doing to his home.

From the edge of the porch he could just about see the window of Jacob's room. Scott crept toward it, watching the rain for any sign of change, alert to the chill that the moisture in the air brought to his skin. The temperature had dropped a good fifteen degrees, but the air still felt thick, as if he was standing inside a hothouse.

There was a metal downspout at the corner of the house. One of the screws that held it together had come loose and a thin stream of water was arcing out over the yard. At the joins, he could see spots where the white-painted metal was starting to turn black. He got as close to the railing as he dared, but he couldn't see the roof above the window, not without leaning out into the rain. Even if he could see it, it might not matter. Once water found its way into the house, it traveled. The leak could be coming from anywhere.

He looked out at the remains of the doghouse. Wilbur must have still been inside when it fell apart, because the pieces had been strewn out around the willow tree as if the thing had exploded. The tree seemed less green now. Its leaves were curled and drooping. The few boards that had been thrown past its relative shelter looked mushy and soft. Scott knew that, if he were to get close enough to touch them, they'd crumble like wet paper in his hands. Whatever the rain had done to them, it had done it quick. But the rain was coming straight down, and the roof was at least two layers of asphalt shingles, the newer one stacked right on top of the old. Apart from the leak in Jacob's room, Scott figured it would be enough to keep the rain out long enough for the storm to finally blow over. At least, he hoped it would be.

The strange, greenish, lightning crackled across the clouds. *No, not clouds*, he reminded himself. *Cloud*. This was no storm front, no natural formation. This was a singular thing, an entity unto itself. The lightning tinged the gray with green, lighting up the cloud from the inside, and in that instant it was almost as if he could see through it, as if the outside of the cloud itself was nothing more than a skin, like paper held in front of a light bulb. He thought that he could see something writhing there, some counter-movement to the thing's incessant churning. Or maybe it was just a trick of the light.

At the edge of the property—what was left of the property—the shed still leaned. It, too, had an asphalt roof, but it had begun to sag in parts and it made Scott wonder if the rain had already gotten inside. He wondered if it had gotten onto his father's tools and all of his father's other things that were stored away there, all the things he could no longer bear to look at. He told himself that he'd take a good look, maybe even clean out the place once the storm blew over, but more and more it was beginning to feel like a promise he wouldn't be able to keep, because a nagging voice at the back of his head was telling him that this storm would not blow over, not soon, maybe not ever.

The tall weeds around the storm cellar door had begun to wilt. He wished that he had thought to try to open it the moment he'd first seen the cloud. More, he wished that he'd gotten it ready after the tornado. But something had stopped him from going near it, and it was still locked up tight. With the rain coming down it might as well be on the other side of the world.

He went back inside and pulled the screen door shut behind him. The front room was empty apart from sheets of paper and Tallie's crayons newly strewn across the floor. He could hear his daughter's voice, high and tiny, coming from somewhere in the kitchen. A jolt of cold fear tingled its way through his body as he remembered the dog. He ran past the stairs, his feet sliding on the linoleum floor as he caught himself on the kitchen doorway.

There was Tallie, holding out a piece of paper in front of her with both hands, showing it to Wilbur. The dog was back on his feet and had moved out from under the kitchen table. Tallie was smiling, pleased that the dog was coming closer. Wilbur's head was down and his tail was tucked under. Scott could see that he was getting ready to pounce.

"See, Wilbur?" Tallie said. "Good boy, Wilbur. Come see."

The dog's teeth were bared in a snarl that showed his bleeding gums. One of his canines had snapped in half, leaving the black root exposed and glistening. He watched Tallie, his eyes as dull and empty as they had been when he'd first come inside, but Scott could still read the intention in the dog's low-slung head, the tightening in the muscles of his haunches.

Scott's breath caught in his throat. He spoke in a whisper, afraid to upset the balance of the scene before him. "Tallie..."

"Look, Daddy! Wilbur's all better!"

Wilbur was most certainly not all better. The scabs along his back were weeping freely now. They had raised up from the dog's skin into thick blisters that seemed to pulse with their own life as he breathed. And he was breathing harder now, his sides moving faster and faster like a bomb about to go off. Scott could hear the low growl building at the back of the dog's throat.

"Sweetie," Scott said. Listen to me. "Just stay still, okay? Don't move."

She didn't seem to hear him. She was smiling at the dog, holding her drawing out in front of her with both hands as if she expected him to sit down at any moment with his tail wagging. This was *her* dog, after all. She had no reason to believe that *her* dog would ever hurt her.

Wilbur wouldn't do that, he heard his daughter say. *Wilbur is a good boy.*

His father's voice answered, gruff and low. *You should have taken it outside and shot it when you had the chance.*

Scott thought of bringing out the gun, but Tallie was too close. He couldn't shoot the dog without the risk of hitting her, too. The growl was still building in the back of the dog's throat, and Scott could see way he was sinking low on his forelegs, those dead eyes fixed on Tallie. He wondered if Wilbur could still see her. He wondered if Wilbur was still in there at all.

The frayed end of the leash still lay coiled on the floor. Scott dove for it and managed to get it wrapped around his wrist just as the dog sprung. The force of its leap jerked Scott along the tile floor, but he caught himself and the rope drew taut. The dog's jaws snapped, just inches from Tallie's face. She screamed, high and shrill, and the sound of it was like a vise clamping down on Scott's heart. The nylon rope was wet in his hands and it dug against his palm as he pulled. The dog lurched, off balance, and fell scrambling to the floor.

Tallie dropped her drawing and ran for the doorway, her high scream trailing behind her. The leash went slack as Wilbur fought his way back onto his feet. Claws clacked against the tile floor. The growl in the dog's throat had given way into a pained whine, a tired whine, as if all he wanted was to stop struggling and crawl back to his place beneath the table. Still, he got his legs beneath him, moving as if by some primal instinct that didn't require intention or will.

The dog shook his head, loosening his collar with a jangle of metal. He was facing away from Scott, and he paused there for an instant, as if he was trying to understand how he got there. The whining stopped then, and the bestial growl returned, deeper and louder than before.

The dog turned with halting steps, like a fawn just discovering how to walk. His tail was tucked between his legs, submissive, even as the warning growl built in his throat. His lips were pulled back, and he snarled with bared teeth that dripped with thick drool, tinged pink with blood. There was pain in that snarl, and between the growls Scott could hear hints of that pained whine, as if he dog he had known was still in there somewhere, begging to be set free.

But Scott knew that this wasn't Wilbur anymore. There was nothing left of Wilbur in those black and unblinking eyes. The scabs on its back were oozing fresh now, oozing trails of black blood through the thick, yellow pus. The dog stepped toward Scott, moving slow, as if the mere act of putting pressure on its paws was a pain that it could hardly stand to bear. Its head swung from side to side, like it was saying no, trying to stop itself. But it did not stop. It came forward, closing the distance between them, dropping lower with each step.

Scott got his arm up just as the dog pounced, crashing into him with more force than he could have imagined, sending them both skittering across the tile. The jaws snapped, just inches from his nose, sending a hot spray of blood and spittle into his face. His arm was at the dog's throat, and he could feel its muscles moving as it growled and snapped.

Scott felt the gun slip free from his belt. He reached for it with his free hand, patting desperately at the floor as he tried to find it. The dog's eyes rolled back, no longer black but now yellow and bloodshot. Its jaws swung wildly, its broken teeth drawing closer with every snap.

The dog was on top of him now, and the strength in Scott's arm began to fade. His fingers brushed against the barrel of the gun and sent it spinning. He gave up trying, and with both hands he shoved at the dog and sent it flailing across the room. It cried out in a high-pitched whine as it fell against the cabinets in a tangle of legs and mud and matted fur.

The thing was back up in an instant. All signs of its earlier hesitation were gone now, but Scott could still see the pain in the dog's every movement, in the twitching of its muscles beneath its scabby skin. It spun around, growling from the corner but hesitating to come back after him. Scott had the dim thought that he had hurt it, even as he dove for the gun. He got hold of it and brought it around. Still lying on his side, he fired.

The dog yelped. The shot had caught it in the flank, just below the largest of its oozing scabs. It shrank back against the cabinets below the sink. The snarl disappeared and for a moment the dog was Wilbur again. With his fur plastered to his body, he seemed small and vulnerable. For a moment, the dull look was gone from his eyes and in its place there was only pain. His tail flipped once in what looked like friendly recognition, or was it only Scott's own wishful thinking?

But the look was gone as quickly as it came, eclipsed by an empty darkness that fell across the dog's face. It turned, scrambling, for the screen door. With a hollow crash it collided headfirst with the metal door, shaking it in its frame. It bounced back in a tangle of feet and gathered itself to leap at the door again. This time the latch gave way. The door banged open and the dog disappeared into the rain. The leash followed, slithering like a snake until, finally, it too was gone.

13

"What the hell's going on?"

Dana was at the top of the stairs, Jacob at her shoulder, Tallie peeking out from behind her legs.

"Just stay up there for a minute, okay?" Scott limped across the front room and took a quick look outside before he slammed the door shut and shot the deadbolt closed. He'd already locked the kitchen door and jammed a chair beneath the knob. Most likely, the dog was long gone, but he wasn't about to take any chances.

"Scott..." Dana's eyes were wide with a level of concern that he hadn't seen there in years, not since that night in the basement with the winds whistling over their heads. It was finally the right level of concern.

Jacob wore the same look. He had so much of his mother in him. "Dad, what's going on?"

The gun was still in Scott's hand. He was gripping it tight, the handle pressed painfully against the fresh rope burns on his fingers, against the splinter and the ragged wound in his palm.

"Did daddy kill Wilbur?" Tallie's voice was stretched thin, and the way she shrank back behind her mother's legs at the sight of him was like a dagger pressed against his heart.

"Wilbur's fine, Sweetie," he said, thinking of how the shot had hit the dog in the flank, how it hadn't even slowed it down. "He just needs to stay outside for a while, okay?"

"I thought it wasn't safe outside," Jacob said.

Scott had already moved on to the windows, pushing up on them to make sure the locks held, snapping the curtains shut as he went. "It's not."

"Scott, did you…" Dana's eyes were wide as she looked at the gun in his hand, not wanting to say it in front of the kids. *Did you shoot the dog?*

"No." It wasn't the rain or even the dog that she was concerned about. It was *him*. He tucked the gun back into his belt. It was still warm, and the faint smell of gunpowder clung to the air. "Wilbur is just sick is all. Very sick. We need to make sure he stays outside right now."

Jacob stared down at him, the doubt plain on his face. "If he's sick, we should get him to the doctor. I told you, I can drive in the rain. I don't mind—"

"Would you just fucking listen!" He couldn't take the way Jacob was looking at him, all that teenage arrogance wrapped in his mother's disapproval. He closed his eyes, tried to bring his breath under control. When he opened them again, Tallie was practically vibrating, her mouth in a wide O because Daddy had said a potty word. Jacob was still staring at him, but the sureness had left his face. It was a child's face again, and Scott could see that there was fear in it. That was good. They should be afraid. He needed them to be afraid.

"Please," Scott said, his voice quiet, his thoughts guilty. "Wilbur is sick. Very sick. And it's too dangerous to keep him inside right now. It's not safe, and—" He felt his stomach drop as he remembered the dog's broken teeth snapping shut just inches from Tallie's face.

"Oh, god," he said. "Sweetie, are you okay?"

Tallie shrank back behind her mother and nodded her head.

"You're not hurt are you? He didn't bite you?"

Tallie shook her head, and clung tight to Dana's leg. Dana looked down at him, doubtful. "Scott, what just happened?"

"I want Wilbur," Tallie said, and the sob that was working its way up his daughter's throat was enough to break his heart.

"I know, Pumpkin, but Wilbur's—"

The television was still on, and something about what the newscaster was saying was enough to cut through his frantic thoughts and make him turn his head. The weatherman was back on the screen, his bald head shining, his throat bobbing. The map behind him was zooming out. At its center was the same cloud formation that was over their heads right now, still almost perfectly round, wide enough now that it seemed to cover half the state. There were other patches of darkness on the map, all of them perfect circles, and Scott didn't need the sound to tell him what they were.

"So, what we're seeing right now are several new formations," the weatherman said breathlessly, "some of them coming together just in the past fifteen minutes or so. One over western Maine, another right there over East Texas, and the largest of these new formations—excluding the original one right here over Illinois—forming right there over the Tacoma area in Washington state."

The map swayed and centered on a swirling mass of satellite-imaged cloud. It intersected a wider swath of gray that cut across the screen like a knife blade.

"And what makes this one particularly interesting," the weatherman said, "is that this new cloud formation appears to be pushing away this front that's coming through from the west, almost as if it were a solid object." His voice was high, almost giddy with nerdy excitement. "So, what we're looking at is a very high-pressure system that seems to resist interaction with these other comparatively low-pressure systems around it. It really is a fascinating phenomenon."

Jacob stood at his side now, watching. "Dad, what the fuck is going on?"

He was almost as tall as Scott was now. Scott wondered how he had missed that happening. He wondered what else he had missed. "I don't know," he said, "but we're all staying inside until it blows over."

"It's just rain." Dana stood in the foyer by the front door, looking down at the muddy pawprints in the hallway with her hands in her hair. "Ugh, this floor."

"No, Mom, it's not." Jacob didn't take his eyes off the screen. His brows furrowed as he tried to make sense of it. "This is really weird. Come look."

Dana disappeared into the hallway. Before she did, Scott saw that her hands weren't just in her hair but over her ears. "And the kitchen! Jacob, could you get the mop out of the laundry room and help me clean this up?"

"Mom," Jacob called after her, "you really need to come see this."

Tallie was climbing the stairs now, moving slow, taking them one step at a time. The picture on the television switched from the map to the news anchor at his desk. He shuffled the papers in front of him, then stared out at the camera, as if he could not bring himself to speak. His eyes were sunken and filled with something that looked like distant dread.

"Jacob!" Dana called from the kitchen. Tallie bounded toward the sound. Jacob moved to follow, but Scott reached out and caught him by the arm.

"So, um." The news anchor shuffled his papers again, then touched his hand to his ear. "I'm being told we're going now to Phil Greer and our Eyewitness News team, who are live and on the scene in Collinsville. Phil, can you tell us what you're seeing on the ground?"

Scott stared into his son's eyes, trying to convey without words the sense of danger that he was feeling, that they should all be feeling. Jacob just looked at him, his eyes darting back to the television, until Dana appeared in the doorway again with

Tallie on her hip. "Can you guys stop messing around and give me a hand? Please?"

The news anchor pressed his finger to his ear again. Jacob watched, riveted. "Mom, you really have to see this."

"No. I don't!"

Dana's words seemed to ring in the air, and in the silence that followed them no one dared speak. The only sound was that of the news anchor, saying, "Well, it appears we're having some technical difficulties. We'll check back in with Phil once we can reestablish the signal."

"It is just a little rain," Dana said, quieter now, but no less serious. "That. Is. All."

"Dana," Scott said, practically pleading, "there's more of them now. If you'd just come look."

"I don't need to look, Scott. I can see it right through the window. Maybe it came on a little suddenly, but it's still rain. That's all that it is."

"It is not just rain," Scott said, gesturing at the television, which had switched back to the map again, little circles of cloud like drops of gray ink all over the screen. "You saw what it did to the dog."

"What I saw was a dog who is sick and needs to be taken to the vet, Scott." Tallie squirmed her way out of Dana's arms, but Dana caught her by the wrist. "Why won't you just let us just take him to the vet?"

"Because it's not safe to go outside."

"Scott, you are scaring the children." Tallie tugged, trying to sneak away, but Dana held her tight. "It's just water. Lord knows we need it for the crops right now. Except we don't have crops anymore, do we, Scott? We don't have anything anymore."

Scott pressed down on the wound in his palm and tried to ignore Dana's dig. "You weren't there," he said. "In the kitchen. The dog. He tried to bite Tallie. He came after me and it was all I could do to fight him off."

Dana laughed. It was a harsh sound, a mocking sound. It cut Scott to the bone because he had never heard her laugh at him like that before. "Are you serious right now? Scott, the dog can't be more than fifty pounds. Are you telling me that you can't keep hold of a fifty pound dog?"

"You saw what the rain did to his back. You saw the look in his eyes. He's not—" Tallie was looking at him, hanging on every word. He lowered his voice to a whisper. "He's not our dog anymore."

"You know you're being ridiculous right now, right? Wilbur is sick. Or he got in a fight and got hurt. I don't know. We won't know until we get him to the vet. But what I do know, Scott, is that the rain out there is still just rain!"

"Mom," Jacob had the remote in his hand, turning up the volume. "It's all over the news. Clouds, just like this one. They're all over the country."

"You too, Jacob?" Dana pressed her fist to her forehead, squeezing her eyes shut, searching for strength. The longer she held it there the more pained her look became. She banged her fist against her head, once, twice, then once more, each time harder than the last.

"Fine. I'll prove it to you." She made for the door, pulling Tallie along behind her. "We'll just go outside."

"Dana, stop!" Scott's heart leapt into his throat as she touched the doorknob. Tallie, tried to pull free, the look on her face telling him that she knew something was wrong, very wrong. Her mother's hand only closed tighter.

"You're acting completely unhinged over a little bit of water. So we'll go outside and you'll see that it's nothing. Absolutely nothing. And we can stop talking nonsense, okay?"

The knob turned in Dana's hand. Tallie struggled to pull free. She was confused, on the verge of tears as she cried out, "Mommy!"

The door swung open. The screen door was still closed. Beyond it, Scott could see the darkened sky, the drooping branches of the willow tree. He stood, frozen, afraid to go to her, afraid of what might happen if he did.

"Dana, stop it!"

The four of them stood, blinking at each other while the voices on the television blared. Tallie stared up at her mother, this change in the air between them enough to open up the flood of tears that she'd only barely been holding back. The sound of Tallie's cries was like the breaking of a spell. It brought a change to Dana's face, and she looked at her daughter as if she'd only just noticed she was there.

Scott chanced a step towards them, his hands at his sides, like he was trying to soothe a wild animal. "Now who's scaring the kids, Dana?"

She looked down at Tallie's tiny wrist in her hand. The hand was shaking, her knuckles turned white. Her fingers sprung open, and as Tallie pulled away Dana could see the red marks she had made in her daughter's arm.

"Sweetheart," Scott said softly, "it's okay. Just come to Daddy, all right?"

Tallie hesitated for an instant before she ran into her father's arms. Dana let her go, blinking as if she were just waking from a long sleep. Scott pulled his daughter into a fierce hug, and the warmth of her tiny body against his was almost enough to start his own tears flowing. Jacob was there, standing beside him. Scott handed Tallie over to him. "Hold onto her for a minute, okay?"

Scott turned then and started toward Dana, but she was already out the door.

14

Dana stood at the foot of the porch steps, the rain soaking into her hair, into her shirt. She watched Scott as he stepped out the door and onto the porch, getting as close to her as he dared without going into the storm. The rain was falling harder now. The light shower had become a torrent, the sound of it like nails falling on the roof, rumbling down the gutters and splashing out onto the muddy ground.

Dana spread out her arms and Scott saw a chill work its way up her spine and through her body. Even as she trembled, she smiled.

"See?" she said, turning her face up to the rain. "Do you believe me now?"

Scott thought of the dog, of the sores weeping across its back. His insides grew cold, and numb. "Dana, please, just come inside."

"All that worry. All that nonsense, and for what? All for a little rain that's going to wash away by tomorrow, and you'll forget that it ever even happened."

"Okay," Scott said, his words catching in his throat. "You're right. You're right, okay? It's just a little rain. Now please just come inside."

Dana didn't seem to hear him. She closed her eyes and let the rain wash over her, bathing in it as it plastered her hair to her neck and her clothes to her skin. She stumbled backward but turned it into a spin, lurching like a drunkard as she came back around to face him.

"Oh, Scott, this feels amazing!" She swayed, hugging her arms around her body, smoothing her wet shirt down with her hands. "You have to come out here. Come out and dance with me, Scott. Please come and dance with me."

Scott tried to speak, but felt something like a sob work its way up his throat. He wanted to go to her, to grab her up in his arms and forget the rain, forget everything else, and just hold her. But then he remembered the face of the kid in the video, the length of wicked steel laid across his handlebars. Dana watched him. She saw him hesitate, and her face turned cold.

"Dana," Scott said, his mouth suddenly dry. "Dana, please. Just come inside. I'll dance with you. We'll get you cleaned up and we can dance all night if you want to. I promise. Just, please. Please come back inside."

"No!"

She stood defiant, arms pulled back and fists balled tight as if she were about to lunge at him. "You can't tell me what to do, Scott. You can't tell me not to feel something if that's what I want to feel. That's not how people are supposed to work."

She turned again, moving like a caged animal, pulling at the collar of her shirt as if it were choking her.

"And I *am* a person, Scott, in case you've forgotten. Even with all the laundry, and the driving an hour each way just to buy groceries, and waiting forever in the parking lot in *my* car to pick *you* up from work. I'm not just some fixture in your life, and you're not the only one who's made sacrifices for this family!"

She slicked her hair back, felt the pleasure of it, and smiled. If he could just get her inside. If he could just get her into the shower and wash all of that off of her, she might still be all right. If he could just get her inside, get her out of that rain, everything could still be okay.

"Do you think I wanted to live in this house, Scott?" she said, riffling her hair until it hung down in her face. "This fucking... museum to misery? Did you ever give me a choice about that? Did you ever let me change one thing—just one thing, Scott—to make even just a little bit of it my own? To make it a home, instead of this monument to dead parents who never gave a fuck about you?"

She laughed. It was a harsh, barking laugh, and she put a hand to her mouth to stop it. She watched his face, and what she saw there must have pleased her because her eyes were practically dancing.

"I'm sorry, Scott," she said, "but they didn't. Your father was a drunk who pissed away every good thing that he ever had. That's probably why your mother left him in the first place."

The screen door creaked and Jacob stepped into the doorway with Tallie in his arms. Scott held out his hand to motion them back. He didn't want them to see her like this, all wide-eyed, pulling at her clothes. He remembered then that the dog was still out here, somewhere, if he wasn't already long gone. He watched the rain drip down Dana's face and thought of the sores on Wilbur's back, the dead look in his eyes.

"But I love you, Scott," Dana said, her voice breaking. "I love you and I'm here *right now*. Don't you see that? I fucked up. I got lonely and I fucked up. I got lonely and I fucked someone else. And you know what, Scott? It was *good*."

Scott glanced over his shoulder for the children, but they had already retreated back into the house. For that, he was grateful.

"It was good," Dana said, "and it felt so good to feel wanted. I'd almost forgotten what that was like, to feel wanted. To do something just because I could, to do something just for me, just that once."

She was crying now. Or was it just the rain in her eyes?

"So yeah. Just that once, I didn't think of you, or the kids, or fact that we can't pay the fucking bills on this stupid fucking house that I never wanted in the first place. But I'm still here, aren't I? I could have left, but I didn't, Scott. I stayed. Here, with you. Shouldn't that count for something?"

"I don't care about the house," Scott said, inching closer to the edge of the porch, close enough to feel the damp wind on his face. "It doesn't matter, okay? Just come inside. For God's sake, please just come inside."

He was trembling now with more than just the cold. He held his hand out as far as he dared, thinking if she'd just come closer he could catch hold of her arm as she spun, thinking he might be able to pull her inside, thinking she might just pull him out into the rain with her.

"Please, Dana! Just come inside. Please? I forgive you, okay? We'll work it out later. It doesn't matter anymore. Just, please. I forgive you."

Again came the laugh, harsh and mocking. This time she did not stop herself.

"Forgive me?," she said, her mouth turned up into an incredulous smile. "It's too late, Scott. And anyway, I don't want your forgiveness. I don't need it. What I need is a life. I don't care about the rest of it. All I want is to just... live."

She stretched her shirt out away from her body. Her clothes were soaked through and dark with the rain. She twirled, and her hair fanned out, sending droplets of water in an arc that shined like amber in the dying sunlight.

"Everything we've ever done has been on your terms, Scott. Every single thing. Not anymore." She tugged her shirt up over her head and threw it aside. It landed with a wet plop on the ground. "I don't need you to tell me how to live on your terms, okay? What I need is for you to start living with me on mine."

"Dana, please."

She worked at the tie on her yoga pants, and with some effort skinned them down past her legs. "My terms, Scott. I'm not going to be controlled. Not by you, not by anyone. And if I want to dance in the rain, then I'm going to goddamn well dance in the rain."

Naked, she stood beneath the swirling clouds. She spread out her arms and threw back her head to meet the rain. In those last rays of sunlight her skin almost glowed, and as she spun—little droplets spraying from her hair, from her fingertips—he thought that maybe he *could* join her. He watched her spin, his wife, in the relentless rain. He saw her small breasts, her skin breaking out in gooseflesh, and remembered the way her breath used to quicken at his touch. He saw the little pucker of the c-section scar just above the tangle of her pubic hair, the history of their life together written in every curve and angle of her body. He saw her then, almost like he was seeing her for the first time. Just for a moment, he thought that they could dance together in the rain and everything would be all right.

"God, this feels amazing!" She ran her hands over her face and down her shoulders, rubbing the rain into her skin. When she exhaled, it was a little shiver of pleasure, and the sound of it made his heart ache for her. "It tingles, and it's barely even cold!"

He watched her from the shelter of the porch, this new Dana, awakening in him so many memories of the old. She held out her arms to him and fixed him with a wicked grin.

"Come and dance with me, Scott. Please. Come out and dance with me."

A shudder went through him. A strange wobble worked its way down his legs as he thought for an instant that he might go to her. It rooted him to his spot, that fear that he might act on the impulse, that he might abandon himself, abandon this place, and run out to meet her in the rain. He pressed his fingers against the wound in his palm and let the pain anchor him to the spot.

"I can't."

All the pleasure drained from her face then, and her arms fell limp to her sides. She stared at him, her lips set in a thin line, and all Scott could think of were the eyes of the dog, cold and lifeless and alien. Those were the eyes that stared at him now out of his wife's face, and they made her into something that he no longer recognized. He wondered if the woman he knew was in there still, some place where the rain could not touch her. He wondered if he would ever see that woman again.

"You're just like your father," she said. "I should have left you years ago."

Her face spread into a smile then, her lips curling, showing her teeth. She looked into Scott's eyes, amused by what she saw there, looking into him and through him, seeing all of him and nothing at all. In that moment he thought that she might come at him, the way the dog had come at him. Worse, he knew that he did not have it in him to stop her.

Then at once the look was gone. The moment forgotten, she turned, laughing up at the rain, spinning with her arms outstretched. Scott watched her go, watched her as she danced away beneath the drooping branches of the willow tree, until he could see her no more.

15

Scott shoved the door closed and fell back against it, his breath ragged, his heart hammering. His legs were shaking, and when they would not hold his weight he let them collapse beneath him and sank down to the floor.

"Dad, what happened?" Jacob stood in the front room holding Tallie's hand, their faces pale and blue in the glow from the television. "Where's Mom?"

Scott opened his mouth to speak but couldn't find the breath to make words. What could he tell them, anyway? That their mother was gone? That the rain had done something to her, that she might end up exactly the way Wilbur had? That they couldn't let her back in the house even if she wanted to, because they didn't know what they might be letting in?

"Dad?"

Scott raised pointed toward the kitchen, caught his breath and said, "The windows. Go. Make sure they're all locked."

Jacob stared back at him, horror creeping across his face as he began to understand what it was his father meant.

"Go!" Scott yelled, with all the authority he could manage. Jacob balled his fists and stomped off to the kitchen. "And make sure the deadbolt's locked!"

Scott stood, chest heaving, his legs still shaking, and shot the bolt across the front door. Tallie watched him with wary eyes. He held out a hand to her, and she shrank away.

"It's okay, Sweetie," he said, knowing it was a lie, knowing that it was not okay and might never be okay again. She had the little toy giraffe and was hugging it to her chest, hugging it so tight that it seemed as if its head might pop off. He looked down at himself, still muddy from his fight with the dog, the wound in his palm bleeding fresh. He breathed deep and tried to stand a little taller, tried to push his worry down somewhere where his daughter wouldn't see. He didn't want her to see any of the relief he felt, knowing that Dana was on the other side of that locked door, or to see any of the guilt that came with it.

Jacob appeared from around the corner, frowning, confused. Tallie leapt into his arms and clung on tight. Seeing the two of them like that broke Scott's heart a little.

"Take your sister upstairs," he said. "Her room. Not yours. Keep away from the leak. And lock the door."

"Dad—"

"I know," Scott said, catching his breath, trying to project calm. "It's gonna be fine, I just... Just, stay with your sister, okay?"

"What about Mom?"

He wanted to tell his son that she would be all right, that she—the real Dana, the real Mom—would be back any minute. But the thought that she might really be back at any minute was the thing that was frightening him the most. "I don't know," he said. "Stay with your sister, and keep that door locked, okay?"

Jacob nodded and started up the stairs with Tallie in his arms. "It's going to be okay," Scott called after them, hating himself for the lie, knowing that it had to be said anyway, even if he couldn't find a way to believe it.

The basement stairs creaked. They had always creaked, but they'd never seemed so loud before. Scott paused halfway down and waited for the frantic rustling of mice to subside. The sump pump surged, and the flush of water through its pipes was like the roar of a jet engine. The air down here was stale, almost fetid. The narrow, frosted windows up by the exposed floor joists were still closed and locked.

He found a yellowed filing box on top of the metal shelves and dumped out the papers inside. He filled it with his electric drill, an orange extension cord, a box of screws. There were votive candles and a few Sterno cans—leftovers from when the tornado had come through. He threw them in, along with some mismatched rolls of tape and a couple of flashlights. These last he tested before he put them in the box, and when they wouldn't light, his first impulse was to find Dana and ask her where the batteries were.

He wasn't prepared for the weight of the thought, how it brought with it the idea that he might never see her again. Worse still was the thought that she *would* come back to him again, and that when she did she would be like the dog, her eyes vacant and lifeless, her skin covered in scabs.

He was breathing too fast, and starting to feel light-headed. He steadied himself against the shelves and pressed his forehead to the cold metal until the feeling passed. His kids were waiting for him upstairs, waiting for him to figure out a way to make everything right again. He didn't know what it would take to make things right, but at least he could keep them safe until the rain stopped. Once the rain stopped, they could figure out a plan. They could find Dana and get her to a hospital. Once the rain stopped, everything would be all right.

He set the box on the kitchen table and tested the chair he'd wedged under the doorknob. The windows were closed but half of the latches were still undone. He snapped the rest of them closed, annoyed with Jacob for not having done it like he'd asked, annoyed with himself for not having checked them first thing. He yanked up on the frames to make sure they were secure before he lowered the blinds, thinking maybe he was asking too much of the boy. The kids had to be as frightened at he was right now. He told himself he'd apologize as soon as he got the chance.

Dana's purse was still on the counter, with her keys peeking out the top of the unzippered pocket. At least that meant she couldn't get back in. Scott felt clenched by a wave of guilt at the thought, at the thought of his wife, naked and shivering in the rain. He forced himself to remember the kid on the bicycle, the dog's dead eyes, and tried to convince himself that he was making the right choice.

The kitchen floor was a ruin of muddy paw prints and streaks of dirt. A wide patch had been rubbed almost clean where he'd fallen with the dog. His shirt had stayed mostly dry, but there were deep scratches in his forearms that he only just noticed, crusted over with dried blood and grime. More blood lay in little droplets near the refrigerator where he'd shot the thing, one red paw print near the door to show which way it had gone.

Yes, he told himself. He was making the right choice. He was making the only choice.

There was a rectangle of paper, face down amid the drying mud. It was Tallie's drawing. Scott picked it up and tried to rub the dirt away. The four of them were there, rendered in loops of bright crayon, a little cartoon Tallie smiling next to a little cartoon Wilbur colored in yellow. She'd drawn Jacob smiling, too, with what looked like an old PlayStation controller in his hand, the wire a single curve of black, trailing off to nowhere. Scott and Dana were there, but their mouths were just straight little lines, and he could read no joy in either of their faces. Tallie had drawn them all close together, but Scott was set apart, taller than all the others. Cartoon Tallie was holding Cartoon Dana's hand, but Cartoon Scott loomed like an afterthought at the edge of the page.

Guilt hit him all at once. He thought about Tallie without
her mother, about the locked doors between them. Tallie
wouldn't know why he couldn't open those doors, even if
Dana did come back. He stared at the windows and wondered
how easy they might be to break from the outside. The longer
he stared, the more his guilt twisted into anger. If she'd only
just stayed inside he wouldn't have to be thinking this way,
thinking of keeping her out instead of keeping them all inside
together. If she'd only stayed inside, he wouldn't have to think
about that part of him that was glad she was gone.

Nothing but a no-good whore, came his father's voice,
bubbling out of memory, the words slurred with drink as he
spat them into the phone in the kitchen. Scott squeezed his
eyes shut to drive the voice away, but that child part of him still
listened from the top of the stairs.

He pressed down hard on the splinter in his palm. It was
Tallie he had to think of now, Tallie who might reach up and
unlock the door when he wasn't looking. Tallie, who might
let her mother back inside, or worse, run out to meet her in
the rain. It didn't matter what Jacob might have to say about
it. It didn't matter that he wanted to go after his mother, too.
Scott couldn't risk it. He couldn't risk what happened to the
kid in the video happening to either of them. He couldn't risk
seeing Wilbur's dead eyes staring back at him from inside his
daughter's face.

Still, he hesitated before he picked up the drill. If he did this,
he'd be crossing a line, taking a step from which there was no
going back. It felt like giving up, like he was admitting that
Dana wasn't coming back, that whatever the rain had done to
the dog it would do to her too. It was admitting that their kids'
mother wasn't their mother anymore. Admitting it to them.
Admitting it to himself.

He put the screwdriver bit in the drill and drove three screws
at an angle through the door and into the doorframe, one at

the top, one at the bottom, and one just above the doorknob. As long as the rain kept falling, and as long as he had anything to say about it, no one was getting into this house. Or out of it.

16

There hadn't been a checklist on that night that the tornado came through, but Scott had been carrying one in his head ever since. He'd found the candles in the cabinets, but only a handful, maybe enough to light one room for a few hours if the power went out. He'd rifled through the kitchen drawers for batteries but only managed to get a faint glow from one of the flashlights before it died completely.

Most of his tools were in the house, but the generator was out in the shed with the lawnmower, which meant that they might as well be on the moon. There were three gallons of spring water on a shelf in the basement. They could stretch that to a couple of days if they had to. He didn't know how much longer they could trust what came out of the taps. There was milk in the fridge and maybe a quart of orange juice. Maybe three days. He didn't think that they'd need it for that long. This was still a storm, for all its strangeness, and storms always passed. Whatever had started it—some kind of climate disaster, chemicals in the atmosphere—the rain had to stop sometime.

He found a box with maybe three or four black garbage bags left in it and brought it to the low table in the front room, along with the tools and the bucket and the candles. He didn't want to have to go back into the kitchen again unless he really needed to. He was angry with himself for not being better prepared but he didn't have time to dwell on it, not with the kids upstairs waiting on him to find a way to fix all this. And

Jacob really was still a kid, no matter how much he might
protest to the contrary. He was probably missing his mother
as much as Tallie was.

Scott kept running it over and over in his mind, looking
for something different that he might have done, some way
of keeping Dana in the house. He didn't think he could have
forced her if he'd tried, and going out in the rain after her
would have left the kids with no parents at all instead of just
one. The kids were what he needed to focus on now, to keep
them inside, to keep them safe. He'd put three more screws in
the front door, just like the ones in the kitchen. If nothing else,
he could make sure that they all stayed put.

The TV had been muted, but the picture was still going.
He caught a glimpse of the anchorman shuffling papers before
they cut back to the weatherman and his map. More circles
had cropped up, one over Florida, two more in Canada.
The whole screen was peppered with them, and where two
of them had formed close together over Kansas, the larger
one was overtaking the smaller, subsuming it like some giant
bacterium, eating it, making it part of itself.

Scott snatched the remote off the table and turned the
volume back on. The bald man was no longer smiling. He
swallowed hard between his sentences, the great Adam's apple
bobbing nervously. "...given the number and uniformity of
these weather systems, we can no longer consider them to be
natural phenomena."

Gee, no shit, Scott thought, remembering the way the green
light had lit up the clouds from the inside. Something had been
moving inside of them, something writhing and alive. It hadn't
just been his imagination, no matter how many times he heard
his father's voice trying to tell him that it was. Scott could
just about picture him, sitting in the recliner in the corner of
the room with a drink in his hand. Scott wanted a drink now,

wanted it more than anything. For once, he was glad that he never kept the stuff in the house.

"Though we're waiting on an official statement from the National Weather Service, we've been told that these formations should be considered severe weather events, and treated similarly to a Severe Thunderstorm Warning. So if you're in one of the affected areas, do your best to stay indoors and limit travel wherever possible, unless it's an emergency—"

The picture switched back to the anchorman, looking serious with his finger pressed to his ear. "Sorry, Don, but I'm being told that we've reestablished contact with Phil Greer on the scene in Collinsville. Phil, what can you tell us about conditions on the ground out there?"

The picture went dark, though not entirely. Scott could see the vague outline of a road, lit by some bright light behind the camera. Lightning blossomed across the sky and in that instant it picked out the silhouettes of tree tops in the distance. But for the little daggers of rain that glinted in the darkness, the scene was empty.

"Phil, can you hear me?"

The record-scratch sounds of a jostled microphone growled out from the speaker. But beneath them there was something else, something low and guttural, and it took Scott a moment to realize that it was a voice. It was muttering, words coming too fast to hear, if they were even words at all. They rose, coming faster and higher until they culminated in a series of giggles that trailed off, lost beneath a fresh burst of microphone static. The road was brightening, rain-slick and shining with the glow of reflected headlights.

The microphone cut off then, and for an instant, there was nothing but the road and the rain, growing bright in the light from the oncoming car. Then the lights tilted abruptly and something came into frame, spinning like a toy helicopter let loose from a child's hands. It wasn't until it hit the ground that Scott realized it was a body.

It bounced once, then twice, landing in a tangle of limbs, all bent at unnatural angles. The car followed an instant later, sliding sideways along the wet pavement, lurching into the air as the body went under the back tire. The man's chest caved in with a crunch, a sound made only more awful by the complete and engulfing silence that came after.

The picture switched back to the anchorman, his mouth open, horrified. Scott mashed down the mute button and reached for his phone. The screen was cracked, probably from when he had fallen with the dog. He thought about calling the police, but what would he even say? That his wife had left him to dance naked in the rain? Would he tell them about the dog? Worse, would he ask them to come out to the house, to get out of their squad car and walk the ten yards between the driveway and the door while the rain was still falling? And if they did come, what would they be like when they arrived?

He called up the video again, expecting it to have ended, expecting the Internet to not be working at all. It was there, the NOW LIVE icon still flashing like a warning sign. He pressed down on it and the familiar view of the awning and the sky filled his screen. Only, now there was more of the sky to see, because most of the aluminum awning was gone, eaten away, as if some great beast had chanced by and taken a bite of it. The bits that were left hung paper-thin and dripped with fat sluices of rainwater. Beyond it, he could see the churning clouds, patches of gray moving at opposites from each other, bulging and swirling, punctuated with flashes of green.

Scott wondered if the kid with the bike was still out there somewhere, wandering in the rain like Dana was probably wandering right now. He wondered how long it would take for the rain to eat through his gutters the way it had eaten through that awning. He thought about the leak in the old bedroom, and wondered how long the roof would hold.

The picture on the television screen dissolved into pixels and froze, fractured by great streaks of white static. When they resolved again, a car commercial was running, a blue SUV chewing up a dirt road beneath a blazing sun. Scott flipped through the channels with the sound off. More static on one. Sunday church shows on another. Mostly just commercials. The world going about its business, at least until it couldn't anymore.

He went to the basement again and came back with a handful of old rags, threadbare and stippled with dried paint. He found an old orange bucket, and he brought that up, too. Even with the drill and the candles they didn't look like much, laid out on the low table, but they gave him something to focus on. Something that wasn't the guilt of not following Dana out into the rain, of not trying to get everyone out into the storm cellar when he first saw the cloud.

More than that, they gave him something to think about that wasn't the gun in his belt, one shot down now but plenty more left in the box in the upstairs closet. They kept him from thinking about when he might have to use it again.

17

The leak in the old bedroom had gotten worse. He'd brought the orange bucket upstairs with the idea of swapping it out with the wastebasket, but the basket was already flowing over, its sides deformed and collapsing. The carpet around it was dark and soaked through.

Scott ran back down to the kitchen and tugged on the heavy rubber gloves. He maneuvered around the wastebasket like he was defusing a bomb, lifting it slowly, avoiding the steady drip from the ceiling as he tipped it over into the bucket. He took the bucket and emptied it into the bathroom sink, not thinking until it was done about what it might do to the pipes. The water drained slowly, and he remembered the tweezers that he'd lost down there. How long ago had that been? It felt like a lifetime. He watched the puddle of rainwater swirl in the bottom of the porcelain sink. It was dark, like amber, and when the light caught it, it glinted like silver stars.

He brought the bucket back to the bedroom and emptied the wastebasket into it again. The water was barely enough to cover the bottom, but it was still more than he'd expected. The water from the ceiling was falling steady now, and had eaten a hole in the plaster the size of a quarter. All around the opening, a black mold clung to the ceiling, radiating out in little spiky blossoms. He got up onto the bed and poked at the growth with a gloved hand. More plaster broke away, sodden and crumbling. When he rubbed it between his fingers, it felt springy, and when he pulled his fingers apart it stringed between them like snot.

At the rate the water was falling, it would probably fill the bucket in less than half an hour. He'd need a better place to empty it, a place that wasn't outside, a place that didn't risk doing to the pipes what it did to that awning in the video, what it was already doing to the gutters outside. He needed a plan, one that didn't involve the kids and didn't put them at risk. Apart from just staying put, the only ones he could think of involved opening up the door again, and there was no way he was ready to risk that.

Dana would have had a plan by now. She was so much better with these things than he ever was. He thought about her, out there, the rain glistening on her skin, raising blisters and scabs on her body the way it had with the dog. He'd left the shed unlocked. Maybe she'd found her way there. Or maybe she was sitting out beneath the willow tree, watching the house with dead, unblinking eyes.

The rain on the window glass blurred the view of the yard, but he could see the willow tree with its branches so wilted now that their tips touched the ground. He could see the old shed that seemed to be leaning even further than it had been just this morning. Nothing was moving, but apart from that he couldn't tell what, if anything, might be going on out there. But for the rain, all was quiet, and the sky had made the whole world bleak and gray.

<hr>

The door to Tallie's room was open a crack. Jacob hadn't locked it like he'd been told. Scott knocked anyway out of habit before he pushed it open. Tallie was curled up by the headboard, asleep in her sweatshirt and jeans. Jacob sat on the edge of the little toddler bed, phone in hand with his earbuds in, the long charging cord drooping off toward the wall outlet.

Scott watched them in silence from the doorway, remembering the time, not so long ago, when the little bed had been Jacob's, before he'd outgrown it. He'd been all about the dinosaurs then, and Dana had found a set of old Jurassic Park sheets at the resale shop that he loved so much that a whole month of bedtimes became as easy as just saying so. It had just been the three of them then, with the whole future stretching out ahead of them. Tallie wouldn't come along for almost seven more years. Everything since then had felt so immediate, so *now*, that he hadn't even noticed the time slipping away. Looking at his son now, he still saw the child, even though Jacob was practically a man.

"911's busy," Jacob said, popping a headphone out of one ear. "I've been trying for twenty minutes. How can 911 be busy?"

Scott pressed a finger to his mouth and pointed to Tallie, who was beginning to stir. Jacob nodded, and followed as Scott beckoned him out of the room. Scott swung the door closed behind him, but not without checking the ceiling first, looking for water spots.

"I don't know," Scott said, his voice still low. "Maybe the system's just overloaded. Or maybe the lines are down."

Jacob leaned in, close enough to whisper. Scott saw the fear in his eyes, felt it like a gut-punch. "How could the lines be down? It's 911."

"I don't know," he said, but he had an idea. He'd seen the way the rain had eaten through the awning in the video, seen how it had pitted the gutters outside. He thought of the overhead phone lines, fragile connections strung with aluminum guy-wires, and wondered how much longer they'd last.

"The phones are working," Jacob said, his voice rising. "The TV's working. 911 should be working, too. Right?"

"TV's on the antenna," Scott said. The cable had been the first casualty of the money crunch. "The antenna's inside. As long as they're broadcasting we'll still get it. Same for the phones, I think." It was all satellites and antennas, things he'd never had to think about before and never had to understand. The not-knowing made him feel helpless, but he did his best to not let it show. Jacob was still looking at him like he was still in charge, like he knew what to do, but his mind was a blank, still reeling from the sight of Dana dancing away in the rain.

"The important thing is that we stay together," Scott said, trying to push the doubt out of his voice and replace it with something like authority. "Once this rain passes we can figure out the rest."

Jacob nodded, and some of the tension left his shoulders until a snap of panic brought it all back again.

"Dad, where's mom?"

Scott opened his mouth, but there were no words. He'd watched Dana disappear behind the willow tree, stepping over the burst and rotting fragments of Wilbur's doghouse. Wilbur was still out there, too. He'd tried not to think about that, but couldn't help it now.

"You didn't leave her outside, did you?"

He *had* left her. He could have gone out in the rain after her. He could have taken her by the hand and maybe she would have even come with him. If he'd only followed her, she could be sitting downstairs, wrapped in a towel, warm and safe and dry.

"We have to go after her," Jacob said, pushing past him. "I'm gonna go after her."

Scott grabbed him by the arm, harder than he'd meant to, but he wasn't about to let go. "No," he said, then leaned in to whisper again. "No. We have to stay here."

"Dad, what are you talking about?"

"We have to wait for the rain to stop," he said, thinking of the kid on the bike in the video, thinking of the look in Dana's eyes as she spun away toward the willow tree. "Once it's over, we'll go out and look for her. It can't—"

"It's just a storm, right?" Jacob's voice was rising, and in it Scott could hear Dana's cadence, Dana's rebuke. "It's not like the tornado. We have to go. We have to find her!"

"We have to stay together." Scott said it with a growl that surprised them both. He took a deep breath, softening to a whisper. "And we have to stay *inside*."

Jacob straightened and shrugged Scott's hand away. His eyes were fixed, determined, and Scott felt a flare of pride beneath the sudden onrush of fear.

"I'll go then," Jacob said, nodding like he was making up his mind as he went along. "You can stay here with Tallie, and I'll—"

The floor beneath them shook and glass rattled in the window panes. A low rumble worked its way through the house, growing louder before it subsided. Scott first took it for thunder, but it was too loud to be thunder, unless it was right on top of them. Maybe an earthquake. Maybe something worse.

Jacob got to the window first. Tallie was stirring in her bed, and Scott hoped the sound hadn't been enough to wake her. He wasn't ready for the questions she was sure to have, and he wasn't ready for two dissenting voices chipping away at his resolve.

In the distance beyond the soybean fields, smoke was rising in a great, black plume, lit from below by a still-burning fire. It roiled skyward, an ashen pillar set off against the gray-green clouds.

"What the hell was that?" Jacob was whispering again, all of his earlier confidence drained out of his voice.

"Fuel tanks," Scott said. Three of the big 10,000-gallon cylinders, one sitting right next to the other. He'd watched the big cranes from the front porch when Ned Colby had them put in, on the last of the land Scott had sold to him.

"Did the storm do that?"

Scott frowned. The tank shells would be thick, thicker than an old aluminum awning at any rate. The lines, though, would be thinner, much thinner, and though the valves would be galvanized, someone would have to be out there to make sure they were all shut off. Out there in the rain. That, of course, assumed that shutting them off was what they had in mind. Even if the tanks had been eaten straight through, all that gas didn't just light itself.

"I don't know," Scott said. He thought of the kid on the bicycle with his dead eyes, the camera in the video turned on its side. "Maybe."

"Dad, what's going on?" All of Jacob's earlier resolve had left his face. In its place was little-kid uncertainty. He was looking at Scott to fix this. He was looking at him to make it right again.

"I don't know," Scott said, "but you're not going out there. None of us are. Not until the rain stops. Is that clear?"

Jacob nodded. His face was slack and there was fear in his eyes. Scott would have given anything in that moment to have the cocky teenager back, to feel as if there might be two adults in the house instead of one. He watched the thick smoke rise high into the air with no wind to carry it. At least the rain would wet the crops enough that the fire wouldn't spread too far. That was something, at least.

"What was that noise, Daddy?" Tallie was sitting up now, eyes squinting and sleepy, stuffed giraffe tucked under her arm. He scooped her up and pressed her to his shoulder, turning her around so she couldn't see out the window.

"It's nothing, Sweetie. Just some noise outside. That's all."

She squirmed and cuddled against him, calming and warm. He pushed his fears aside, if only for her sake.

"I want Mommy," she said, and punctuated it with a yawn.

"I do too, Pumpkin," Scott said, bouncing from foot to foot, rocking her the way he had when she was a baby. "I do too."

18

He carried Tallie down the stairs, holding her tight with one hand while he negotiated his way in the dark, moving by feel and memory. Without the lights on, it was as if it were the middle of the night, the bright sunlight of just a few hours ago gone and forgotten. He could see the flicker of the television in the front room, throwing shifting shadows onto the walls, and wondered how much longer the power would stay on.

The light was on in the kitchen, tracks of mud and wet leading out from it down the hall and all the way to the front door. His father's voice in his head told him he needed to clean it up, and soon, before any rot set in. He was grateful for the voice this time, because it gave him something practical to think about, something small enough that he could get his mind around.

Jacob was right behind him, breathing hard, heavy footsteps squeaking the risers. When they reached the bottom of the stairs, Scott turned and pressed Tallie into his arms, Tallie who was already dozing again. "Take her back to the front room, okay? If she wants to sleep, let her sleep, but keep her in there for now, okay? And watch where you're stepping."

Jacob nodded, and Scott could see in his eyes that he was grateful to have something simple to do, too. He tiptoed over the mess and Scott caught him by the arm, taking care to be gentler this time, doing his best to be reassuring. "It's going to be all right," he said. "I promise."

Jacob nodded, but Scott couldn't tell if the boy had believed him. It didn't matter if he believed him though, as long as Jacob did what he asked, as long as they all stayed in the house. Scott listened to the rain, heaver now against the siding, great plops of it sluicing down and over the tops of the gutters. It couldn't go on forever, he told himself. It had to stop sometime. It just had to.

He followed the light into the kitchen, stepping around the muddy pawprints, the little puddles of drying blood that led to the door. The air was thick here with the smell of wet dog, but beneath it was something else, the sharp, earthy smell of ozone, of stones after a rain. Petrichor. He could still hear the word on Dana's lips, sitting out on the porch at night, when Jacob was still small, still sleeping with his dinosaurs, when Tallie wasn't even a thought yet. That had been a different rain, a light fall shower, barely more than a drizzle. They'd been sitting together on the chain swing that had rusted so much since that Dana had made him take it down. He could remember the feel of her head on his shoulder as it swayed, the gentle curve of her hip beneath his hand.

Scott pushed the thought aside. The floor was a mess and all he wanted to think about was cleaning it, that he could clean it, that he could do at least that much. Maybe once that was done, he'd be able to figure out the rest.

He pulled a trash bag from the box and grabbed the roll of paper towels. He stretched Dana's rubber dishwashing gloves back over his hands and knelt down, trying to ignore the stench that got so much worse the closer he got to the floor, the petrichor scent sharper now, more like acid in his nostrils.

The worst of the mess was beneath the table where Wilbur had tried to hide himself, a rough oval of brown streaked with trails of yellow-white. There was something strange about the mud, something that he couldn't quite place until he tried to scoop up the mess and brought bits of the linoleum tile up with the dirt. He held up one of the bigger pieces to examine it. It was pitted through, with great holes through the middle of it like Swiss cheese.

He pressed a gloved finger to the exposed wooden subfloor and felt it give like a sodden sponge. With a little more pressure, he pushed right through and pulled back chunks that crumbled in his hands like wet fall leaves. The bits were shot through with rubbery fibers that wobbled as he rolled them between his fingers. They were dark and reddish, almost black, but as they caught the light he could see arcs of color within them, flecks of silver-green.

He tested the floor around the spot, afraid to use too much pressure for fear that his hand might go all the way through. The subfloor was weak, almost mushy, in the spots where the mud was the thickest, in the spots where Wilbur had left the most water on the floor. Where the floor had stayed dry, there was no give at all.

A sinking dread crept through him as he followed the muddy footprints back through the hall to the front door. The water had fallen onto the hardwood in a trail of coin-sized circles, and he could see without touching them that they were pitted and worn. Dark branches wound through the boards where the water had found cracks in the varnish and soaked through. When Scott bent low to touch them, they felt weak and rotted, as if years of neglect had been conferred on them in the space of less than an hour.

He thought of the splintered remains of Wilbur's dog house, the pitted and rotted look of the sodden bits of wood, but when he went to the window, it was too dark to see anything but the smoke still billowing up from the propane tanks, lit from below by the glow from the dying flames. The branches of the willow tree drooped low, as if they were burdened by some unseen weight. He hoped that Dana had taken shelter beneath those branches, somewhere where the water could not touch her. The shed would be better. Through the dark, he could just make out that the door was ajar, but he couldn't recall if he'd left it that way.

Scott ran to the basement stairs, doubling back to grab a candle out of the box on the low table. He heard muffled splash of water as the sump pump ran, but the tone of the vibration was off. It was hollow, sluggish, and went on for far too long. When the check valve thumped shut the pump sputtered and wheezed to a stop. All through the basement was the faint smell of smoke and machine oil, of water soaking into dusty concrete.

He found the dark spot beneath the kitchen floor and held the flame up to it. A spongy patch bulged from the wood between the floor joists, moist and glistening like moss on a rotting log. Black tendrils suffused it, branching out in irregular paths, stretching across its surface like veins beneath the skin of a hand. When the light hit them they shined, translucent and suffused with silver-green.

The rain streaked against the narrow windows and pooled against the paint-slopped frames. How long would it be before the frames rotted away and the glass fell out? How long would it be before it happened to the windows upstairs? He thought again of the metal awning in the video and wondered how much longer the roof would hold. The water was already finding its way in, cutting pathways through to the ceiling of the old bedroom and who knew where else. *All rot starts from the inside*, he heard his father say, so vivid and so clear that it might have been a whisper in his ear. And even if he could believe that the shingles would hold, could he believe the same for the wooden joists that held it up? How long would it be before all of it went to pieces?

Something rustled behind the boxes on the storage shelves. Scott heard the brushing of furry bodies against cardboard, the clipped gnawing of tiny teeth. He swung the candle around, spilling wax and dousing the flame. He swore, and the sound abruptly stopped. The mice were getting restless. Scott wondered if it was because they could sense the rain outside or if they'd already been out in it.

He thought of Daisy the mouse, safe and dry in her little box beneath the earth. Wilbur was still outside. For all he knew, the dog had already clawed Daisy out of the ground, eaten her in one bite like a wolf in a fairy tale. The sump pump kicked on again, taking too long to get up to speed. He wished again that he had thought to take them all to the storm cellar, on its little patch of high ground, before the rain ever started. He wished that Dana was still here, that the four of them were huddled in the dark, together.

But Dana was in the shed now. That's what made the most sense. He hadn't left the door hanging open the way it was. He was almost sure of it now. It had to mean that she was inside. It had to mean that she was out of the rain, and if she was out of the rain, then maybe it wasn't too late. Maybe she'd gotten there quick enough that whatever had happened to Wilbur wouldn't happen to her. There were rags and tarps in the shed, and half a roll of paper towels. If she'd managed to get dry, then maybe everything would be okay. Maybe.

He went back up the stairs and followed Wilbur's muddy tracks back to the front door. The worst of the mess was right in front of the door. A throw rug had sopped up most of it, but when he bent down to test the floor, he found that the wood had gone spongy. He tried to roll up the rug to get it out of the way, but the fibers had become stiff, and bending it only forced the water out. In the end he just pulled it to the side and hoped that no one would step on it.

Outside the little window in the door, he could see the water sluicing over the tops of the metal gutters. And through them. The shed door might be open. Then again, it might not. There was no way to see through all the rain. He pressed his face to the glass and cupped his gloved hands around his eyes to block out the light of the hallway. He let his eyes adjust to the dark, but still he couldn't make out the door. All he could see was the outline of the shed, and the shed was leaning.

19

The television was quiet, but the light from it still flickered and danced on his children's faces. He should have thought to tell them to turn it off, but at least Tallie wasn't watching. She was on her back on the sofa, holding the little stuffed giraffe up at arm's length, its limbs and long neck bouncing and flopping with boneless energy. Jacob sat next to her, his eyes wide, his face pale as he stared at the screen.

"Hey," Scott said, trying to keep the fear out of his voice, trying to sound casual. "Let's you and Tallie stay out of the kitchen, okay? The floor's not safe in there."

"Dad!" Jacob seemed to come to life when he saw Scott standing in the archway. "You have to see this."

The picture on the screen was frozen, and shot through with pixelized artifacts, like another signal was trying to bleed through. The camera was out of focus and cocked at an odd angle, but Scott could still make out the stop sign in the lower left corner, the wooden utility pole just beyond it. The rest of the picture was sky, billowing gray and lit from within by glowing green. There was no blue to be seen, no break in the roiling clouds for as far as the camera could show and, Scott knew, for so much farther beyond.

The picture wasn't moving, but every few seconds it would shift, and the pixel breakup would move to a different part of the screen. Scott watched as each image overlaid the last like a slideshow, the green light in the clouds growing brighter, then fainter, as if the whole of the sky was pulsing and alive with strange energy, lightning that seemed unable to strike the ground.

"What is that?" Jacob whispered, darting a nervous glance toward Tallie to make sure she wasn't listening.

Scott shook his head. It was the same green glow in the clouds above the house, in the clouds in the video on his phone, but this seemed so much brighter. So much more alive. "Nothing good," he said quietly.

He sat down next to them on the sofa, and until that moment he hadn't realized how much he had wanted to just sit down, to do nothing and catch his breath for a minute, just long enough to quiet his racing thoughts and get his head right. He smoothed Tallie's hair beneath his hand, and for a moment the splinter in his palm didn't hurt anymore. She kicked at Jacob's leg as she bounced her giraffe, but Jacob didn't seem to notice. Scott could almost see the wheels turning behind his eyes as he watched the screen, a subtle anxiousness that Scott found worrying.

The image came to life for a few seconds before it froze again. In those seconds he watched the stop sign bend and flex in a way that made it look more like paper than steel. A dark line bobbed against the utility pole and it took him a few moments to realize it was the one of the high-tension lines, fallen to the ground. A few of the spots that he'd taken for blurry artifacts were wet streaks on the camera lens. They made him remember that there ought to be someone behind that camera, made him wonder what had happened to them.

He pulled his phone out of his pocket to check the video feed. The little loading icon spun and spun, taking its time, taking too much time. It probably wouldn't be much longer before it didn't spin at all. He wished that he'd stopped Dana from getting rid of their land line. At least those lines were buried and shielded, and might last longer than a cell tower. She'd been right about the money, but money seemed like such a distant worry right now that it barely seemed worth thinking about at all.

When the profile page for KING_CAESAR91 finally loaded, the icon at the bottom of the video thumbnail told him that the live feed had ended. The little picture was frozen on the feed's last frame, a view that looked up at the green gray sky, the awning mostly gone. Scott tried to pull up the recording, but the icon spun so long that he finally gave up. He thought about the man in the knit cap with the rust-red beard and felt a twinge of worry for this man he'd never met. He hoped that it was just that the man's phone had finally died. He hoped, but he knew better.

"What are you looking at, Daddy?"

Tallie had grabbed onto his arm and was in the process of climbing up to his shoulder so she could see his phone. He angled the screen away. "Nothing, Sweetie," he said. "Just grownup stuff."

She reached for the phone anyway, and he held it back out of her reach. She stretched for it, pushing at his face, smiling because she knew it was a game, and they had played it a hundred times before. He held her around the middle and tickled her ribs and the gleeful sound she made was maybe the best sound he'd ever heard. Tallie gave up the struggle and threw her arms around her father's neck. He was glad for her warmth, the sheer aliveness of her. He held her close, and didn't want to let go.

The picture on the television came to life again, a wash of blue light against the stop sign, against the utility pole, followed by a splash of red. Police lights. Had they been there before, when the picture moved? He couldn't be sure.

He looked to Jacob, his face slack in the glowing light. As he stared into the flickering screen there seemed to be more of the boy he was than the man he would become. How long would it be before he could see nothing of the boy at all? He wondered what Jacob would do if he reached out to comfort him. His entire existence seemed caught up in pulling away these days, and when Scott thought about trying, he found that he didn't know how.

The image on the screen crackled and froze, only to unfreeze, advancing half a second at a time. He saw someone enter the frame and hang there, half obscured by pixel-static, a digital version of an old Victorian ghost photograph. His back was to the camera, but as the picture unfroze once, then again, Scott could make out the dark police uniform he was wearing, his gunbelt hanging low and shining in the flashing lights, the fabric of his uniform clinging wet to his skin.

The scene started moving again and Scott watched the cop lurch toward the utility pole, teetering like a monster in an old black-and-white movie. He hung there, off-balance, as the picture froze again. It hung like that a while, long enough for Scott to wonder where the picture was coming from, long enough to try to read the patch on the side of the policeman's sleeve.

When the picture finally started up again, the policeman stood next to the utility pole with both hands on it like he was trying to push it over. Scott sat up with a start. The policeman swung his head into the pole, over and over, like some mad woodpecker. Again and again the head crashed into the wood, rapid-fire, like a hammer against a nail, until the image froze again, the head blurred in mid-swing.

"Ow. Daddy, you're squeezing!"

Scott's hands sprang open out of reflex, but he managed to keep Tallie pressed against his chest as he fumbled for the remote. He turned the TV off, but not before the picture changed a final time, the policeman crumpled on the ground and glistening in the rain, a smear of blood, black as oil, dripping from the wooden pole where his head had struck it.

The room went dark, but the haunted look on his son's face stayed burned like an afterimage onto Scott's eyes.

Tallie took his face in her hands, the way she did when she wanted to talk about something important. "Daddy, why did you turn off the TV?"

The light was on in the hallway, and it put her face in shadow. They were nose-to-nose, just inches apart, and he could see on his daughter's face the beginnings of another shadow, one he didn't know how to drive away.

"The TV's not working right, Pumpkin."

"Is it because of the rain?"

"Yes, baby. It's because of the rain."

Her face scrunched, like she was smelling something bad. "I want the rain to stop," she said.

He pulled her into a hug, holding her close, holding her tight. "So do I, Sweetie," he said. "So do I."

She stiffened and pushed away from him, one hand on his neck, the balls of her feet digging painfully into his thigh. He struggled to keep her from falling over. The splinter in his palm throbbed.

"The reason," she said, frowning. "Daddy, listen. The reason I want the rain to stop is so we can have a picnic in the sunshine when the TV is working again, but the *real* reason I want the rain to stop is so we can go outside and look for Mommy."

Scott tried to pull her to him again, mostly out of fear that she might look at his face, that she might see in it how helpless he was. But she twisted away and jumped down to the couch, landing hard on her knees. She found the stuffed giraffe and bounced it in her lap, and for a moment Scott thought that maybe she'd already moved on, that it might be the end of it, at least for a little while.

"Daddy, why won't Mommy come inside?"

She didn't look up from the giraffe when she said it. Scott held his breath, hoping she'd forget, but he could tell that she was listening. He could feel Jacob's eyes on him in the darkness, waiting for him to answer, waiting for him to make things right.

"Because Mommy doesn't want to come inside," he said.

"Then I want to go *out*side." There was a pout in her voice that told him she'd been thinking about this for a while, that she wasn't going to let it go. It told him that she only saw it as a choice that he was making for her, a choice she didn't want, just another of childhood's unfathomable indignities.

"We can't, Sweetie," he said. "It isn't safe."

"Why?"

"It just isn't, Sweetie."

"But why, Daddy?"

He rubbed at his eyes. A little spot of pain was blooming right between them, just above his nose, and now that he noticed it, it seemed to be spreading.

"Because it's raining, Sweetie. It's not safe."

"But I've been out in the rain lots of times!"

"This rain is different, Sweetie. This rain might hurt you if it gets on you."

"Is that why Mommy took all her clothes off?"

The pain between his eyes flared. The pain in his palm answered it. "I don't know, Sweetie," he said. "Maybe."

"But if Mommy's out in the rain, is the rain gonna hurt Mommy?"

"I don't know!"

The words came out louder than he'd meant them to, but they kept on coming. "I don't know why Mommy went outside. I don't know what's happening and I don't know why the rain is different. I don't know when it's going to stop and I don't know when Mommy is going to come inside. I don't know if Mommy is ever going to come inside. Sometimes, that's just life, okay? Sometimes people just don't come back and they never say why."

The room grew quiet. The pain was pulsing across his forehead now, marking time with his quickened heartbeat. His fist had closed around the splinter, and it was shaking.

He could hear Tallie's breath hitching in the dark, on the verge of crying, and it shamed him. The words had just come out of him, not his own words but his father's words, and he could hear them echoing in the silence even as he squeezed his eyes shut and tried to push them away. *They don't come back and they never say why.* That was what he had told Scott, all those years ago, and they'd never spoken of it again, apart from once, when his father had been deep in his bottle and caught little Scott as he'd tried to tiptoe past. *I'm sorry*, the old man had said, raising his head off the table just long enough to get the words out. *Scotty, I'm sorry.*

"I'm sorry, Sweetie," Scott said, but he could already feel her retreating toward her brother. Jacob gathered the little girl up in his arms and settled her in his lap.

"It's okay, Tallie," Jacob said. "Dad just wants to make sure we all wait here until Mommy comes back."

"I want Mommy," Tallie said, with so much sadness in her voice that it felt like a fist closing around Scott's heart. "I want Wilbur."

"I do too," Jacob said. "But you see how dark it is out there, right? We have to wait for the sun to come out or we'll never be able to find her. Then we'd all be lost and that's no good. Right?"

He punctuated it with a little tickle that made Tallie giggle, and Scott was grateful. He was grateful that Jacob was stepping up, that Jacob *got it*, that he was finally understanding how dangerous the situation was. But beneath the gratitude was a twinge of envy at how easily Jacob was calming Tallie down, how he was able to connect with her instantly in a way that

Scott could never seem to manage. It was something that Dana did all the time, and the tone of Jacob's voice was an almost perfect copy of hers. Realizing that only made the twinge worse.

"Besides," Jacob said, "I'm sure Mom is totally safe. Right dad?"

He sounded *exactly* like Dana now, lying, making him complicit in that lie. "Yeah," Scott said meekly. "She's probably just out in the shed is all. Totally safe."

Tallie let out a frustrated sigh that made it sound like she was deflating. Scott watched her little body relax and take all the tension out of the room with it. He watched her pull the little giraffe into her lap, but she didn't bounce it. She only held it there.

"What do you say we get some light in here, okay?" Jacob leaned down until he and Tallie were nose-to-nose. "Okay?"

Tallie nodded, vigorously enough for Scott to know that the moment had passed. He breathed, and found that he *could* breathe. He could hear the white-noise drum of the rain falling outside, steady, almost comforting, punctuated by the occasional plop of dripping water.

Jacob reached over to the lamp and the light came on, so bright that Scott had to squint. Still, he could see something glistening on the wooden end table, something that banished the calm in an instant and set his heart thundering again.

"Jacob, stop!" Scott lunged and grabbed Tallie by the arm. She screamed as he pulled her to his chest, the sound muffled against his shirt as Jacob stared at him, his arm still poised below the lampshade. The shade was wet, melted out of shape, and a puddle had formed below it on the end table. Above it, drops of water bulged from a dark brown patch on the ceiling.

20

The bucket in Jacob's room had overfilled and run over. The carpet all around it was sodden and dark. Scott stood in the doorway—Tallie still crying, still pressed to his chest—and stared at the ceiling. The drip had grown into a steady, pencil-width stream. All around the spot, the ceiling had turned gray, the plaster bulging, suffused with a roadmap of dark tendrils just under the paint, like varicose veins.

Scott lifted Tallie into Jacob's arms. "Stay out of there," he said, and started back down the stairs. "Keep her out out of there."

He took the steps two at a time, and landed hard at the bottom. The heavy rubber gloves were on the coffee table where he'd left them. He snatched them up and made it partway up the stairs again before he stopped and reversed himself. The bucket wasn't going to be enough, not with the way the water was coming in. He careened into the kitchen, throwing open cabinets, searching under the sink. He would have given anything for another of the big buckets, but he had left them in the shed with everything else that was out of his reach. He settled on the box of black garbage bags and hoped it would be enough.

"All right, stay back," he said, and Jacob backed away down the hallway. Tallie was quiet now, and that was something. He'd talk to her as soon as he was done, apologize for being so rough. *Daddy was just scared*, he'd tell her, and it wouldn't be a lie.

The bucket was full to the brim with cloudy gray water, it's sides bulging out of shape, melting. When he grabbed it with his gloved hands it buckled and the water sloshed over the side. It couldn't be helped, but he sound of the water plopping onto the already-wet carpet still made him wince. He carried the bucket out, trying to go slow but still moving too fast, his arms out in front of him like he was holding something on fire. Heavy drops splashed onto the hallway floor, and he took dancing steps to keep from getting his feet wet.

When he got to the bathroom he dumped the bucket out in the tub, wincing again at the thought of what the rainwater might be doing to the drainpipes. They were ancient, probably made of lead, and he didn't know if that was better or worse. It was a problem for later, though. The problem for right now was still coming down from the bedroom ceiling. He got the bucket back under it, yanking his hand back when the first few drops splashed up from the bottom.

"Did you get any on you?"

Jacob stood in the doorway, bouncing Tallie to calm her, the way Dana always did. He stared at Scott, not comprehending.

"Downstairs!" Scott said. "Did you get any water on you?"

"No."

"Are you sure?" he lunged closer, looking over his son's hands, looking for spots of wetness on his shoulders, on his sleeves.

"Dad! I'm sure!"

Scott caught his breath, listening to the water drumming into the bottom of the bucket, the sound of it so steady it was almost soothing. Tallie and Jacob watched him from the doorway, safe enough for now, at least.

"Towels," Scott said. "I need towels."

"What kind?"

"Any kind. Big as you can find. Hurry."

Jacob disappeared around the corner and took Tallie with him. That was good, he thought. Keep them away from all this. Keep them dry. He pulled a garbage bag off the roll and shook it open. The opening wasn't wide, but it was enough to make a little reservoir around the bottom of the bucket. He'd just managed to slide it into place when Jacob appeared again in the doorway, Tallie on his hip, a stack of mismatched towels draped over one arm.

"Great," Scott said as he took the stack with both hands. Some of them were the good towels, barely six months old, and he could hear Dana in his head, complaining bitterly. *That's fine*, he thought. *If she wants to complain she can come right back in from the rain and do it*. Only, he didn't want that either. Not really. Not anymore.

He spread the towels out around the bag and pressed down on them with his gloved hands. It took a while, but before long they were dark and soaked through. The floor beneath them was solid, at least for now, but the carpet was still wet. He wondered what it would take to pull it up before the water got too deep into the floorboards, but decided it was all right for now. It would have to be.

"Okay, keep back," he said as he gathered the first towel into a ball, careful not to squeeze out its contents, careful not to let it drape past the edge of the gloves and onto his bare arms. One by one he carried them out to the bathroom and laid them into the tub. He thought about wringing them out, but didn't want to risk getting himself wet. He didn't want to send all that rainwater rushing down the drain.

All the while, Tallie watched him from the safety of her brother's arms, watching him do this new thing, this desperate thing, with wide eyes beneath a furrowed brow. Scott had worked so hard to keep her insulated from this, from all of it, but there was no hiding it now. Did she understand what was happening? The fear was plain on her face, but was she scared in spite of what he was doing, or because of it?

He wiped the gloves on a dry corner of a towel and peeled them off before he went back to the kids. His breathing was back under control now, and when he turned back to his children, he put his hands on his knees to stop them from shaking.

"Are you sure you didn't get any on you?"

"Yeah, Dad," Jacob said, a note of annoyance creeping into his voice. "I'm sure."

"How about you, Sweetie? Did any of the water get on you?"

Tallie only frowned and retreated beneath Jacob's arm.

"Sweetie," Scott said softly, making his voice calm, doing everything he could to project quiet authority. "I know Daddy scared you, but everything's okay now." He frowned a little at the lie, and hoped neither of them would notice.

"You hurt my *arm*." She spit the last word at him, her face scrunched up as mean as she could make it.

"I know, Sweetie." His voice cracked a little as he said it, and he cleared his throat to bring it back in line. "Daddy got a little scared is all, and I'm sorry. But everything's all right now. I just need to know if any of the water dripped on you, okay?"

She softened a little at this, and rubbed her hands together. She frowned, as if she had only just noticed that they were empty. "I want Gilbert."

"Who's Gilbert, Sweetie?"

"It's her giraffe," Jacob said. "She must have dropped it downstairs."

Scott did his best to smile. "Sweetie. Look at me, Pumpkin, okay? I'll go downstairs and get Gilbert, but first you have to tell me if any of the water got on you. Okay?"

Tallie raised her chin and made a show of shaking her head from side to side.

"Does that mean you didn't get wet, or that you don't want to tell me?"

"I didn't get wet." She said it with such an air of finality that it sent a shudder of relief all through his body.

He took a deep breath, forced himself to slow down. "Okay, Sweetie. You stay here and I'll go get Gilbert."

"Daddy?"

"Yes, Pumpkin?"

"Is our house gonna fall down?"

He opened his mouth to tell her no, but stopped. *Holy shit. Was it?* He'd been thinking in terms of leaks and superficial damage, things that he could fix once the rain passed. But what if the rain didn't pass? And even if it did, what if it went on so long that it left nothing behind to fix?

"No, Sweetie," he said. "The house is going to be fine. It's just a leak is all."

Her look softened and he could tell that she believed him, even as Jacob's faraway stare told him that his son did not.

"I want Mommy," she said, burying her face in Jacob's shirt.

"I do too, Pumpkin," Scott said, relieved at last to be able to tell her something that was true.

"Keep her here for a minute," Scott said. Jacob nodded his head. "And if the bucket starts to get full, come get me. Do not touch it. Clear?"

Again Jacob nodded. His wide eyes gave him a shell-shocked look. Scott wanted to pull him into a hug, but could only bring himself to settle a hand on his shoulder, holding it there until his son looked him in the eye.

"It's going to be fine," Scott said. "I promise."

Jacob nodded again, and this time he seemed to deflate a little, as if the weight he'd been carrying had finally fallen away. Scott knew that Jacob wanted his mother back as much as Tallie did, maybe even more so because he could understand the implications of what was going on outside. He played at being an adult so much that Scott had taken to treating him like one. But he was still just a kid, and he was still looking to his dad to make things right. Scott knew that he had to pretend that he could still do that, for as long as he could manage.

The stairs creaked as he went downstairs. This wasn't the dry-wood squeaking that was so much a part of this place that he barely noticed it was there. This was a new sound, a weary sound, as if the boards had grown tired and were threatening to give way beneath his feet. He stepped around the mess on the hallway floor, keeping his distance, not wanting to take chances.

The lamp was still on in the front room, and it flickered as the power bottomed out, only to blaze up again an instant later. It wouldn't be long before the electricity failed entirely. Above the lamp he could see the wet patch on the ceiling. The drip was coming slower now, or at least he imagined it was slower. From where he was standing it looked like any old leaky ceiling. There was no sign of the dark tendrils he had seen upstairs and in the basement, at least not yet.

He didn't have to look long for Gilbert. The little giraffe had fallen onto the end table beneath the lamp. Its stuffed legs were in the air, pointed skyward. Its head lay in the little puddle of water, and when the ceiling dripped again the water splashed up into its black marble eye. Scott thought of the mouse again, lying in its shallow grave, the little box probably soaked through by now. Had the dog dug it up, the way Dana had said he would? Probably not. If anything, the dog was long gone by now. Or dead. Maybe both.

Scott picked up the giraffe by one of the legs. It's head drooped, heavy and waterlogged. He knew then that he'd have to get rid of the thing. The thought clenched down on his insides, that Tallie would never hug the little giraffe to her chest again, and filled him with a deep sense of mourning that he couldn't account for. The toy seemed as much a part of her as her arm, and he had failed to protect her, even in this. How could he expect to keep her safe, keep any of them safe, when he couldn't even protect her favorite toy?

Another drop fell from the ceiling, a wet slap against the wooden table. In that moment he could almost see the blue tumbler sitting there, close to the edge. It had been made of plastic but molded to look like cracked glass, and it had always been his mother's favorite. He kept in on a high shelf in the cabinet where it never got used. Someone had gotten it down. Dana. It had to be.

A memory flooded back to to him then, a smaller Scott with smaller hands reaching up for the thing, his mother pulling it back with a smile. *No, no, Scotty*, she had said softly, the memory so clear that he could almost hear her now. *That's not a drink for little boys.* It had looked like orange juice, but the smell it stirred into the air was sharp and made his nostrils tingle. He'd found the tumbler in the cabinet a few days after mother had left, and he'd taken it down and drank his juice from it at breakfast that morning. His father had stared at it the whole time, frowning. Scott never saw it again, not until after his father died.

He'd forgotten all about that until just that moment, but now the memory was so vivid that it may as well have been an image on the TV screen. And yet, in all of it, he could barely picture his mother's face. He could remember her smile, white teeth behind faded red lipstick. Why couldn't he remember her eyes?

The rain drummed against the siding, against the windows. The sound was making him nostalgic. Or was it just soothing? He wished that he could lose himself to it, that he could hear nothing but the rain, feel nothing but the rain. The fire in the distance had mostly died out, but the smoke was still billowing, getting lost amid the low clouds. The kids were still upstairs, waiting for him, depending on him, and yet, with the heavy sound of the rain he could almost imagine that he was the only one left in this world, that everything would turn out all right if he could just close his eyes and listen.

But it wasn't just the rain he was hearing. There was another sound beneath it, a new sound, halting and mechanical. An engine running rough. It rattled in the distance, somewhere up the road. With it came the rumble of gravel crunching beneath big tires, and it was getting closer.

21

I t was definitely a vehicle of some kind, old and on the verge of breaking down. Its engine struggled, belts whining, muffler barely doing its job. It was out on the road, hard to say how far away, but it was getting closer. It wasn't the police. If it was, there'd be sirens, and he'd never heard a cop car that sounded on its last legs the way this one did.

Whatever it was, it was moving fast, fast enough that Scott figured it would pass them right by. He hoped it would pass them right by and ignore this old farm house in the middle of nowhere, being eaten by the rain. The stuffed giraffe was still in his hand, its sodden head drooping low, dripping onto the armrest. He dropped it behind the sofa, where it landed with a soft plop. The sound made him think of the cop on the television, bashing his own brains out on the telephone pole. He felt the weight of the gun in his belt, and hoped that he wouldn't have to use it.

He crept back toward the hallway, careful to not let his shadow fall across the windows. The curtains were drawn but there were enough gaps that someone wouldn't have trouble seeing through them if they got close.

But they're not going to get close, he told himself. Whoever they are, they're just passing by. They're not going to stop at some old farm house, even with the lights on. He cursed himself for leaving them on, but turning them off now would be worse. Turning them off now would be as good as telling them someone was inside.

The engine was louder now, straining like some overclocked old hot rod. Something popped, a sound as loud as a gunshot, followed by a high-pitched whine as the whole engine changed pitch and began to sputter.

Jacob was at the top of the stairs, Tallie still balanced on his hip. With the flat of his hand, Scott motioned for them to stay back. Jacob's eyes were wide with fear and questions, questions that Scott silenced by bringing his finger to his lips. He listened to the approaching engine, waiting for the sound to recede. He told himself that, whatever it was, it would pass. It would have to pass. He listened and waited for it to move on down the road so he could breathe again.

But it didn't move down the road. Its brakes screeched and he heard the thing skid. The sound was followed by a heavy clunk, like something in its suspension snapping, like a wheel falling off. Scott felt his insides tighten as it turned onto the long, gravel driveway. He crouched low and crept to the window, listening as it drew closer. It was heavy, and its wheels slipped against the gravel like it was fighting for traction. Up close, the sound of it was enough to rattle the windows, enough that he could feel its vibrations shaking their way up through the floorboards.

Headlights played across the windows as the truck lurched to a stop. Scott could see it now through the gap in the curtains, a familiar black pickup truck, though the black was peppered with lighter patches where the paint had worn away. The front tire on the driver's side was flat, the wheel canted inward as if the suspension had snapped.

Smoke rose from the engine, almost blue against the dark gray sky. It was hard to believe that this was the same pickup he had seen just this morning, shining like new. The door swung open with a loud creak, and as if to remove any doubt, a hunched figure stumbled out, a cowboy hat still perched on top of his head.

"Scott!" Ned Colby called. "Scotty! Scotty my boy! Come on out! I wanna talk business!"

His voice was hoarse and cracking, wet, like he was gargling spit. In the light from the headlights he stood out in silhouette, shirt plastered to his skin, hat drooping. His steps were heavy as he lumbered to the porch, his boots thudding hollow against the decking.

"Come on out here, Scott!" He punctuated the words by banging against the door three times, hard enough to rattle it in its frame, loud enough to make Scott flinch.

"I know you're in there, Scott." Ned's voice was softer now, conspiratorial. "I know you ain't got nowhere else to be, not until this rain clears up. Hell, maybe not even then."

Ned tittered at this, giggling in a high pitch that Scott wouldn't have thought the big man was capable of. He banged against the door again, not with a knock this time but with his shoulder. "Git on out here, damnit! Come out on the porch where we can talk a while. Maybe that fine wife of yours can even bring us some lem-o-nade!"

He shouldered the door once more, colliding with a thud. Scott thought he heard the doorframe crack. The screws he'd put in at the top and bottom were long, and he figured they'd stay put longer than the latch would. At least, he hoped they would.

Heavy footsteps creaked, moving slow, stalking the length of the outside wall. The light in the front room might be enough for Ned to peek inside if he got a mind to, enough to find Scott crouching there. And yet, Scott couldn't bring himself to move for fear of giving himself away. Scott couldn't see Ned through the gap in the curtains, but he could smell the sour tang of gasoline, and beneath it the scent of burning, like charred meat left out in the rain.

"Aw, Scott. Don't be like that," Ned said, sounding like he was right on top of him. "I just wanna talk about those twelve-point-six acres of yours. Though if it's one blade of grass over eight I'll be dipped in shit and dance like a monkey."

The decking creaked again, boot heels on rough wood, as if Ned had broken into some kind of shuffling two-step. It ended with a series of stomps, like he was trying to put his foot right through the the porch. From the sound of it, he came close to succeeding.

"You see, Scotty," Ned said, breathing heavy, his throat full and rattling. "I haven't been a hundred percent honest with you. And I believe that honesty is the only way for two men to do business, don't you?"

Ned's shadow fell across the gap in the curtains as he backed away from the windows toward the railing. In the headlights, Scott could see the man's arms, bare, with the sleeves rolled up to his elbows. They were covered with scabs that oozed yellow against his rain-slick skin. The shirt was burned away at his shoulder. The skin beneath it was charred and peeling up in papery, black flakes.

"I lied, Scott. I lied to you about wanting this land. Not that I lied about wanting it, because oh, Scotty, I absolutely do. And I mean to have it, too. But I did lie to you, Scott, even if I only lied about why."

He put his hands on the railing to steady himself, his chin to his chest, like it was hard for him to breathe. "You see, this land..." Here he paused to work a wad of phlegm up from the back of his throat and spit it down onto the decking. "This land, Scott, it's like a great big puzzle. And you're sitting on the very last piece. The last piece, Scott! And you know how it is with the last piece of a puzzle. I know you do. It just sits there, mocking you, and all you can do it stare at it and worry about it like you're tonguing a loose tooth all day long until you finally just pop the damn thing in!"

Ned squeezed down hard on the rain-soaked wood. His fingers sank into it, and wet splinters came away in his hands.

This seemed to put him in a rage, and he pounded his fists against the rail, swinging his arms in great, wrecking-ball blows against the slats, breaking them easily, sending them spinning into the yard. Scott scooted back from the curtain. He could still see Ned through the gap. A piece of rail dangled from his forearm, pinned there by a length of nail. The big man didn't even seem to notice.

Ned stood huffing, looking out at his truck, looking out at the yard as if he'd forgotten where he was. Scott sat holding his breath, watching, willing the big man to get back in his truck and just leave. But the big man did not leave. He gathered himself up and threw himself at one of the support beams that held up the porch roof. The sound of the impact reverberated through the house, shaking the walls. From somewhere upstairs, he heard Tallie cry out, only for the sound to be abruptly muffled. Jacob's hand over her mouth, he thought. That was good. If he could keep her quiet, he could keep her safe.

Ned slammed against the pillar again, and this time Scott heard something crack as the house shook, only he couldn't tell if the sound came from the pillar or from something inside Ned. He hoped it was the latter, and a distant part of him hated himself for the thought. Ned took one last run at the pillar and staggered backward, shaking his head. He stood, panting, standing taller with each breath, collecting himself. The rotted board still hung impaled against his arm.

"Sorry about that, Scott." For a moment, his voice seemed almost normal, like they were back to this morning, the two of them just talking in the rising heat of a cloudless day. "I just get a little passionate when I think about you taking away what's mine. And I'm gonna have the whole place plowed down to the ground anyway, so just think of it as a head start."

He giggled again at that, a high, percussive tittering that seemed too light, too childlike to come out of an adult mouth.

He turned back toward the house, and in the harsh glow of the headlights, Scott could see his eyes, how the whites went all the way around. He didn't think that Ned had seen him, not yet at least, but Scott didn't imagine that he'd stop with just breaking the railing. Again, he thought about the gun at his back, about how much longer it might be before he had no choice but to use it.

"Cause the land, Scott... The land ain't worth nothin' all by itself. You know it. I know it. You know I know it, and I know that you know that I know..." Here he giggled again, high and sinister, like a villain in a cartoon. "But what's under this land? What's been under it all this time, just waiting for me? Well, Scotty my boy, it's more money than you've ever dreamed of. It's more than money. It's *wealth*. The kind of wealth that changes lives. The kind of wealth that buys entire towns with plenty left over."

He pulled off the hat and ran a hand across his rain-slick scalp. It was then that he finally noticed the board dangling from his arm. He regarded it curiously, scrunching his face like he was trying to figure out how it got there. He pulled it away, and when the nail slid out of his flesh it had to be three inches long, maybe more. A rivulet of blood rolled down from the wound, black in the dying glow of the headlights.

"Course, they have to do all kinds of pumping and fracking and cracking just to get it up out of there, but as long as they do it from *my* land, I get what's mine, you see? Easy peasy lemon squeezie. Only, I got to thinkin', what happens when they get it in mind to do it from *your* land, from this land? Maybe you'd let 'em do it cheaper, given you're one step from the poorhouse. What happens to all my *wealth*, then? I'll tell you what happens. You stick your big-ol' drill in the ground and drink my whole future away like a big goddamn mosquito!"

Ned doubled over then, as if he'd been punched in the gut. With the big man's back turned, Scott moved back from the gap in the curtains and pressed himself against the far wall. Ned's shadow staggered in the glow of the headlights as Scott pulled the gun from his belt.

"Well, I can't have that happen, Scott. I just can't. I was driving over this way to tell you so, but then it occurred to me, just like a flash. It's simple, really. You can't take what's mine if I just take what's yours first."

The broken board was still in Ned's hand, and he swung it experimentally at the window glass. It made a wet smack, not strong enough to break the pane but enough to set it shaking. The nail squeaked a crooked path down the glass. The scratch it left behind was tinged with blood.

"I figure you ain't got no next of kin." Ned traced the scratch with one dirty finger. "Not with your daddy in the ground and your mama run off to who-knows-where, maybe still whorin' around, probably dead. Ain't no one gonna come askin' questions if a man and his family dies all accidental-like, not in a storm like this."

He swung the board against the glass again, harder this time. Scott jumped at the sound, his heart in his throat, the gun still behind him, his fingers curled around the grip.

"Then again, I figure, maybe it doesn't have to be the four of you. Maybe you is all I need. I've seen the way that pretty wife of yours looks at me, Scott. And I see the way she looks at you, all disappointed and such. Can't say I blame her." He raised his voice, rough and croaking. "Are you in there, sweetheart? A fine woman like you, I'd bet you'd appreciate the chance to trade up. Get yourself some attention from a man of means!"

Another strike on the glass. The board broke into splinters and fell to the ground, but not before Scott heard the sharp snap of cracking glass.

"And don't you worry about those kids, Scott. I don't think they'll mind at all. Hell, I'll bet they'd be happy to get themselves a new daddy."

Ned laughed, wheezing, trailing away into a cough. Even when he was done, Scott could hear him huffing on the other side of the wall, his chest rattling and thick with phlegm. The porch boards creaked beneath his weight as he shifted, and for a moment Scott thought that he might have forgotten again, that he might be moving on. Scott's muscles started to unclench. His grip on the gun loosened. But the moment was gone in an instant as the window glass broke, great shards of it snapping off to shatter against the floor below.

A length of pitted wood jutted from the upper pane of the window, wagging back and forth, attempting to clear the glass from the frame but not succeeding. The sharp edges dug into the wood until, after a few tries, it fell apart. A hand darted in to replace it, swollen, with scabs across the knuckles. Fingers curled around the jagged glass and pulled. The glass didn't budge, and when the hand came away it left behind streaks of red.

Scott scrambled back on all fours toward the hallway as Ned's face appeared in the opening. His eyes were wide and he was wearing a lopsided grin. A vacant smile. An elevator doesn't go all the way to the top smile. His skin had gone gray and barely looked like skin at all apart from the way it clung loose to his cheekbones. The ear above his burned shoulder was shriveled and blackened, like meat left on a grill too long. A crusty sore, cracked and weeping, blossomed along his cheek.

"I would have paid you, Scott." Ned's eyes were unfocused, and he was calling out to the empty room. Scott held his breath. Ned didn't even seem to know he was there. "I would have paid you and you could have left this place behind months ago. Started fresh, put your whole worthless life in the rear-view."

Ned's face retreated, and a meaty arm felt its way through the break, searching for the latch. It, too, was covered with scabs, and Scott could see traces of silvery-black tendrils working their way below the skin.

"You could have just been *reasonable*, Scott." The arm was in up to the shoulder now, the broken glass catching on the rolled-up shirt sleeve. "It takes effort to be unreasonable. At least, that's what my Daddy used to say to me. 'Ned,' he'd say, 'you show me a man who's being unreasonable and I'll show you a man who's working way too hard,' Well, Scott, you're making me work pretty fucking hard right now. So, I guess I'm going to have to show you just how *unreasonable* I can be."

His fingers found the latch in the center of the windowsill and yanked it open. The arm drew back, catching on the broken glass as it went. One jagged edge sliced deep into the scab across the forearm, spilling a thick run of snotty yellow pus onto the dusty windowsill.

Hands pressed flat against the lower pane, squeaking against the glass, trying to slide it upward. When it didn't move, they reached inside, pawing at the frame, grasping with clumsy fingers. The window gave out a screech as it slid, first by an inch, then more, until a gap opened up beneath it. The hands retreated past the jagged glass, only to reappear as the tips of probing fingers, reaching in over the sill.

Scott gripped the gun in both hands and held it steady. Ned grunted and the window slid up another inch, protesting with a squeal as the swollen wood gave way. Scott pulled the hammer back, wondering if he could make Ned leave with just a warning shot. The gun shook in his grasp. He'd shot at the dog out of reflex, but this? This was different. He'd never shot a human being, and Ned was still a human being, despite what the rain had done to him.

A thump came from upstairs, the sound of a door closing. Scott thought of Tallie huddling against her brother, afraid, maybe even crying. He thought of Jacob trying to keep them both safe, knowing all the while that their father could not.

The gun grew steady then. He sighted down the barrel at the dark gap beneath the window and held his breath.

With a harsh groan of wood against wood, the window went up the rest of the way. The hands retreated, and for an instant there was a terrible, all-encompassing quiet, no sound but the steady droning of the rain. Again, the hope rose in him that Ned—what had used to be Ned—had wandered away and wouldn't come back. Then the head—that terrible head—inched its way through the opening. The absurd cowboy hat was gone, the rain-slick scalp singed black and peeling up like old paint. The skin was a minefield of sores, the topography of some other planet in some other time, volcanoes oozing, pushing up mountains.

Scott steadied the gun. His finger tightened around the trigger. Ned turned his head and stared at him, not Ned any more but some crazed parody of Ned, wild the way a rabid animal was wild. It stared at him, and it smiled.

"I'm taking it back, Scotty," it said, its voice almost still Ned's voice. "I'm taking it all back!"

He struggled over the windowsill, pulling himself inside by his bloody hands. Scott imagined Ned knocking the gun aside and cracking his head open on the hardwood floor. He imagined him lurching up the stairs, Jacob meeting him at the top only to be thrown down to the bottom, his bones crunching. He imagined Tallie, helpless, those bloody fingers closing around her tiny neck.

Before he could squeeze the trigger, what was left of the window glass shattered, exploding over Ned's back and onto the floor. The wooden frame splintered and the crosspiece fell away with a hollow clatter. Ned slumped over the sill, half inside the opening. He let out a wet rattle of breath that trailed off into a sigh, and then he grew still.

A curved handle of polished wood stood up from his back, the head of an axe buried deep between his shoulder blades.

22

Something moved in the light from the pickup truck that spilled in through the broken window. Its shadow fell across Ned's body, across the handle of the axe jutting out from the man's back. The gun trembled at the end of Scott's outstretched arm. Through the opening, he could hear faint music coming from the truck's radio, Ned's boot-scoot honky-tonk, draining down the last of the battery. The axe was sunk so deep that he could barely see the head of it at all. It had severed Ned's spine, and probably found his heart in the process. Whoever—whatever—had swung it was strong, unnaturally strong. They would have to be to get that old, dull axe through so much meat and bone.

"Sweetie?" a voice called from just beyond the opening. "Scott, honey? Could you come outside for a minute? I think it's time we talked."

Her voice was low and throaty, the way Ned's had been low and throaty, but there was still enough of Dana's old musicality in it to make Scott's heart give a hopeful lurch. And yet, he found himself backing away, pointing the gun into the empty space beyond the broken window.

"It's safe now," Dana said. "I made sure of that, didn't I?" The axe listed toward him, its handle smooth with wet and wear. He hadn't sharpened it in years and it had still gone through Ned's back like he was made of butter. As if she had sensed Scott's thoughts, the thing outside the window gave out a laugh, a high titter that descended into a low chuckle, like the croaking of a frog.

"You see how I protect you, Scott? Even though you turn me away, lock me out of my own home? You see how I still protect you? How I protect our children?"

A pale hand reached in through the opening. It picked idly at the broken glass that had fallen onto Ned's back, flicking it away like bits of lint on a sweater. The fingers seemed too long, the knuckles too bony. Along the bulging tendons, he could see a raised roadmap of veins, almost black beneath skin so pale that it seemed translucent.

"I'm not going to let anything hurt you, Scott. If you'd just come outside, you'd see that."

A breeze drew the curtain back, revealing a bare shoulder, the same pale skin stretched taut across the thin blade of her scapula. A large scab trailed along the ribs and disappeared beneath her rain-soaked hair, not weeping, but caked solid, like packed-on mud.

"You're afraid of me, aren't you? That's why you're stuck in there, hiding. Isn't it?"

The slender arm rose. Fingers found the axe handle, tracing it with a lover's touch.

"Is it because of this? This was never meant for you, Scott. I could never do that. Oh, no."

From behind the curtain, she let out another high giggle, accompanied by a throaty warble, as if two voices were coming out of her at the same time.

"Of course, I thought about it," the low voice said. "How easy it would be to just... chop the door down. Just like that."

The head slid past the curtain and into the opening, face shrouded in dripping hair. He checked his grip on the gun as it slipped against his sweating palms.

"I could drag all of you out kicking and screaming if I had to." She was looking down at Ned's body draped over the windowsill, admiring her handiwork. Her hair hung low, obscuring her features. Fat drops of water dripped from it to mingle with the blood on Ned's back. "I could force you, Scott. I could make you see."

The head turned, slowly, inch by terrible inch, until at last she was facing him. A fall of hair draped over sharpened cheekbones, across a nose that had become too pointed. One eye stared out from the tangled mess, cloudy blue stippled with red.

"I wouldn't even have to break the door down anymore. Do you see how easy it would be? You see that, don't you?"

The lips split into a crooked smile, baring teeth. The eye shifted from Scott's face to the gun in his hands and then back again. Above it was a thin crease, like a puckered wound across her forehead. She caught him staring at it, and somehow the smile grew even wider.

"But I don't want that, Scott," the thing in the window said, retreating slowly back behind the curtain, taking its time. "And I know you don't want that."

When he couldn't see her anymore, Scott let out his breath and felt himself deflate. His arms were shaking again and his legs had begun to wobble. But she wasn't gone. He could hear her on the other side of the wall, long nails tapping and scraping at the siding as it moved.

"You think I'm a bad mother, don't you? You think I'd do something to hurt our children? Do it on purpose? Is that it?" The voice was muffled now, almost lost beneath the sound of the driving rain, as if her mouth were pressed to the siding, pressed to his ear, whispering for him alone. "That man would have killed you, Scott. Killed our *babies*. But I saved you. I saved you when you couldn't even save yourself."

She was at the front door now. Scott shifted, moving back against the stairs where he wouldn't have to see that terrible eye staring in through the little window above the doorknob.

He held the gun in both hands. The barrel trembled in front of his lips, close enough to kiss.

"I wish you could see yourself right now," the voice said, louder now, almost spitting the words. "Cowering inside that ridiculous old house, afraid of a little rain." The doorknob rattled in emphasis, turning back and forth so violently that he thought it might fall off. He edged back against the railing and pointed the gun at the door. The screws he had driven into it were loose, but they were holding, at least for now. The doorknob turned once more, and grew still.

"That's all it is, Scott," the voice said, almost pleading, sounding so much like Dana that it made his heart ache. "Just a little rain. And if you'd just come outside, you'd see that it's beautiful! It's so beautiful that I can't even describe it, so beautiful that it almost hurts. I want you to see it, Scott. I want the kids to see it too."

Behind him, the curtains bellowed with a gust of wind. He spun toward it, imagining that pale, almost skeletal hand reaching for him through the broken window, but there was nothing there. When the voice spoke again, it seemed to come from everywhere at once.

"And you *can* see it, Scott. You all can! And once you do, we'll be a family again. Don't you want that, Scott? To be a family again? We can do that if you'll just *come out and look with me*, Scott. All you need are the right kind of eyes. I can help you find the right kind of eyes, Scott. You won't need the old ones anymore, I promise. All they ever saw was pain."

All was silent for a moment, silent except for the patter of the rain and the rush of his own pulse in his ears. He didn't know where one ended and the other began. When the voice spoke again, it carried to him in a low growl.

"Would you *please* just come outside, Scott?"

Silence again, so thick that it felt as if the very air was choked with it.

"Damn it, Scott! Would you just come outside!"

The voice boomed and Scott fell back, tripping and scrambling against the stairs. He held the gun, arms stiff, pointing it at the window, at the door, at the window again. But nothing came. He listened to the rain, knowing that Dana—if it was still Dana—was standing just on the other side of the wall, just feet away but so far apart that the two of them might as well be in different worlds. He could feel her presence there, listening for him the same way he was listening for her. He heard the porch boards creak as her weight shifted, footfalls soft and wet against the old wood.

And then, all at once, she was gone.

He sat for a while, listening to the rain and to the sound of his own breathing before he crept to the window to look for her. He took his time, stepping softly around Ned's body as the wind billowed the curtains, bringing with it a sickly-sweet smell, like rotting leaves. The engine on the pickup truck had quit, and its headlamps were dimmer now, the honky-tonk music silenced. Light flashed across the sky, and for an instant he could see the old shed, collapsed to ruins, its roof sunken in on top of splintered walls that had grown too weak to hold it.

23

Scott tried to take the stairs at a run but tripped on the second step. He came down hard, twisting to catch himself on his shoulder, sending an electric jolt down his arm that turned his fingers numb. The pain drove the panic from his mind, and as it faded he found that he could think again.

He listened for sounds from upstairs, but there was nothing. There was no way Dana could get up there from the outside, not without him hearing. And anyway, she was long gone, back to her hiding place. Beneath the willow tree, most likely, now that the shed was gone. She wouldn't be back. Not right away.

I could drag all of you out kicking and screaming if I had to. That terrible eye came back to him, framed in a tangle of dripping hair. *I could force you. I could make you see.*

He forced himself to breathe. His chest loosened a little with every exhalation. The gun was still in his hand, his finger still curled around the trigger. *Jesus, it could have gone off*, he thought. He could have shot himself, shot one of the kids. He reached with his free hand and eased the hammer back, untangling the grip from his trembling fingers as he set the gun down on the step. He didn't want to touch it anymore, didn't want to even look at it, because all he could see there were his father's hands, the muzzle of the stray dog as it thumped its tail.

His forehead was wet. *Sweat*, he told himself, *not the rain*. He'd been careful to stay away from the window, away from the drip in the ceiling. And yet, there was a part of him, a part he'd shoved down so deep, that wanted it to be the rain, that wanted to follow Dana out into the storm. That part of him wanted to dance with her in his arms, to feel the water falling on their bare skin. They'd argued, but he could barely remember what it was about. She'd hurt him once, but that hurt seemed like such a nothing now.

From his place on the stairs he stared at the front door. He could almost see himself taking a hammer and yanking the screws out like rusty old nails. The thought was like a magnetic pull that sent an icy tingle down his spine. It rooted his legs to the spot. It would be so easy though, just the work of a few seconds to take out those screws. Then he could follow her. The thought of it being just that simple terrified him.

Old photos stared down at him from the wall along the staircase, pictures of his father, of his father before that. Aunts and uncles whose names he could no longer remember. His grandmother, her lips thin and unsmiling. She'd only lived to be forty-three, but she'd died in this house. There was a plot in Mount Hope Cemetery where he could visit her body, though he'd never been moved to. There wasn't a picture of Scott's mother, but his father was there, leaning against the side of his old car, staring out at him from the crooked brass frame. He could no longer picture his mother any more, but he could never forget his father's face.

Scott felt the weight of his gaze, the way his eyes seemed to follow his every move. It occurred to him then that he could have taken the picture down. He could have taken them all down, thrown them away or put them in the shed with the rest of his father's things where he'd never have to look at them again. These were his father's memories, the same way this was still his father's house, the same way he slept in his father's bedroom and ate his meals at his father's table.

Dana had been right. There was nothing of her in this place, but there was nothing of Scott in it either. There should have been pictures of *his* kids on that wall, pictures of *his* wife. Maybe if Dana had been able to see herself in these walls, see everything the two of them had built together, she never would have strayed in the first place. Maybe he never would have driven her out into the rain, and she'd be safe inside with him now. They could have waited here, together, for the storm to pass. When it was done they could have walked out into the sunlight, the four of them, together.

But instead of filling the place with life, he'd left it to wither and die. He hadn't touched a thing, not the curtains, not the pictures, not the wood splintering away from the railing. He'd never realized why until that moment. It was because that's the way it had been when his mother left him. Because if he kept it all the same, maybe this place could be a beacon to lead her back to him.

Scott reached out to straighten that crooked picture of his father, but took it down instead. How long had it been since he'd thought about the stray dog? Years, maybe more than a decade. He'd barely remembered it at all until he and Tallie had buried that mouse. He hadn't remembered, until now, how this man in the picture had taken the belt to him when he'd cried over his missing mother. The old man hadn't even let him grieve.

Jacob and Tallie hadn't had a chance to grieve either. There hadn't been time. Scott hadn't stopped to consider, even once, that they might be hurting too, that if the rain didn't let up soon they might never see their mother again, either. He could fix that, too. All of it. It would be easy, so easy, just to go outside, to take them all out into the rain. He'd be lying to himself if he said that he hadn't wanted to do that too, that maybe he'd wanted it from the beginning. Otherwise, he would have used more screws to seal up the door.

His father stared out at him from the photograph in his hands, watching in silent judgment, finding him lacking. It was as if he had already made up his mind all those years ago about a son who hadn't even been born yet, as if he knew what would happen to this house that had stood for almost a century, only to crumble to pieces under the care of his hapless only child. Scott resented that stare. He'd withered under it for his whole life, and hated that he withered under it still.

He couldnt stand the sight of that picture anymore, couldn't stand the weight of it in his hand. He flung it away, and sent it spinning across the hallway. It hit the wall with a thump and the sharp tinkle of breaking glass. The sound was loud, loud enough to drown out the old man's voice in his head. It made him want to find more things to break.

The picture had hung over faded wallpaper, and it left behind a rectangle of green that probably hadn't seen the sun in over forty years. Only, now there was something behind that old wallpaper that made it bulge in odd places. Now that he was really looking, Scott could see that the other pictures weren't laying flat anymore, that many of them had also gone crooked. One by one, he took them down, following the irregular lines that bulged along the wall. He found the seam in the wallpaper and worried at its edges with his fingernails. When it came away, the backing was wet.

Black tendrils snaked their way through the age-brown plaster, descending from the ceiling like the branches of upside-down trees. He pulled again and a length of wallpaper fell free in a long sheet to coil on the stairs at his feet. Plaster flaked away, and he picked at its edges, exposing still more tendrils whose pathways forked and fractured into almost mathematical patterns, like the veins on a leaf, like frost crystallizing on an icy window. He followed their meanderings with his eyes. His fingertips skimmed their surfaces, and where he touched them they reacted, pulsing with a glow of silvery light. The pulses lingered even as he pulled his hand away, flashing and fading in patterns that seemed almost deliberate, as if they were a message meant for him to understand, if only he had enough time to decipher them.

All you need are the right kind of eyes.

A thump came from upstairs, followed by the creak of footsteps. At once he remembered Tallie and Jacob, waiting up there, wondering where he was, probably still afraid. He climbed the stairs and pushed aside the door to Tallie's room. His daughter's bed sat empty in the corner, sheets rumpled and askew. The kids weren't there. A dark patch had spread along one corner of the ceiling, paint stretching over swollen plaster, as if it were waiting to give birth. A fat drop of water plopped onto the pillow.

His stomach gave a nervous flip at the thought that the the kids might have gone out a window, that even now they might be out there in the rain, looking for their mother. He imagined Dana, her long fingers curled around their wrists, dragging them both beneath the willow tree.

The door to the old bedroom hung open. The ceiling was covered in black branches from end to end now, little traces of silver light streaking beneath their surfaces. The bucket was bent almost in half and spilling into the trash bag, but the trash bag was still holding, and that was at least something. It wouldn't last much longer. Half an hour. Maybe less. One more thing to add to the list, he thought. *One more thing to screw up*, his father's voice added. Scott pushed the voice aside and closed the door.

He found them in the big bedroom, huddled against the wall next to the headboard. Tallie was curled up in Jacob's lap, sucking her thumb. She hadn't done that in at least a year, and seeing her like that made Scott remember when she was barely big enough to fit across one arm, their little surprise baby, wrapped up tight in a blanket. Jacob stared up at him, searching for reassurance. Scott made a gesture with the flat of his hand, trying to tell him it was all right. Tallie's eyes were open, staring past the curled fist at her mouth, staring out at nothing.

The ceiling was dry here. Scott checked it for drips as he crossed the room, looking for bulges on the wall, for pools of water beneath the windows. There was nothing, at least for now, and knowing that felt like a weight being lifted. He bent down and scooped Tallie into his arms. She looked at him, as if she were realizing just then that he was there, and her mouth curled into a smile around her thumb.

Jacob got to his feet, too, and moved in to lean against him. Scott tensed. How long had it been since Jacob had come to him like that? Years, at least. His kids were regressing right before his eyes, and once again the flood of emotions threatened to overtop him the way the water had overtopped the wastebasket. He thought of his father, wondered if the old man had ever held him the way he was holding Tallie now. He wondered if the thought had even occurred to him.

He shifted Tallie to his shoulder, hoping to free up an arm for Jacob, to pull him close, but Jacob pulled away before he could manage it. He'd waited too long, and now the moment was gone. How many more moments would they have like that? How many more chances would the boy give him? How many more chances would the storm give either of them?

Tallie's hair fell back from her ear, and Scott saw then that she was wearing Jacob's earbuds. Her foot was marking time and he could hear the music, tinny and distant, bleeding out from the little speakers. He'd expected to find her crying, expected to have to explain why he wouldn't let her mother back in the house, but she was in another world. Jacob was the one looking at him with haunted eyes, Jacob who was looking to him for answers when he had none to give.

"How much did you hear?" Scott asked.

Jacob hesitated, as if he sensed a trap in the question. "All of it, I think."

Scott nodded, frowning. With Tallie in his arms, his heart wasn't beating quite so fast and his breath was coming under control. He could think again, or at least he was getting there.

"That leak in Tallie's room. How long has it been there?"

Jacob shook his head. "I don't know," he whispered. "It was fine when we got there. Then I saw it dripping, so we came in here. That's when we heard the glass break downstairs, so I gave Tallie my headphones and we hid behind the bed."

"It didn't get on you, did it? Didn't drip in your hair, splash on your clothes?"

Jacob's eyebrows furrowed. "No."

"You're sure? It didn't splash on Tallie? Not even a little?"

"Dad." Just like that the child was gone. He was seeing adult Jacob now. "What happened downstairs?"

Scott opened his mouth. *Nothing*. That's what he almost said. It was what he wanted to say. It's what he wanted to be true, for Jacob's sake, for Tallie's. But he couldn't bring himself to lie, not to his son, not while he was missing his mother, not while he was doing the very adult job of keeping his sister safe.

"It was Ned. Mister Colby," Scott said, talking low, checking to make sure the headphones were still in his daughter's ears. "The rain got to him, I think. Just like..."

Just like the guy on TV, he almost said, but he didn't want to think about the policeman beating his head against the utility pole. He didn't want to think about the shards of window glass digging into Ned Colby's bloody hands.

"Dad, what's—" Jacob stopped himself and checked Tallie's headphones. When he spoke again, it was in a whisper. "What's going to happen to Mom?"

What's already happened to Mom, he thought, picturing the long, pale fingers, the skin stretched tight over her bones.

"I don't know," he said.

Jacob watched the rain streaking down the window, and Scott could see that he was working his way up to another question, the real question. "Is she going to be okay?"

Again, he wanted to lie, as much to himself as to the boy. But he couldn't, not when it was so painfully clear that they both already knew the answer.

"No," Scott said. "No, I don't think she will be."

Jacob didn't look at his father. He only stared at the window, the two of them listening to the rain driving down on the roof, relentless and inevitable. Scott watched his son, saw him getting older right before his eyes, his spine straightening, adjusting to this new reality, a reality that would never let him be a child again.

"So, what do we do now?"

Scott had no answer. He hated that he had no answer. He shifted Tallie onto his other shoulder. She snuggled in, warm, falling asleep. He had no sense of how much time had passed. Was it her naptime? Was it her bedtime? The cloud-dark sky seemed to render such distinctions meaningless, as if time were standing still and moving too fast all at once. Maybe the rain would stop. Maybe it would never stop. He listened to the sound of it, steady and soothing, threating to lull him to sleep too, threatening to lull him into giving up. It would be so easy to give up, if not for the child in his arms, if not for the way Jacob was looking at him, as if he too were slowly giving up on the idea that there might be an answer at all.

Scott took a deep breath. "Just keep your sister up here a little longer."

"Dad, are you kidding me?" Jacob was bouncing on his heels now, pent-up energy bursting out with no place to go.

"Just for a little while," Scott said, thinking of Ned Colby's body hanging in the window with the axe sticking out of his back. "It's not safe downstairs and I don't want Tallie running around where she might get wet."

"Dad, I can help."

Scott put his hand on the back of Jacob's neck and pulled him close, until their foreheads touched. "I know you can, son. But the best way to help right now is to keep Tallie safe, for *you* to stay safe."

Tallie squirmed in his arms and pulled the headphones from her ears. "Daddy, I'm hungry," she said.

"I know, Sweetie," he said. "Daddy's going to get you something to eat, but I have clean up downstairs first. It's not safe." He watched Jacob as he said it, looking for signs of dissent. Jacob tensed, as if gearing himself up to protest, but the moment was gone as quick as it came.

Scott lifted Tallie up by the armpits until they were nose-to-nose. She was heavy, and he felt the strain of the effort in the small of his back. It wouldn't be much longer that he'd be able to hold her like that, even if they made it through this. He pushed that thought away. They *would* make it out of this. They had to.

"I need you to stay up here with your brother for a little while longer. Can you do that for Daddy?"

Tallie nodded solemnly, though her eyes told him that she did not want to. He hugged her close. She squirmed, but he didn't want to let go.

"Just for a little while, okay? Let me get things set up downstairs and then we'll get you some lunch, and then..." He had no and then after that, no ideas, no plan. He had nothing that would get them out of this, just a head full of fears that were running roughshod over any chance he had to get his thoughts straight.

"I want Mommy," Tallie said, her voice soft, her cheek pressed against his shoulder. Scott knew that voice well. It was the voice she used when she already knew she wasn't going to get what she wanted.

"I know, Pumpkin." He handed Tallie off to Jacob, who promptly sat her down on the edge of the big bed, its covers still bunched up in the middle.

"Don't let her out of your sight, okay?" Scott held his gaze on Jacob, forcing him to meet his eyes. "And watch the ceiling. If you see a leak, if something new starts to drip, you let me know right away. Okay?"

Jacob nodded, but Scott could see that his thoughts were someplace else, someplace out beyond the rain-streaked window. It would have to do.

"It's going to be all right," he told them, pausing in the doorway, burning the sight of them into his memory. He went downstairs, past the black vines bulging behind the old photographs. The whole way down, the gruff voice in his head chided him for being a fucking liar.

24

Ned Colby's body lay draped over the windowsill, his arms outstretched, his bald head almost touching the floor. There was no sign of his outsized cowboy hat, so there was nothing to cover his singed and peeling scalp, or the crop of yellow-gray sores that spread down his cheek and into the collar of his shirt. The cracks in them had dried a little, and the liquid they dripped had turned crusty. The handle of the axe stood up from his back like a ship's mast, its head sunk deep into the bones of his back.

Scott's first thought was to push the body back out the window. At least then he wouldn't have to look at it any more. An exploratory shove at the meaty shoulders told him that there was no way it was going to be that easy. The body wouldn't budge, and even when it did, the axe handle wouldn't clear the broken window frame. The steady drip of water from the ceiling plopped onto the coffee table, marking out the time like a metronome. The axe would have to come out, and he'd have to be quick about it.

He remembered the rubber gloves and put them back on before he touched the body. Everything was still wet from the rain, and it took him a while to find a good grip on the handle. Ned's body jerked and swayed as Scott pulled, like he was working the yoke of some grotesque, oversized marionette. It took his foot on Ned's shoulder for leverage to even make the thing budge, and three more sharp tugs before it came loose, wrenching free with a great screech of metal against bone.

He leaned the axe against the wall and took a moment to catch his breath. The lights of the pickup truck had all but died, reduced to two dim eyes that stared in at him through the broken window. They weren't the only eyes that were watching him. He could feel Dana still out there, beyond the broken window, somewhere out beneath the willow tree. Was she waiting to see what he'd do next? Was she waiting to see if he'd go out in the rain and join her? He wanted to join her. He wanted it more than anything. Did she know that, too?

He gave Ned's shoulders an experimental shove. Even with the gloves on, Scott was careful not to touch the sores that ran down Ned's neck. He'd already seen what the rain could do. He didn't want to think of what might happen if he got any of that pus on him, any of that blood. The arms hung limp, fingertips making little trails in the pool of blood beneath the body as Scott pushed. It would not move.

Something thumped against the outside wall. Scott startled, and the tip of his boot slipped on the edge of the spreading blood. He caught himself on the arm of the sofa and listened for the sound, but it did not come again. It had come from high up on the wall, but it hadn't come from inside. Something on the roof, maybe. A fallen tree branch. He didn't want to think about what else it might be.

Ned's body was stuck, probably pinned in place on a shard of glass. That would account for all the blood, since there was barely a trickle from the axe wound. The best way to get him off of it would be to pull him back out the way he came in, but to do that, Scott would have to go outside, onto the porch. He was pretty sure he could stay out of the rain if he did, assuming the roof of the overhang hadn't already been eaten through. It was hard to tell in the dark.

But worse than the rain was whatever might still be out there in the rain. Dana, sure. Maybe Wilbur too, if he hadn't run off. But Ned had only been the tip of the iceberg, if the TV had been anything to go by, if everyone out there was like the cop beating his own brains out on a utility pole. Who knew who else—what else—might be coming? Scott listened again for the sound on the roof, but all he could hear was the rain.

He settled on sliding one of the big plastic garbage bags over Ned's head and shoulders to cover up the scabby skin and wet clothes enough to make it safe to lift the body. He felt a pang of guilt at this, wrapping Ned up like he was so much garbage. Then he remembered the way Ned had looked at him through the open window with all that murderous glee in his eyes, and suddenly he didn't feel guilty any more.

He got underneath the bag and heaved, trying not to slip in the pool of blood, trying not to think about the way Ned's head rolled and nodded against his shoulder. A final shove cleared the glass and heaved the body out through the opening. It landed with a thud. The broken glass in the window frame was slick with blood, a single length of intestine still looped over one of the shards.

The breeze hit Scott through the open window. It was cool and moist, and on it he caught the smell of brimstone and the low scent of rotting leaves. There was nothing left of the dry-oven heat of this morning. The morning was nothing but a distant memory. The rain was part of the air now. He could feel it on his skin. He could taste it as he breathed. Soon enough, it would be inside them all, no matter how careful he was, no matter how much he tried to stop it.

He listened to the sound of raindrops falling against the roof, steady and relentless. It had to end sometime. No storm went on forever. Except, maybe this storm would. Maybe this wasn't a storm at all. Maybe it was his father's gun to the stray dog's head. Maybe this was every bad thing mankind had ever done coming back to bite them in the ass. Maybe this was no less than they deserved.

He could see the looming shape of the willow tree at the edge of the yard. Its branches were almost unrecognizable now, a thick mass of spiraling growths, drooping like dreadlocks, heavy and wet. They were red, the same deep red as an open wound. Green lightning flashed across the clouds, and as if in answer, those sagging fronds coursed with silvery light.

In the flash, Scott glimpsed the low mound of earth and the rusted door of the storm cellar. If there was any safe place in all of this, it was there. If they could just get there, get the door shut behind them, they could wait out the storm there as long as it took. But the door was chained shut, and had been ever since he was a little boy. Even if he had a way to stay dry walking fifty yards through the rain, there was no way they were getting in there. He picked up the axe and used the edge of the blade to nudge the loop of Ned's insides off the broken glass.

Again the gentle breeze came to him. The chill of it seemed to penetrate all the way to his bones, and he shuddered. This time, the wind brought with it the iron tang of blood and the wet-shit smell of opened guts. A distant part of him felt bad about leaving Ned on the porch to rot, but there was nothing for it. It wasn't his fault that the rain had turned him into the scabby, raving thing that had tried to force its way into their home. Or maybe it was. Maybe the rain didn't change people. Maybe it only revealed them.

He thought again about Dana watching him from beneath the pulsing willow tree. He had to board up the window. There was nothing for that, either. Of course, any boards he had were out in the shed and probably reduced to mushy splinters by now. He doubted that a few two-by-fours would be enough to keep anyone out anyway, not if they really wanted to get in. He thought again of the strength it must have taken to bury that axe in Ned's back. The blade was dull and rusty, and probably hadn't been whetted since before his kids were born. No, boards wouldn't be enough, but at least they'd be something.

Another thump sounded high against the outside of the house, followed by a frantic scratching, like a scrabbling of claws. He held his breath and waited for the sound to come again, but all he could hear was the dripping water. The silence should have calmed him, but it didn't. This wasn't the only window, and when he got right down to it, there was no way to fortify this place. Not enough, anyway. If something really wanted inside, it would get inside, and there was nothing he could do about it.

All at once, the sound of dripping water was too much to bear. He carried the axe into the kitchen and leaned it against the wall before he slumped into a chair. His head was pounding, and the splinter in his palm throbbed. He stripped off the rubber gloves, and as they turned inside-out he found a tear in the left one between the thumb and forefinger. His skin was glistening, but the gloves had been warm and it had to just be sweat. It had to be. If the rain had gotten in, if it had gotten onto him, he would have known. He would have felt it.

He figured he must have cut it open on the glass when he was heaving Ned's body out the window. He counted himself lucky that he hadn't cut himself, too. Still, they were the only pair he had, and he had no idea how he was going to empty the bucket upstairs with just one. Just like he had no idea how to board up the window, and no idea how to stop the ceiling from leaking.

If Dana was here, she'd know what to do. Dana was the one with the plans. Dana was the one who cut grapes in half for Tallie and made sure that Jacob got on the bus to school every morning. Dana was the one who kept this place running, but now Dana was outside, probably watching through the broken window from beneath the willow tree, watching him fail. She was probably watching and laughing, knowing that sooner or later she'd be right, that eventually they'd have to come out in the rain and join her.

He put his elbows on the table and held his head in his hands. It occurred to him then that he'd seen his father like that, so many times, in those days after mother left them. The old man had fallen asleep that way, more than once, always with the bottle half-empty in front of him. Scott wished that he could do the same, and felt the pull towards the bottle, stronger than he had since those days before Tallie was born.

Dana had kept him running then, too. She'd given him a reason to kick the stuff, kept him on a path so narrow that there was no room for him to stray. There'd been days that he'd resented her for that. He resented her for that now, and wanted nothing more than to lose himself until the rain stopped, so he could worry about picking up the pieces of whatever was left after it was done. But there was nothing stronger than orange juice in the house. She'd made sure of that, even on those days when he wasn't strong enough to make sure of it himself. She'd protected him. Even now, probably without even realizing it, she still was.

He stared through his fingers at the scratches on the table. He wondered how many of those scratches Tallie had put there, how many he'd put there himself after years of eating all his meals at this faded wooden rectangle that he'd all but turned into an altar. How many had his father put there, dragging the bottle along its surface to fill his glass? He could all but picture the old man standing over his shoulder, telling him that he should have taken better care of it, that he should have gotten it refinished, that he should have fixed the railing on the staircase, that he shouldn't have sold what was left of his land to a vulture like Ned Colby. How old was this table, anyway? He'd never seen it new. It had been old and scratched all his life, damaged before he was ever even born.

He stood and took up the axe in his hand. The splinter in his palm sang, but the pain only made him grip the thing tighter. He ran his fingers over the ragged table, over this piece of junk that he'd allowed his memories to turn into a museum piece. Its joins were old. It creaked and swayed when he put his weight on it. When he told himself it was worth keeping, it was his father's voice telling him so, not his own. With the mess on the floor and the drips from the ceiling, that voice seemed suddenly so absurd. It had always been his father's table. It was strange now that he'd ever thought of it as something worth preserving.

He raised the axe, and swung.

25

The power went out before he got the last screws in. The living room turned dark all at once, leaving afterimages of the broken window, a world in negative. While he waited for his eyes to adjust, he listened to the fall of the rain and the irregular plop of water dripping from the ceiling behind him. Another thump sounded, high against the outside of the house. He held his breath, but the sound did not come again.

He finished his work in the dark, grateful that the battery in his drill had enough juice left in it to do the job. He hadn't thought to plug it in until now, until it was too late. The gruff voice in his head had things to say about that, but he chose not to listen.

The broken bits of the kitchen table weren't enough to cover the whole window, but they were enough to keep anyone else from coming in. At least, so he hoped. Now that they were in place, they seemed almost comical, a Band-Aid stretched across a gaping wound. What would happen when the next window broke, and the next one after that, he didn't know.

Once the work with the axe was done, Jacob had come out to watch him from the top of the stairs. He stood there in silence, neither of them saying a word as Scott put the boards in place. Even now, in the dark, he could feel his son looking down on him, maybe wondering if Scott was losing it, maybe wondering if it meant that his dad would end up like his mom, naked and raving in the rain. He had to be wondering how they were all going to get out of this. He had to be wondering if his dad had a plan.

And he did have a plan, or at least the beginnings of one. While he hung the boards, he kept an eye on the door set into the little hill, estimating the distance in his head, figuring how many steps it would take to get there. They could make it in less than two minutes, he was pretty sure, as long as they had a way to stay dry. They only had one umbrella, and that was in Dana's car. Sheets wouldn't keep the rain off. They'd just soak through. Coats might help, but there was no way to cover up completely, and if the rain got on their faces or on their wrists where gloves didn't cover, they'd might as well be going out there in nothing at all.

Or, maybe not. He'd gotten the rain on his skin, and he was still okay. Or at least, he thought he was okay. Dana probably thought that she was okay, too, but at least he wasn't out there dancing in the stuff. But it had only been a few drops, and the rain had been so much lighter then. He was fine now, but with the way it was coming down, heavy and relentless, could he afford to risk getting wet, to risk the kids getting wet? If they could dry off as soon as they got to the cellar, and not let it soak into their skin, then maybe they could.

He thought of the blue tarps that he'd left out in the shed, and wished that he'd thought to keep one of them—just one—in the basement where he could get to it. Dana was still out there. Maybe she was back in the shed, or even out beneath the willow tree. He had the absurd thought to call out to her, to tell her to bring one of the tarps and slide it in through the gaps in the boards. He began to laugh at the thought, and the laughter threatened to overtake him. Then he remembered the way she had smiled at him, wet hair across her face, leaning in through the broken window. Then he didn't feel like laughing anymore at all.

The drill screeched in protest as he hurried to drive in the last few screws. Jacob was still at the top of the stairs. Scott could hear the sounds of his breathing, could feel him there, looking down on him. He probably *did* think Scott was losing it. Maybe he was even thinking about the gun tucked in Scott's belt, thinking how he could sneak up and take it from him in the dark. Scott made a fist, and the pain in his palm pushed the thought away. It left him feeling absurd and more than a little guilty. He couldn't blame the kid for being worried, not when he'd seen everything that had happened in the past few hours. Not when he'd just heard his dad chopping the kitchen table to bits with an axe.

"Jacob?"

"Yeah, dad?" His voice seemed so far away. Jacob wasn't sneaking up on him at all. At least not yet.

"How much charge is left on your phone?"

"Seventy-three percent." He said it right away, like it was top of mind. Like he was two steps ahead. "But the Internet's down and I can't get a line out."

"Keep it on you, but don't use the flashlight unless you absolutely have to." Scott wondered how much charge was left in his own phone after he'd wasted so much battery watching that stupid video. "I have some candles in the kitchen. As soon as I finish up here, I'll bring some up for the bedroom, okay?"

There was silence for a moment, and in that moment, all Scott could hear was the rain.

"Jacob! Did you hear me?"

"Yeah, dad." His voice was shaky, and immediately Scott felt bad for shouting. "I mean, yes. I heard you."

"Where's your sister?"

"Sitting on the bed. I told her not to move."

"Make sure she doesn't, okay?" He made an effort to keep his voice low, to show that he was calm. To show that he was still in charge. "Don't let her wander in the dark. I'll be done down here in a few minutes. Until then, listen for drips. If you hear anything, find out where it is and stay clear of it. Understand?"

Another pause, and then, "Yeah. Yeah, I understand."

Scott listened for the creak of the floorboards, the familiar squeak of the hinges on the bedroom door, but they did not come.

"Dad?"

"It's going to be okay, son." He was lying out of reflex now, lying out of necessity. "I have a plan. It's just... I just need a little time, is all."

More silence. The boy standing in the darkness at the top of the stairs, watching him, judging him.

"Just tend to your sister now, okay?"

"Okay, dad."

"I'll be up there as soon as I can."

"Okay, dad."

The candles were tea lights, the kind Dana used to burn at the bottom of a wine glass on nights when she wanted dinner to feel fancy. It took him forever to find the matches in the dark and his hands shook as he lit the flame, but once he saw its light, felt its heat, he began to find his calm again. He lit another off the flame of the first, and wanted to light a third, but there were only six left in the box with no telling how long they'd last. He wanted to take one upstairs to Jacob and Tallie, but there was a part of him that wanted to leave them in the dark, just for a little while, just long enough for them to know that they still needed him.

He left one of the candles burning on the kitchen counter and held the other in the palm of his hand as he crept down the basement stairs. He paused halfway, struck by the oily smell of machine smoke and the unexpected silence of the place. The sump pump had quit working long before the power went out. He could see the pit in the deep shadows cast by the candle, the water shining and almost all the way up to the top. The stairs groaned as he took another step, and he heard the mice rustle frantically from their hiding place in the wall.

He didn't know what he was looking for. He only knew that, if he was going to find an answer to their problem at all, he'd find it down here. He'd already brought up everything he thought would be useful, but he hadn't had the whole picture then. He hadn't imagined that they'd need to abandon this place, that he'd have to find something that would let them go out in the rain and not end up like Dana. He hadn't been desperate then. He was desperate now.

The shelves were packed full from floor to ceiling along the far wall, stacked with sagging cardboard boxes and mismatched plastic bins. None of them were big enough for Tallie to fit inside, but that didn't stop him from imagining himself carrying her, like an animal in a crate on its way to the vet.

He set the candle aside and pawed through the boxes, turning them out, dumping their contents onto the floor. Old baby clothes. Christmas decorations. Box after box of old papers and receipts. All of it precious once, but all of it completely useless now. He rummaged through an old milk crate full of odd-sized screwdrivers and electrical switches that looked so old they were probably made before he was born. He found a dusty light bulb inside a lone boot. He flung it at the wall and found an instant of satisfaction in the sound it made as the pieces rained down to the concrete floor.

A half-used tube of caulk. A deflated basketball. There was nothing but old junk, nothing that could possibly be of any use to them. He swept the shelves empty, and when they were bare he grabbed at the empty shelves and shook them. All his frustration came out in a growl as he slammed them back and forth, shaking them so hard that they threatened to topple over.

Then he noticed what was on the wall behind them.

He tugged at the shelf, more gently this time, and found that he could slide it with some effort. Then he kicked the mess aside so he could slide it some more. The wall wasn't bare concrete like the rest. Cheap wood paneling had been nailed into wooden shims that were glued to the outer wall. A corner of one panel was torn away near the floor, its edges chewed down by mice over many years. There was something behind the panel, though. Something that *shined*.

Scott brought the candle closer and bent down to get a better look. With his free hand, he tugged at the edge of the panel, holding his breath. Suddenly it was hard to swallow. He was almost afraid to believe what he was seeing, but he could feel it there beneath his fingers, smooth and real, even beneath the dust of ages.

A plastic sheet.

He moved so quickly that hot wax dripped onto his palm. The flame guttered, and threatened to leave him in the dark. Scott placed the candle gently back on the shelf and set to work with both hands. The nails that held the panel up were short, and it came away easy. Once it was free he set it aside and went to work on the next one, taking his time, willing his hands to stop shaking for fear of ruining the delicate plastic.

It took long minutes of work, but when it was done the panels were stacked neatly off to the side and what was left of the wall nearly glowed with reflected candlelight. There were tears in the surface here and there, and he'd have to patch the nail holes somehow, but there was still enough of it to keep the rain off of them—off of all of them—for a few minutes, and a few minutes was all they'd need. He laughed then, and this time he let himself laugh. He laughed so long that it turned into sobs.

26

By the time he remembered to check on the kids, the little candles had burned down almost halfway. He'd lit them all to work by, and placed them all around the front room, on end tables and bookshelves, on the coffee table he'd shoved in the corner. It hadn't been enough light, not really, but he'd managed. He took up one of the candles and held it between two fingers, careful not to let the wax drip, careful not to burn himself as he crept up the stairs, past the spreading growth on the wall whose branches had thickened through the cracked plaster and visibly pulsed now with their strange silver energy.

He found Tallie sitting on Jacob's lap, their faces lit by the glow of Jacob's phone. As the door creaked open, the glow abruptly vanished, but there was still enough light from the candle for Scott to see the sheepish look on his son's face.

"Sorry, Dad," he said, defensive, like he was bracing for a scolding. "It's all I could think of to keep her busy."

"It's fine, son," Scott said. It wasn't fine, but it didn't matter anymore. If they had to sit in the dark once they got to the storm cellar, then so be it. They could sit in the dark for days and days if they had to. There'd be plenty of time then to lecture his son about listening to his old man, plenty of time to remind him which one of them had the answers.

Scott waved them tover. There was a dark patch on the ceiling over the bureau, not a leak yet, but it would be soon enough. "Come with me."

He led them down the stairs, holding the candle out at arm's length. He wished that he'd thought to leave at least one of the things unlit so they could take it with them to the storm cellar. They wouldn't have time to let them cool, so they'd most likely have to leave them all behind. That was alright, though. They didn't need them. They didn't need anything but each other.

Jacob walked behind Tallie, herding her down the steps one at a time. He stopped when he saw the growth on the wall and stared at it with his mouth open. "Dad, what the hell?"

"Don't worry about it," Scott said. "There's nothing we can do about that right now." There wasn't anything they could do about it right now, but the rain couldn't go on forever. Once it was over, they'd rebuild. He'd find out which outfit wanted to drill on his land and he'd let them, even if it meant taking pennies on the dollar. Even then it would still be enough to start fresh someplace new. He'd believed Ned about that much. Or even better, enough to tear this place down and start all over right here. Maybe he'd find some way to help Dana, and the four of them could build a new home together, a place that was all theirs. Only theirs.

Tallie reached out a hand, fascinated by the light pulsing through the branches in the wall. Scott caught her by the arm, a little too quick, a little too rough. He saw it in the way she looked at him, and he relaxed his grip.

"Don't touch, Sweetie, okay? It's not safe." She didn't nod, but Jacob pulled her back, bending over her and crossing his arms over her chest the way that Dana sometimes did, protecting her. From the stuff in the wall, Scott thought, but maybe from him, too.

He led them, candle guttering, around the muddy mess on the hallway floor until they were beneath the archway that joined it to the front room. "It's not perfect," he said, "but we won't need it for long. Two minutes, maybe three. It'll hold for that long at least."

The plastic sheet lay spread out over the floor, glinting in the candlelight. There had been two of them hung up behind the panel boards, but the other was badly torn and had been chewed through by mice in half a dozen spots. This one, however, was in workable shape. Scott had spent the better part of a half-hour going over it inch by inch, patching the rows of nail holes with little bits of duct tape, accounting for every little defect that might let the water pass through.

"You're kidding, right?" Jacob's voice was rising. Scott could hear the panic in it. "We're not going outside, are we? Not with just that?"

Tallie was picking up on his tone of voice, and Scott could see the the worry starting to form on her face. He scooped her up, swinging her as she went, just enough to bring her smile back. "Of course we are," he said, keeping it as light as he could. "It's just gonna be like a big umbrella."

"Dad." Jacob caught the look his father was giving him, and lowered his voice to almost a whisper. "Dad, where are supposed to go?"

"Not far," Scott said. "Just out to the old storm cellar. Maybe fifty yards, that's all."

"We've never even been *in* the old storm cellar. The door's all chained up, probably rusted shut."

He'd thought about that. He'd thought about all of that. Why did Jacob think that he hadn't thought of that? He'd seen what the rain could do to metal. He'd seen it in the gutters outside, in the pockmarked hood of Ned Colby's pickup truck. The door would be like tissue paper by now, if it was still there at all. And if the door was somehow still solid? If the chain still held? Well, Dana had solved that problem for them. Even a dull axe would be enough to break the chain, to knock the door off its rusty hinges.

"It'll be fine," Scott said. He'd expected this to go differently, for his son to see the simple effectiveness of his plan right away.

He'd expected the kid to be *on board*. They didn't have time to waste with a bunch of pointless questions.

"And even if we get in, how do you know it's safe? It's probably all flooded by now. It'd be worse than if we just stayed here!"

Scott took a deep breath and collected himself. When he spoke again, his words were slow and deliberate. "It won't be flooded, Jacob." That much he knew for certain. His father had built the thing before Scott was even born. He'd been down there once, as a little kid, and remembered it like it was yesterday. The ladder set into the concrete wall. The gravel floor that sloped up into the side of the little hill. His father never went halfway, not when he built something, not in those days before the bottle, before his mother left them. "Could you just... I just need you to trust me on this, okay?"

"Are we going out in the rain, Daddy?" Tallie put her hands on his cheeks. He turned his head and kissed her fingers.

"Yes, Pumpkin," he said. "We're going out in the rain, but we have to be very careful and you have to do as I say. Can you do that, Pumpkin?"

Tallie nodded solemnly, but Jacob's face looked stricken. "Dad, we can't."

"We can, and we have to." Scott pressed Tallie's head to his chest and covered her ear with his hand. He lowered his voice to a whisper. "Look, you were right. We can't just wait, and we can't stay here."

Jacob said nothing. His eyes had found the patch of floor beneath the broken window and he was staring at the pool of dried blood that still glistened in the candlelight.

"Jacob!" At the sound of his name, Jacob's attention snapped back to his father. Scott could see the beginnings of fear in his son's widening eyes. Scott hated to see him that way, but a part of him was grateful for that fear. Fear meant he was finally taking this seriously. Fear meant that he would do as he was told.

"You see what's happening," Scott said. "This place is getting worse and worse, and sooner or later the leaks are going to get so bad that there won't be any way to avoid them. This whole place could come crashing down on top of our heads. And what then?"

Jacob nodded, but his eyes still flicked toward the stain on the floor. He was coming around, though, and that was good. Scott didn't want to think about what might happen if it came down to a choice between staying in the house and leaving his son behind.

"We have to stay dry. And right now the best place to do that is the storm cellar. It's not perfect, I know. But if we can keep the rain off of us long enough to get out there, it'll be enough to keep us dry until the rain stops. And after that, we'll find your mother. We'll get help. We'll—"

"But what if it doesn't?"

Scott watched his son's face. The fear had taken hold of him now, and turned his eyes glassy.

"What if the rain doesn't stop?" Jacob's voice was thin and his eyes were threatening to brim over. "What if it never stops? What if we go out there and end up stuck the same way we're stuck here? What if something..."

Again his eyes darted to the stain on the floor. "What if there's something out there?" he whispered. "Something waiting for us, like that guy on the TV?"

Tallie squirmed in Scott's arms as his stomach tightened around a little bubble of self-reproach. Of course Jacob was taking this seriously. He'd been taking it seriously all along. Jacob had watched the whole thing unfold, same as he had. He'd been on his phone the whole time, and probably knew more about it than Scott did. He'd been holding onto all of that fear, all of that doubt, and never said a word. Scott hated himself for not seeing it sooner.

"What if the whole world is like that?" Jacob asked. His eyes were pleading now, a child's eyes, looking for the simplicity of a child's answers. "What if there's nobody left? What if the rain never stops and nothing's ever going to get better?"

Scott bounced Tallie to settle her down, and smoothed her hair down over her ears. He was pressing too hard, and she tried to wriggle out of his grip. He shifted her to his other shoulder, but he couldn't bring himself to let go of her.

"I don't know," he said. "All I know is that we can't stay here, not for much longer anyway. The cellar might be dry. It might not be. I don't know. But I do know if we try to wait…"

He couldn't bring himself to say the rest. *We'll end up like your mother. We'll end up like Wilbur, like Ned Colby. We'll walk out into the rain and bash our brains out on the side of a utility pole. Or worse, we'll find metal pipes and bash out each other's.* He couldn't say that, but he didn't have to. He could see that Jacob understood. He watched his son's face, and watched whatever was left of the child inside him die. He'd mourn for that child later. They both would, when there was time. If there was time.

Jacob nodded. "Okay," he said, reluctant, but growing in resolve. "Okay. Let's do it."

27

The drill whined in protest as it backed the last of the screws out of the door. It went slow, getting bogged down, and Scott knew there was no way there'd be enough juice left in the battery to get the screws back in. That was all right though. It meant the drill was useless now, and that meant they didn't need to think about taking it with them. It was one less thing to carry. One less thing to slow them down.

They'd talked it through, and decided on one backpack—Jacob's book bag from school—and one day's worth of food, mostly leftovers from the fridge and a few cans full of things they wouldn't mind eating cold. It didn't make any sense to take any more than that. If the rain went on for more than a full day, the extra food wouldn't matter. Scott felt the weight of the gun at his back and tried not to think about having to use it.

They'd rehearsed it, the three of them under the dusty plastic sheet in the darkened front room, getting Tallie used to the weight of it on her shoulders, making it a game. Tallie smiled through it all, her mouth smeared with chocolate as she munched the Nutella sandwich that Jacob had made for her. Scott had watched them from the hallway, watched Jacob smear the bread with the knife that Dana had left on the edge of the kitchen sink. He watched him take care of his sister, and thought about how proud his wife would have been of their son.

They'd agreed that Scott would carry Tallie while Jacob took the backpack. One slip, one misplaced foot, and that could be the end of it, so they'd go slow, take their time, with Scott in the lead and Jacob's hand on his shoulder. Dana was sure to be watching them from somewhere out there, but Scott didn't think she'd try to stop them. If she wanted to take the plastic sheet away from them, there was nothing he could do about it anyway. They'd all get wet, and that would be that. Scott added that to the list of things he wasn't going to worry about until he had to.

Tallie didn't like the plastic, and kept trying to pull at it no matter how many times Scott told her not to. He'd settled on carrying her in a way that kept one of her arms pinned down at her side. It made it harder for him to keep hold of Tallie and the plastic at the same time. That meant that Jacob would be responsible for keeping a grip on it, for keeping all of them dry. It was more of a burden than he'd wanted to put on the boy, but Jacob seemed up to the task. Or maybe he was only grateful to have something to focus on, so he wouldn't have to think about his mother outside, about the leaking house, about any of it.

Scott swung the door open and peered out into the yard. The smell hit him full in the face, all brimstone and vegetable rot, as if the whole yard had been turned into a compost heap. He'd expected the sky to be darker, but the lightning arcing across the low clouds bathed everything in a greenish hue, as if the night were lit by fireworks. He had to remind himself that it wasn't night at all, that only a few hours had passed since he'd seen that first cloud in the sky, that the sun was still up there somewhere. At least, he hoped it still was. It had to be.

He stepped onto the porch, testing the boards as he went, getting as close to the stairs as he dared to without the plastic to cover him. As far as he could tell, the steps were still intact, and showed no sign of the wet rot that he'd seen in the wooden floor, in the broken planks of the dog house. He'd given them a fresh coat of paint just two years before, and he'd slopped it on thick. Maybe that had been enough to protect them from the damage the rain would have done. Or maybe all it was doing was masking the rot, and once he put his weight on it his foot would go clean through. Either way, it was the most dangerous part of the whole journey, getting down off the porch and onto solid ground. If they could make it past those first few steps, the rest should be easy by comparison.

Tallie and Jacob watched him from the doorway, Tallie growing restless, Jacob following his every move as if he was committing them to memory. Scott saw the furtive glances that his son cast at Ned's body. It lay at the end of the porch beneath the broken window, its head and shoulders still tucked in the garbage bag, the wide gash in his back glistening in the darkness. Whatever thoughts Jacob had about that, he was keeping to himself. It was just as well, Scott thought. He had no answers to give, and they were running out of time.

"Okay," he said finally. "When we go down these stairs, I want you to stick close. But make sure you don't put your weight on a step until my weight is off of it. Understand?"

Jacob nodded. Tallie nodded too, her face grim, as if she was beginning to understand that this wasn't a game at all. Scott looked down at their shoes. With his work boots on, he was pretty sure his feet would stay dry. Jacob and Tallie were wearing their snow boots with their pant legs stretched over the tops of them. He didn't think he'd have to set Tallie down, not if everything went right, but if he did, the boots would be enough to keep her feet dry, at least for a while. A little ember of hope began to kindle within him. This might just work out after all.

"Once we're on the ground it should be easy going, but we're not going to rush it. We take our time, one step at a time, okay? We can't afford to trip or stumble. If anything goes wrong, we turn back, but we do it together."

Jacob nodded. Scott went back to them and leaned in close enough to whisper into Jacob's ear. He pulled the gun from his back and pressed it into his son's palm. "You know how to use this, right?"

Jacob looked down at the gun. His eyes went wide for an instant, but he covered it well. He was shaking a little, just enough for Scott to notice, just enough to think that giving him the gun was a bad idea. But he didn't have much choice and waiting wasn't going to make it any better.

"Jacob," Scott said, softly but firmly. "It's going to be fine. I don't think you're going to need it, but I want you to have it just in case. I'm carrying Tallie, so my hands will be full. It has to be you. All right?"

Again Jacob's eyes darted to the body crumpled beneath the window. He swallowed hard and nodded. He took the gun and tucked it into his waistband at the small of his back. *Just like his dad*, Scott thought, and the thought was enough to bring out a grim little smile.

"Just don't drop it, okay?" Again Jacob nodded, more certain this time. Scott chewed at his lip, not wanting to say the rest of it. "It's just a precaution, but if you do have to use it, don't hesitate. Your job is to stay safe and keep Tallie safe. No matter what. Do you understand?"

Jacob stared at him, and in his eyes Scott could see that he did understand, that he understood all the parts of it that Scott wasn't telling him. *Stay safe, even if I get wet. Even if I turn into a raving lunatic like Ned Colby and try to drag you into the rain. Stay safe. Use the gun and keep Tallie safe.*

"And no matter what happens, we stay dry. If the plastic starts to slip, or if you lose your grip on it, say so right away. We'll stop and fix it, then we'll keep going."

The distant look in Jacob's eyes was gone now. He was looking out at the yard, at the little door set into the hill that now seemed so impossibly far away, at the drooping willow tree, whose shadows were so terribly deep.

"Are we good?" Scott asked the question, and he could see in Jacob's face that they were not good, that they might never be good again. Jacob nodded anyway.

✆

Jacob shrugged the backpack on in silence, the axe dangling heavy from a loop at his side. Scott tried not to notice when he shifted the gun to the front of his waistband, tried not to think about it being there at all. Tallie was already sweating inside her winter coat, and when the plastic went over their heads he didn't think she was going to let it stay there. He bounced her and petted her hair smooth against the back of her head, wishing she'd just grow tired and fall asleep. This would be so much easier if she was asleep.

Scott kept the short end of the plastic sheet in front of him. He'd kept just enough of it to reach down over his feet, but there was a long train of extra material that trailed out behind Jacob. Scott had thought to cut it down, but didn't want to get out there and find out that they needed it, so he'd left it alone. Now he just hoped that it wouldn't snag. It was dark beneath the porch roof, and so dark beneath the plastic that he could barely see out into the yard. There'd been the light from the candles when they'd tried it in the house, but outside there was nothing more to light their way than that odd glow in the sky. He could see now that it wouldn't be enough.

He lifted the sheet to get his bearings. Three steps to the stairs, four more to get down to ground level, and after that, nothing but the long trek across the yard. All he could do then was hope that they wouldn't stray too far off course, and hope that there wasn't anything out there in the dark to stop them. He squinted through the rain into the black depths beneath the willow tree. The drooping fronds pulsed again, sending trails of light coursing up along its branches like some deep-sea jellyfish, but the light was not bright enough to give up the tree's secrets.

Tallie squirmed in his arms, trying to get down. She was running out of patience, and Scott couldn't blame her. He shifted her weight and got a solid grip around her legs, solid enough that she couldn't wiggle free.

"Put me *down*, Daddy," she said, putting a little lilt in her voice that she only used when she really wanted something. "I want to go see the glowy tree."

"We can't go see the glowy tree right now, Pumpkin." She squirmed again, but his grip didn't give her much room to maneuver. "Remember what we talked about? We have to get all the way across the yard or else we lose the game, remember?"

Tallie had been all nods and wide eyes when he'd first told her about the game, but now she was having none of it. She tried to push away from him, but Scott held her tight. "Ow, Daddy! You're *squeezing*!"

"I'm sorry, Pumpkin." He relaxed his grip a little, but not enough for her to get free. "You have to stay up here for a while, okay?"

Tallie went limp, defeated. "I want Mommy," she whispered, her voice on the edge of tears.

"I know, Sweetie," Scott said. And then, before he could stop himself, "we'll see Mommy after we're done with the game, okay?"

He felt like a bastard the moment the words were out of his mouth, and more so as he felt Jacob shifting restlessly behind him. But Tallie laid her head on his shoulder and didn't struggle anymore. That was worth feeling like a bastard, knowing that he wouldn't have to fight her. He'd set things straight once she was safe. Once they were all safe.

He called back over his shoulder. "What do you say? Are we ready?"

Jacob didn't answer. Scott could feel his son close behind him, the faint heat of breath on the back of his neck. *Don't wimp out on me now*, came the voice in his head, but whether it was his father's or his own, he could no longer say.

"Jacob," Scott said softly, and this time he could tell that the boy heard him. "Are we ready?"

"Yeah," Jacob said, and as he spoke his voice was trembling. "Yeah, I'm ready."

Scott stared out again into the inky darkness beneath the willow tree, through the long branches that drooped low, the light pulsing down now toward the wet ground. For an instant he was sure that he could feel another set of eyes staring back at him from behind those branches. He wasn't ready. None of them were. But they couldn't wait for ready. They couldn't wait even a minute longer.

28

The first step held his weight. He'd expected the thing to crack right through, but it didn't even even sag. *Thank God for that sloppy paint*, he thought. Still, he didn't trust it, and got both feet on the first step before he even tried the second. When that one held too, he felt the beginnings of hope start to kindle in his chest. *This is going to work*, he told himself, and to help believe it, he told himself again.

He paused as his feet touched the muddy gravel walkway. He held his breath and listened, but all he could hear was the drum of rain against the plastic sheet. Jacob had kept his hand on his father's shoulder the whole way down, and Scott feared that if he went any farther his son would overbalance and go stumbling onto the wet grass. "The steps are safe," he said. "Just take it slow."

Jacob listened a little too well, because his halting footsteps gave Scott time to think about those eyes staring at him from beneath the willow tree. He didn't want to think about Dana still being out there somewhere. All she'd need was one tug on the plastic sheet and they'd all be soaked by the rain, just like she'd wanted. But he knew somehow that she wouldn't. For all that the rain had done to her, she was still Dana, and Dana would never force them. She wanted them to make the choice on their own. She wanted them to join her of their own free will. She was waiting because she believed that, eventually, they would.

As he reached the ground, Scott felt Jacob take hold of his belt and squeeze down on it until the leather creaked. His hands were shaking.

"We're going to walk slow and you're going to follow my lead," Scott said. The plastic sheet amplified the sound of the rain, and he had to raise his voice just to be heard. "Just like moving a couch, okay?"

Jacob said nothing, but Scott felt him nod. It would have to do.

Now that the sheet was getting wet, the thin coating of dust had turned into dark, muddy streaks that were impossible to see through. He hadn't planned for that. He shook the bit that he held wadded in his fist and tried to knock the streaks loose, but that only made them worse. It was hot under the sheet, and had gotten hot almost instantly, the warm rain and the humid air conspiring to turn their makeshift tent into a sauna. Tallie poked at the plastic with her fingers but Scott didn't have a hand free to make her stop. All he could do was to shift her weight and hope that her little fingernails weren't sharp enough to rip through.

He shook the sheet again and sent enough water running to make a clean streak about an inch wide, right in his field of vision. It didn't last long, but while it did, it was enough to let him find the willow tree and use it as a landmark to point himself toward where the storm cellar ought to be. Between the dirt and the falling rain, he wouldn't be able to see much, but that was okay. The shadows beneath the glowing branches were still, and all they had to do was walk in a straight line.

"All right," he said. "One step at a time. You ready, Pumpkin?"

Tallie stopped poking at the plastic and nodded, grinning.

"All right. Eyes open and stay close."

His boot squished in the muddy ground, and water welled up around the outsole. The grass at the edge of the path was woven through with a rubbery web the yellow-white color of snot. Peppered in amongst it were new growths, like tufts of spiky black hair stretching skyward to catch the rain. He toed the web and it felt felt spongy beneath his foot. When his boot came away it made a squelching sound as sticky tendrils clung to the sole, stretching and snapping, fighting to keep hold.

Another step. Then another. Jacob tugged at Scott's belt, lagging ever so slightly behind until the two of them fell into a rhythm. The streaks of mud on the plastic were running clearer now, but the sheet was fogged and covered with scratches, and he could barely see two steps in front of them. The rain was a relentless patter that drove all other sound away. It made him feel like they were deep-sea divers, like astronauts marooned on another world.

With each step he checked the inside of the plastic, looking for leaks. The little patches he'd made with the tape were holding, but he didn't know how long they'd last. He didn't know how long the plastic would last either before the rain managed to eat right through it. He hoped it would be enough to get back to the house when all this was done, when the kids were safe in the storm cellar. As long as the plastic held, he could go back as many times as he needed to. He could bring more supplies and he could patch the holes if he had to. If he had to, he could even reach the willow tree.

Something brushed against his leg, moving fast, but by the time he looked down it was nothing more than the leftover swaying in the drooping stalks of tall grass. There came a distant rustling amid the ground cover that ended as abruptly as it started. Scott thought that he heard a crunch, but with the sound of the rain he couldn't tell for sure.

"Doing okay back there?" Scott said, loud enough to be heard. Louder than he'd wanted to.

"Yeah," came Jacob's voice, still trembling but not as much as before. Their footsteps squelched in the sodden ground, each step taking them farther and farther from the porch. Scott tried to keep his head straight, his eyes focused on that distant, unseen point where he'd judged the storm cellar door to be. Again he thought of astronauts, overshooting their orbits, spinning off into the cold of outer space. He thought he was still headed the right way, but with Tallie squirming in his arms there was no way to be sure. He'd already lost count of the steps they'd taken since they left the porch. As hard as it was to see, they might pass within five feet of the door and never even know it.

It was all he could do not to lift the sheet to get their bearings. It was hard to breathe now, and each pull of air was so heavy that he felt like he was sucking it through a straw. He watched the condensation dripping down the inside of the plastic and wondered how much of the rain was still getting to them through the humidity in the air, trapped now and concentrated, filling their lungs, soaking into their clothes. He could smell the thick, sulfurous stink of it rising up from the ground beneath their feet. With it came the clinging smoke of the distant fire and the deeper, iron tang of blood.

Tallie stopped poking the sheet and put her head down on Scott's shoulder. Already she was growing bored and soon she'd be restless. Scott felt his steps starting to quicken and forced himself to slow down. How far had they come? It couldn't have been more than fifty feet, but it still felt as if they'd been under the sheet for an eternity. He wanted to go faster but knew that would only make it easier for them to overshoot the storm cellar and get lost in the rain. He listened to the sound of it, listened for anything else that might be out there in the dark. All he could hear was the steady tapping of the rain, drowning out everything, even his own heartbeat.

He shifted his steps to avoid one of the black thickets and the strange webbing that coiled around it. There was a dark lump caught inside the web, and scattered shapes around it that he took for feathers. The plastic brushed against his leg and clung there. He tried to shake it free but his foot collided with something solid, something large enough that its outline was lost beyond the narrow range of his vision. The surprise of it brought him up short and sent Jacob stumbling against his back. Scott felt the tug at his belt as his son struggled to stay upright, and had to remind himself that the heavy backpack had left Jacob overbalanced. It wouldn't take much to topple him over, and if he toppled over, all this was for nothing.

"Dad, what? Why'd you stop?"

Scott lifted the plastic enough to see a curved metal fender, dented and pitted by the rain. Beneath it, remnants of rubber sagged like hanging moss around the pitted rim of a wheel.

"It's Ned Colby's truck," he called back. They weren't where they should have been. That meant that they hadn't been walking in a straight line at all, but instead had veered off to the right by a good ten feet. It also meant that they hadn't come nearly as far as he'd hoped that they had. Still, it was a good thing because at once he knew exactly where they were in relation to the house and to the cellar door. Finding their way from here would be easy. He could see the trip unfolding like a map in his mind. From here it was a straight shot—a hundred feet, maybe less—and they'd be right where they needed to be.

"Dad?"

"It's okay, son." Scott's voice was almost giddy. *This was going to work.* "Just getting my bearings again. Let's get moving."

"*Dad.*" Jacob's voice was a low hiss that barely registered beneath the drumming of the rain, but Scott could still hear the fear in it. Tallie raised her head, and he could feel her little body tense with excitement. Scott tried to turn around to see what had frightened them, but froze as he heard a low rumble beneath the sound of the rain, a low rumble that resolved itself into a growl.

Tallie's voice was an excited squeal that drove a chill through his body like a knife.

"Daddy, it's Wilbur!"

29

A gain the low growl came, a ragged rumble beneath the white-noise patter of the rain. Through the streaks of water on their plastic shroud, Scott could see a dark shape moving, a black hole in the landscape that the glow from the clouds had transformed into a sea of pale green. It was moving sideways, not quite circling, but keeping its distance, as if it were taking measure of this new thing that had entered the yard, this lump of rain-streaked plastic that inched and stretched so haltingly. Scott thought he could see the thing's tail flipping lazily as it watched them, and as the lightning flashed silently above their heads, he saw the pinpoints of eyes, blurred and multiplied through the plastic sheet, glowing back at him in the darkness.

Jacob was next to him now, his face obscured by the tented plastic. They had both turned toward the sound and stood shoulder-to-shoulder, neither one moving. Tallie squirmed with newfound energy, and almost tumbled from Scott's grasp. He let go of the sheet to grab her up in both arms, and held her tight against his chest.

"Ow! Daddy, I want to see Wilbur. I want–" Scott pressed a hand to her mouth to silence her and felt a raw sting as the splinter in his palm pressed against her mouth. She grew still at once, her eyes widening at this new roughness, this sudden urgency.

He took his hand away slowly, waiting to see if she would cry out. When she didn't, he pressed a finger to his lips. She watched him, her eyes shining with the threat of tears. Scott realized then with a sting of resentment that it was him she'd turned afraid of. Not the dog, but *him*. Still, her fright had made her quiet, and that was good. She could be afraid of him, just for a while, if the fear meant that she would listen. If it meant she'd be safe, she could be afraid of him for the rest of his life.

In the distance, the dog grew still. No, not *the dog*. Not anymore. Scott could see that it was bigger now. Its movements were predatory, almost wolf-like. The low growl came again, but in a different register this time, a sound that seemed curious, almost playful. It was stalking them.

After a moment, it shrank down on its haunches, its silhouette so much larger than it ought to be. Its tail flipped lazily through the air. Had it gotten their scent? Did it remember who they were? Scott doubted that it did. He thought of the way the thing had looked at him from beneath the kitchen table, its eyes dead like glass marbles set into its skull. Whatever Wilbur had been then, it was something worse now. Something much worse.

"Jacob?"

His son swallowed hard. He was breathing quickly now, fogging the plastic, making it harder to see. Scott met his gaze, then dropped his eyes to the pistol handle jutting out from Jacob's belt. Without a sound, he mouthed, *The gun*.

With a shaking hand, Jacob pulled the pistol out and tried to hand it over. Scott shook his head. He wanted to take it. It made sense for him to take it, more sense than leaving it in Jacob's unsteady hands. But he couldn't chance it. He couldn't risk Tallie squirming free with only one arm to hold her. He couldn't risk her twisting away and having the gun go off accidentally, or having it drop in the wet grass where they might as well have never had it at all.

"Keep it ready," Scott whispered, hoping that the rain did as much to muffle their voices out there as it did in here. "Don't shoot unless you have to."

Jacob nodded, and held the gun out in front of him, tenting the plastic. It was hard to judge how far away the thing that used to be Wilbur was. Fifty feet? Probably less. How long would it take to close that distance if it wanted to? Not long at all, Scott thought.

The dog was sitting right in their path, right in the way of the cellar door. Had it been Dana's doing, setting Wilbur in their path like that? Was she watching them even now from her spot beneath the willow tree? If he called out to her, would she whistle for the thing to let them pass? If he joined her there, in the shadows beneath those pulsing branches, would she let the children go? Was she still their mother, even now?

Tallie stared at him. Her little face was scrunched up in pain and betrayal and Scott could not bring himself to look at her. "Stay close," he whispered to Jacob. "When I move, you move."

Jacob nodded and the two of them crept along the side of the pickup truck. Jacob kept the gun pointed at that black shape out in the distance, but the way he was shaking he might hit anything or nothing at all. At least Tallie wasn't squirming anymore. She lay defeated with her head against his chest. He could feel that something fundamental between them had been lost, something he didn't know if he'd ever get back. He'd have time to think about that later, he told himself again. Once they were safe, they'd have all the time they needed.

Lightning flashed across the sky and once more Scott could see the thing's eyes—too many eyes—watching them. He grasped the plastic sheet in his fist as they circled around the back of the truck, shifting positions to keep the dog in Jacob's line of fire. Scott fought to keep the plastic from slipping, fought to keep Tallie from falling into the grass. His arm had been locked in the same position since they left the stairs and was starting to cramp. He tried to shift her up higher but managed to let her slide farther down.

As they reached the far side of the truck, the dog raised its head. The black shape of the thing seemed to grow as it rose lazily to its feet. It was bigger than it had been the last time Scott had seen it. He was sure of that now. Through the obscuring screen of dripping plastic it no longer looked like Wilbur at all. It looked like part of the roiling gray sky that had torn free and fallen to the Earth. It looked like a part of this new world. It looked like a monster.

The thing turned and sniffed at the air. Scott watched as it padded in a circle, and saw the pain that trembled through its shoulders with every movement. Jacob could shoot it right now. With the thing distracted as it was, it would be quick, as easy as a gentle squeeze of the trigger. Killing it would be a mercy. What's more, it would show Dana that they were willing to fight, that they were still themselves, and not whatever it was that she wanted them to be.

They crouched low behind Ned's truck. Through the sheet Scott could see that the paint on the hood had been eaten away and the metal had turned as brittle as old paper. There was a rifle hanging in the back of the cab, but the water had gotten in beneath the window and done the same to the barrel. He was almost grateful, because it meant he didn't have to choose between taking the rifle or holding his daughter. But it left their fate in the boy's hands, and the boy's hands were shaking.

"It'll let us pass," he whispered to Jacob. "Just walk. Don't run. We'll take it slow and we'll be fine. Okay?" Jacob didn't answer. He was peering, wide-eyed, over the bed of the truck, watching as the great shadow turned its head toward them again, as if it had heard the sound of Scott's voice.

"Jacob!" Scott hissed, and the boy turned his widened eyes toward him. Scott saw the fear in them, and knew that he had lost all chance at reasoning with the boy. The fear had taken root, and the fear was in charge now.

"We have to go back," Jacob said, spinning around so quickly that the handle of the axe flew up and hit Tallie in the leg. She squealed, and the plastic went taut as Jacob began to drag it away. Scott caught hold of his backpack and hauled back on it, pulling as hard as he dared. His son collided with him, and they fell back against the pickup truck, the brittle metal giving way beneath them.

"Stay *close*," Scott hissed, but whether or not the boy heard him, there was no way to know. He chanced a look over his shoulder. The thing was padding toward them now, its movements gaining intention, its dark bulk drawing closer. Tallie squealed again, and the thing stopped in its tracks, its ears pricked toward the sound.

"We stay together," Scott said, but he could see that the boy wasn't listening. If they went back now it would all be for nothing, and they were close now, so close. He could hand Tallie to Jacob. He could take the gun and do it himself. Once the dog was gone, there'd be nothing to stop them, not even Dana. If he had to, he would shoot her, too.

But Jacob was already up and moving, and it was all that Scott could do to hold onto Tallie and the backpack at the same time. He didn't have a hand on the plastic. Neither did Jacob. The sheet started to slip sideways. He couldn't risk grabbing for it, couldn't risk letting go of Jacob because if he did, panic would take the kid out from under its shelter and into the rain. The plastic slid again, and all at once a thought shuddered through him that he would have to let his son go if any of them were going to make it at all.

The monstrous shadow had lowered its head, but through the streaks of rain Scott couldn't tell if it was moving closer. He shifted Tallie's weight as she struggled against him. He tried to stretch his fingers to snag the plastic sheet, but all he managed to do was to brush it farther away.

Jacob surged toward the house and pulled Scott and Tallie along with him. His gun arm trailed behind him, his aim wild. Scott stumbled, tripping over his own feet as he fought to stay upright. He lost his grip, and at once the backpack was just out of reach. Scott grabbed at a fold in the plastic sheet and tried to keep up. Jacob inched ahead of him, seeming to not care about the rain, seeming to care only about staying ahead of the dark shape that was loping toward them now, and getting closer.

The gun went off. Tallie screamed, the sound like an ice pick against his eardrum. Had she been shot? He didn't know, and couldn't stop to check. He threw a quick glance over his shoulder and saw the dog, unhurt, still gaining. It had circled around behind the truck and was close enough now that Scott could see the sharp teeth lining its open mouth, the black tongue that lolled beneath eyes that were too big, and too many.

It leapt for Scott, and he put his hand over Tallie's head, wanting to protect her, knowing that he couldn't. He felt the heat of the thing at his back as its paws came down on the plastic sheet and pinned it to the ground. Scott felt their protection sliding away, but there was nothing he could do as the dog worried at the sheet with its jaws, as if confused by this new obstacle in its way.

Jacob was already out of reach, lost beyond the blur of rain-streaked plastic that had sagged across Scott's eyes. His foot hit something hard and at once he was falling. He twisted in midair, not wanting to land on Tallie's little body, not wanting to end up with her between him and the dog. His shin barked against something sharp but he barely noticed, because in an instant the plastic sheet slipped behind him, and was gone.

His shoulder came down hard on the wooden decking, and all at once Tallie slid out of his arms. His eyes were closed, and when he opened them, he saw Jacob pulling his sister through the open door. They'd landed on the porch, on the boards that were dry but for Jacob's footprints. Scott was dry too, at least as far as he could tell. The plastic had held just long enough. What was left of it lay behind them on the ground, gathering the rain.

Scott could see the black shadow clearly now for the first time, hairless, its muscles taut and rippling beneath gray skin. There was no mistaking its size now, with its elongated front legs, the wide paws that splayed like stunted fingers. It might have been another animal entirely but for the length of chain that still sagged around the straining tendons in its neck, if not for the the familiar tuft of white that still clung to its muzzle.

It let go of the plastic sheet, now torn to shreds between those weirdly-fingered paws, and raised its head. The lightning flashed silently above them and the light from it played over the thing's rain-slick hide. A low growl rose from its throat, and Scott scrambled to his feet, fighting past the pain that lanced through his leg. He heaved himself through the door and kicked it shut behind him.

30

Inside the house, Scott was overcome by the sound of falling water. He had left the candles in the front room burning, and in their flickering light he could see that the leak above the sofa had become a steady stream that had opened up a gaping hole in the ceiling. Through it he could see the plastic bucket, lying on its side, drooping as if it had been melted by fire. The dripping garbage bag sagged down into the room. Dark tendrils spread across what was left of the cracking plaster like lightning strikes, glistening with strange energy.

Jacob huddled in the kitchen doorway, sitting with his back to the wall and Tallie curled up in his lap. He had the gun pointed at the door, his finger on the trigger, ready to fire again, almost as if he didn't see Scott standing there in the way.

Almost like he didn't care, came the gruff voice.

Tallie was crying softly, a sound that cut through the fog of panic and brought clarity to Scott's mind. He held up his hands and motioned for Jacob to lower the gun. Jacob hesitated, his eyes wide, fixed on the door. At last, the gun wavered, and Jacob lowered his arm.

Scott pointed to the stairs but it took the heavy thud of the dog colliding with the door frame to get Jacob moving. He scooped Tallie up in his arms and mounted the steps two at a time. Tallie's tears turned to startled screams as the door banged again, hard enough that Scott could feel the vibration of it beneath his feet.

The growth of tendrils behind the photos had sprouted new roots that spilled out over the stairs. It left an obstacle course of broken glass and crumbling plaster, and when their footsteps ground the debris into the black outgrowths, they reacted with urgent pulses of light that surged all the way up to the ceiling.

They got the door to the big bedroom closed behind them just as the front door slammed open with a crash of splintering wood. Tallie screamed, and Scott pressed his hand to her mouth, again feeling the dull ache of the splinter in his palm, using all his restraint to keep from pressing down too hard on her tiny jaw. He could hear the dog snuffling at the base of the stairs. He knew that if the thing followed their scent up the steps there would be no way of stopping it from breaking down this door, too.

They stood in silence, listening to the steady drip of a new leak in the far corner of the room, listening for the sound of the dog padding up the stairs. But the dog only sniffed again and huffed as if it had grown tired of the chase. The chain at its neck tinkled as it dragged along the hardwood floor. Scott strained to listen as his heartbeat pounded in his ears, as the sound of the chain gave way to the click of claws on the kitchen tile. Then there came the heavy thump of a body lowering itself abruptly to the floor. After that, everything grew still.

Tallie had stopped screaming, but her eyes were full of tears and they tracked Scott's every move. He could see how afraid she was of him, afraid because he'd hurt her, never mind that he hadn't meant to, afraid because she didn't understand that all he was doing was trying to keep them safe. The thought turned into a shadow of resentment that fell across his thoughts like a rain cloud. He had to remind himself that she was only four years old, that she had no way of knowing what the rain meant, no way of knowing how much danger they were in. He took his hand away from her mouth, and the tears spilled from her eyes as her lip started to tremble.

His father's voice bubbled up out of memory. *Stop crying, or I'll give you something to cry about*, it said, in a voice that sounded so much like his own that he couldn't be sure the words hadn't come from his own mouth. Scott squeezed his eyes closed to will it away. His hands were balled into fists and they were shaking. Tallie didn't understand and he couldn't make her understand. There wasn't time. The water from the ceiling was coming in faster with each passing second, and there was no telling how long it would be before the whole roof came crashing down on their heads, no telling how long it would be before the rain got to them and changed them the way it had changed Wilbur. The way it had changed Dana.

"Give me the gun," Scott said, and held out his hand. Jacob looked at it doubtfully. The revolver was sticking out of his belt and he placed a protective hand over it.

"What are you going to do?"

"Just give me the gun," Scott hissed. If only his kids would just listen to him, if only he could make them understand that everything he was doing was for them. *Ungrateful.* That was the word that floated into his thoughts, floated in on his father's voice and hung there no matter how much he tried to push it away. His hand shook, the splinter a black speck at the angry red center of his palm. Jacob hesitated, but Scott held his gaze, almost daring him to disobey. At last, the boy blinked and pressed the gun into his father's hand.

Scott cracked the door open. Its hinges creaked as he strained to see beyond the stairs. The few candles that were still lit in the front room cast odd shadows, but he could see nothing of the dog.

A dark puddle of water had spread out from beneath the door of the old bedroom. He tiptoed around it as he stepped into the hall, mindful of the sharp popping sounds he heard beneath his feet. The wood was swollen and mushy. He could feel the way it sagged through the soles of his boots, the uneven tread of boards warped and bulging out of true. The water had made its way into the bones of the house. Nowhere inside it was safe.

He paused at the top of the stairs. The dog—if it still was a dog—was in the kitchen, in its accustomed spot beneath the table, or at least where the table used to be. Scott was sure of that much, and though he couldn't see the thing he could smell the thick scent of it, wet fur and dead leaves wrapped in the cloying smell of rotting meat.

He crept back to the big bedroom on tiptoes. They couldn't stay here. They had to risk it, and it had to be now.

"Okay," he said, taking a deep breath, gathering himself. "We're going to go. Quiet as you can, but we have to hurry."

"Dad, are you serious? There's no way."

Scott didn't like the way Jacob had said it, all rebellion and snotty indignation. *Ungrateful*, came his father's voice again. *Ungrateful*. He closed his eyes, tried to push it away. All they had to do was get outside. The dog wouldn't even know they were there if they did it quietly, and once they were out the door, they could get to the storm cellar without any trouble. The plastic had been a mistake. It had only slowed them down, kept them from splitting up, kept them from making a run for it. Their winter coats would be enough to keep the rain from soaking through, and they still had those on. It wasn't perfect, but it would work. It had to.

"Wilbur's down there. He'll tear us apart." A flash of realization crossed Jacob's face as he said it, and in that look Scott could see the part of it that his son dared not say out loud: *He'll tear one of us apart, at least.*

Ungrateful.

Something hit the window with a loud thump. Tallie screamed, and this time Jacob picked her up and tried to quiet her. The thump came again and Scott turned in time to see something dark slide down the glass. It left behind a rain-streaked smear of blood.

The drips from the ceiling were coming faster now, so fast that Scott could imagine the roof, pocked with holes like Swiss cheese. Tallie was crying into Jacob's shoulder, but at least she was doing it quietly now. Maybe the dog hadn't heard. Maybe it didn't care. For all Scott knew, it had crawled back inside the house to die. He didn't think so, though. It seemed healthy enough, healthier now than it had been when he had put a bullet in its flank. Healthy enough that it barely seemed like the same animal, if it was still an animal at all.

Scott eased the door open, his ear pressed to the wood, every creak of its hinges magnified. Another thump sounded from somewhere outside, quieter this time. Birds. That was what had made the thumping sounds he'd heard downstairs. The rain had gotten to them, too. The rain had gotten to everything.

Another creak and the door swung open enough for Scott to see down to the base of the stairs. The dog was there, a black shadow against the flickering candlelight. It stood with its paws on the first step, staring up at him with two sets of eyes, the old dead ones and new ones just opening above them, seeing nothing, seeing everything. Scott froze there in the doorway, not sure if he should retreat, not sure if he should stay still and hope that the thing would move on its own. He still had the gun in his hand. He imagined raising it at the end of his outstretched arm, pressing it to the thing's forehead as its tongue lolled from its mouth.

Something banged against the window once more, this time hard enough to crack the glass. Jacob jumped and Tallie screamed again. Scott pulled the door shut out of reflex, but not before the dog turned its head toward the sound. Scott listened to the thing's heavy footsteps as it pulled itself up the stairs. He could hear the chain dragging along the floorboards like nails on a chalkboard, and could hear its labored breaths getting louder and louder.

Tallie was crying, making too much noise. Scott waved a hand to shush her, but she didn't stop.

Ungrateful.

All was quiet outside the door. He could hear nothing beyond the sound of his daughter's cries, beyond the steady fall of water that was spreading across the floor and down into the cracks between the floorboards. Jacob was bouncing Tallie, whispering to her, whispering far too loud. If they would just stop, just long enough for him to know what was happening outside that door. If they would stop being so

Ungrateful.

loud, he could find a way out of this.

Two more thuds sounded against the side of the house in quick succession. Tallie's crying was like a siren in his ears. They were trapped. He couldn't think. They had to get out of there. *He* had to get out of there.

He raised the gun and flung open the door.

The dog was waiting for him on the other side of the hallway. It was down on its haunches, lapping at the water that had spilled out from beneath the old bedroom door. Scott stood frozen in the doorway, the gun shaking in his outstretched hand. He watched the long tongue descend, brushing past sharp and irregular teeth, moving slow, cupping water into its mouth. For an instant he thought that the thing hadn't noticed them, that it might let them pass by and not bother with them at all. Then the tongue pulled back, and the great head turned, jaws dripping, to face him.

Scott brought his other hand up to steady the gun. It barely helped. He felt Tallie and Jacob behind him, watching him, judging him for what he was about to do. But this wasn't Wilbur anymore. They had to know that. It wasn't Wilbur, just like it hadn't been Ned Colby breaking in through the window. He wasn't his father, standing over a helpless animal, gun pressed to its forehead, never knowing that his son was there watching. He wasn't that child anymore either, waiting for his mother, waiting for his old life to come back, even when he knew it never would.

All these thoughts came and went in the space of time that it took for the dog to lower its head and growl. Its breath rattled and popped deep within its lungs as it took a step toward him. Scott pointed the gun at the thing's head and curled his finger around the trigger, but it was too late. It was already leaping for him, jaws snapping at his throat, and he was falling.

31

The gun flew from Scott's hand as he threw his arms up and only just managed to keep the beast's teeth from closing down on his shoulder. Together, they fell against the wall and the thing's weight bore Scott down to the floor. Its paw pressed down on his chest, the weird, paw-fingers flexing as it drove the air from his lungs. He tried to push it away, but it was too heavy. His arms felt like wet rope and all his strength was gone. He tried to fight it, but there was no fight left in him.

Jacob stepped out from behind the door, holding Tallie in his arms, shielding her eyes. Scott wanted to yell to them, though he couldn't muster the breath to speak. *Get her out of here. Get to the storm cellar. Run and don't look back!*

He tried to say these things but the dog's weight on his chest would not let him. The points of its claws popped through the fabric of his coat and dug into his skin as he watched Jacob set Tallie down on the floor. Tallie scrambled back as Jacob unslung his backpack and found the long wooden handle of the axe. *No*, Scott tried again to speak, but the effort brought stars to his eyes. *Take Tallie and go. Just go!*

Jacob swung. The axe hit the beast in the shoulder, the blade glancing off the bone to lodge in the meat of its foreleg. The thing spun around, and the force of its movement wrenched the axe from Jacob's hands. He fell, sprawling, to the floor, sliding as he went. Scott pulled in a ragged breath as the beast's weight left his chest. The thing growled, its head low, its dead eyes fixed on Jacob as it readied itself to pounce.

Jacob struggled to right himself as he slipped along the floor, hid legs pumping uselessly. The dog's muscles tensed, the axe still dangling absurdly from the wound in its side. Scott grabbed at the chain that still hung from the thing's throat and wrapped his hand inside it. The dog leapt, and Scott hauled back with all the strength he had left. The chain pulled taut, and ground the bones of his hands against each other as it pulled him along the floorboards. The dog reared back, halting in mid jump as it let out a high-pitched whine and fell, scrambling, to the floor.

Scott yanked back on the chain, and he felt the sharp stab of broken bones as it pulled taut around his hand. He pushed the pain aside as he fought for leverage, setting his feet against the dog's back. His shoulders strained as the beast's legs flailed wildly, and in that moment Scott could almost feel bad for the thing, because the pained noises it made sounded so much like the old Wilbur.

Somewhere in the distance, Tallie was screaming, but the rush of blood in Scott's ears was too loud for him to tell where she was. His vision was a tunnel of red and he could not see her. All he could see was the dog, confused by this reversal, fighting to get away. He pulled back harder on the chain, and watched it constrict around the beast's neck. The gray-pink tongue fell limp across its jagged teeth, and its body grew still.

Then all at once, the chain went slack as, in one motion, the beast flipped itself onto its feet and turned on him. Scott watched, helpless, as it gathered itself, shaking its head to loosen the chain. It stared down at him, those empty eyes suddenly filled with intent, filled with hate, and growled.

Scott pulled once more on the chain, but all he managed to do was drag himself closer. The beast's claws dug long furrows in the wooden floor as it lowered itself to pounce, its teeth bared, its lips pulled back and dripping. Scott tried to raise his arms, but he couldn't. He had nothing left. The thing leapt for him, and in that moment all he could do was hope that Jacob had gotten Tallie away from there. He couldn't see either of them anymore. He supposed that was a good thing.

Then came a loud snap, like two pieces of wood being smacked together, like a firecracker popping on the Fourth of July. The dog slumped in mid-leap and fell onto Scott's chest, driving the wind out of him once more. A spray of blood and brains lay in a comet tail of wet chunks on the wooden floor. More oozed from a ragged hole in the dog's head and onto Scott's chest. Revulsion overcame him and he heaved it away. The body seemed so much lighter now that it was dead weight, and it tumbled down the stairs to land at the bottom with a heavy thump and the snap of cracking bones.

A thin tendril of smoke rose from the gun as it trembled at the end of Jacob's arm. His eyes were wide, as if the sound of the shot had startled him, and his face was drenched with sweat. His other arm was wrapped protectively around Tallie, her eyes squeezed shut, her fingers in her ears. The gun shook. He was pointing it at nothing, pointing it at the space where the dog had been, as if he expected it to come bounding back up the stairs. Scott's chest was covered in blood. He could taste it in his mouth. He surveyed himself, but the only damage he found was in his crushed and throbbing hand.

He could have killed me, Scott thought.

In response came an older, coarser voice. *You would have been dead anyway.*

He worked his way back up onto his elbows, watching the shaking barrel of the gun, watching Jacob struggle with the weight of it. Another bird thumped against the side of the house and it made the boy jump. His finger was still tight against the trigger and Scott waited until the gun was pointed at the floor before he tried to move again. Jacob didn't seem to notice him. His eyes were still fixed on that empty space on the top of the stairs, his head tilted as if he could still see something there. His lip began to tremble.

"Jacob."

The boy's eyes snapped into focus at the sound of his name. Scott had made it to his knees and he froze as the gun swung back up and hovered there, pointed at his chest.

Scott held up his hands. Purple bruises were beginning to bloom where the chain had been and it hurt to flex his fingers. "Easy now, son," he said softly. "It's okay. Everything's going to be okay."

"No. It's not!"

Tallie buried her face against her brother's leg and put her hands over her ears. Jacob held her there, as if he expected Scott might try to snatch her away. His chest was heaving and Scott could see the whites all the way around his eyes. Another thump sounded against the wall of the house. Jacob didn't seem to hear it.

"Look around, Dad," he said. "Look at this place. You keep saying that everything's going to be okay, but nothing's okay. Nothing's ever going to be okay again!"

Jacob's hand was dripping and his hair was soaked through. In the dark, Scott could see the glint of the puddle, smeared now, beneath Jacob's door. He could see the trail of wet shoeprints that led to the spot where Jacob stood, the water pooling around his feet.

"Mom was right," he said. "We can't fight it. We shouldn't even try."

Scott took a step toward them, but stopped short as the gun grew steady. The arm around Tallie's shoulders pulled tighter.

"We can't stay here." Jacob's voice was rising, hysterical. "There's nowhere else to go. The only safe place is out there in the rain."

More thumps sounded against the outside wall, against the bedroom window. Scott heard the faint tinkle of glass beginning to crack. He inched forward. "Jacob, let go of your sister."

Tallie shrank behind her brother, shaking her head. She squeezed her eyes shut and pressed her hands against her ears, as if she could drive the whole world away. Her coat seemed dry. Maybe she hadn't gotten wet, but in the dark it was hard to tell for sure.

"That's why Mom went outside," Jacob said. "She knew it wasn't safe to stay, and if we'd just gone with her in the first place, everything would be fine now. Just fine!"

"Please, Jacob." Scott could hear the trembling in his own voice. "Just let Tallie go."

"Why? How's it going to help, Dad? Just tell me that. How's it going to help?"

Scott tried to answer, but all he could think of was the cop beating his own brains out against the utility pole, of the burns on Ned Colby's face.

"If we get to the cellar, then what? How long can we stay there before we have to come out? Two days? Three? The rain's not going to stop, Dad. Don't you get it? It's never going to stop."

The thumps from the bedroom were coming rapid-fire now. Or was it just the beating of his own heart?

"Sooner or later, we have to go out there. We can't wait it out and hope it's going to get better. It's *never* going to get better. You can see that right? Why can't you see that?"

Scott took another step forward. Jacob tightened his grip on the gun. They were close now, barely an arm's length apart. Even in the dark, there was no way Jacob could miss.

"So we're going to find mom now," Jacob said. There were tears in his eyes. Or was it only that his cheeks were wet from the rainwater? "I'm sorry, Dad, but we have to go."

He took a step toward the stairs, dragging Tallie by the shoulders, but Scott stepped forward to put himself in the way. "I can't let you do that, son."

Tallie looked fearfully from Scott's face to Jacob's and then back again. She was pushing at Jacob's leg now, but he held her there and wouldn't let her go. Jacob stared at his father, confused for a moment, and in that moment Scott thought that the boy might let the gun drop. But the gun didn't drop. It only started shaking again, still pointed right at his chest.

"You can come with us, Dad." The gun was shaking harder now, but Jacob's grip was still strong. "Why won't you just come with us, Dad? Won't you please just come with us?"

Scott was close enough now to see the tears cutting fresh tracks down his son's cheeks. Tallie whimpered at his side, Jacob's fingers clutching her coat, trapping her there. Scott looked into his son's eyes and knew that he was already lost. He'd have to think about that eventually, but now all he could think about was standing in his way, about getting him to let go of Tallie. There wasn't enough room in the narrow hallway for Jacob to go around him, and Scott would be damned if he was going to move.

"Dad, please."

The little-boy pleading in his son's voice was enough to break Scott's heart, and in that moment he wanted nothing but to pull Jacob into his arms and hold him, the way he hadn't held him since he was a child. He could still see that child now, the gun trembling in his hand. Scott wanted to go to him despite the gun but he couldn't bring himself to move. He had missed his chance, and now that little boy was lost to him, washed away by the years like so much rain.

Tallie pushed at her brother again, both hands balled into little fists, but Jacob held her there, squeezing her shoulders as they inched closer to Scott, to the stairs. There was a grim sort of determination in his eyes, and Scott could see that Jacob wouldn't stop until he got around him, or through him.

"Daddy!" Tallie's cry was like a knife in his heart, and with it came the sound of shattering glass. The bedroom windows exploded, and he could hear the frantic sound of flapping wings, the thud of small bodies against the inner walls. Jacob's head snapped around toward the sound, and the gun faltered. Scott saw his moment, and lunged.

From the door of the big bedroom spilled a black cloud of blurred wings and snapping beaks. They buffeted Scott's face as he tried to wrench the gun from Jacob's hand. Little claws raked at his back and scratched his arms as Jacob fought back. The gun was between them now. Scott tried to close his hand around it, struggling through the pain, through the grinding of broken bones. Jacob fought to keep his grip, holding on tight with both hands. Tallie was no longer at his side, but Scott could still hear her screaming somewhere out there in the dark.

The rush of wings batted at their heads, but the tide was subsiding now. Something sharp grazed against his cheek, and he felt it draw blood. His hand was over the gun's cylinder now but he could not close his broken fingers. All he could do was push, and it wasn't enough. The barrel tilted. He pushed once more and the metal beneath his hand grew hot in an instant. He felt the echo of the gun's report reverberating through the air. He saw the muzzle flash reflected in his son's face.

All at once, the strength left Jacob's arms and he slumped away. Scott caught him as he fell, and lowered him to the floor. A bird lay near them, broke-necked and flapping, half its feathers gone, one wing beating uselessly against the wooden floorboards. Jacob's breaths came quick and shallow. Scott could hear them gurgle in his chest as more birds fell croaking around them. He smoothed back his son's hair as a dark patch spread from the hole, still smoking, in his coat.

Jacob coughed, and blood sprayed from his lips across his father's face like misting rain. He stared up into Scott's eyes, the little boy once more, confused, afraid. There was betrayal there too, as if he was asking his father why he hadn't just let him go, asking why he hadn't saved them. Through the broken windows, the rain fell, the sound inevitable, like an oncoming train. Jacob coughed once more before his eyes lost focus, and his body grew still.

32

Birds were dying all around them. One lay on the floor by Scott's side, still working its broken wings like a mechanical toy that was winding down. Its head lay doubled back against its neck, its throat creased, bones stretching against skin that barely held any feathers. It stared up at Scott, a crop of new eyes clustered around the large, original one. That middle eye had gone blind and milky-white, but the others were clear as glass and he could feel them watching him, even as the thing died.

The gun lay next to him, too. It still had three bullets in it, if he'd counted right. There were more still in the little box in the bedroom closet. Enough bullets for whatever else might come. Enough bullets to not have to face it at all.

The boy had more guts than you, came the low voice growling out of the back of his mind. *The boy didn't flinch when he knew what needed to be done.*

Only, the boy was gone now. Scott laid a hand on his son's chest, waiting for it to move again, even though he knew it would not. The blood had soaked through Jacob's coat and his skin was already growing cold. His eyes were open, like the bird's eyes were open, and Scott could see in them the echo of his son's last thoughts before dying. There was an accusation in them, and he had no words to refute it.

He took up the gun, still warm from the shot it had fired. His hand was reluctant to close around the grip, but he forced the broken bones to do it, forced himself to feel every bit of that pain. He could still pull the trigger if he needed to. Once, and then once more. Simple. Final.

Scott struggled to his feet. The dying bird watched him with its weird eyes. Its beak—too long and too thin—scissored open and shut as it gulped for air. It might have been a crow at one point, but now its head was as bald as a buzzard's, its bare neck long and snakelike. Sharp claws had erupted from the bend in its wing and there were gaps in the feathers that made him wonder how it had managed to fly at all. That cluster of eyes, like a spider's eyes, stared up at him. He wondered what it saw when it looked at him with those new eyes. Was there some new spectrum of light that allowed it to see something in him that he could not see himself? Or did each eye see him only as he was, over and over again, his failures magnified in their repetition?

He brought his foot down over the thing's head and leaned his weight down onto it until he felt it break, fragile, like a Christmas ornament. The wings flapped wildly and he brought his foot down again and again and again until at last it lay still. He found another one pinwheeling around a broken wing in front of the door. He came down on it with both feet, savoring the sound of hollow bones cracking in a puff of dust and feathers. He followed the trail of little bodies into the bedroom, stomping each one that he found, grinding them beneath the soles of his boots until the floor was slick with blood and rainwater and the gray insides of things that no longer made any sense to him. He picked them up from the bed and threw them against the walls and out the broken window. Where they struck, they left wet smears of red, tufted with down feathers. When he was done, he fell back against the bed and dug at the splinter in the middle of his broken hand until it started to bleed. The pain made his ears ring, but he welcomed it because it meant that, in that moment, he could feel only that and nothing else.

And yet, beneath the ringing there was another sound, high and mournful, and it cut all the way through to the core of him, helped him remember where he was, and who he was. It was the sound of a tiny voice crying. He staggered to his feet, the soles of his boots slick now with guts and feathers, and followed it out into the hallway.

He found Tallie curled in a darkened corner with her knees up to her chest. A bird-thing flapped and thumped in front of her and he kicked it away to kneel at her side. She shrank back against the wall and flattened herself against it. Scott realized then that he'd brought the gun with him, that he still held it in his good hand, his finger light against its trigger. He flung it away and it clattered down the stairs, but still she would not look at him. He pulled her close and she pounded his chest with her little fists until at last she gave in and went limp with sobs.

With his broken and bloodied hand he shielded her eyes as he carried her past her brother's body on the floor. The water from beneath the door of the old bedroom was pooling around him now, and Scott could hear the steady flow of the it falling on the other side. The sound was almost soothing. Jacob's eyes were still open and Scott wished that he'd taken the time to close them, but he could not do it now, not with Tallie in his arms. Now that he had hold of her, he was afraid to ever let her go again.

The branching growths all but covered the stairs now, their black tendrils shining wet in the dark. Scott carried his daughter down the steps and whispered in her ear, *I'm sorry, I'm sorry, I'm sorry.* With each step, a new pulse of light raced up along the wall, illuminating their way. He saw them reflected in the faces of long-dead relatives that still hung there, like ghosts looking down on him through the fog of time.

Two candles still burned in the front room. The water had taken the rest. It poured from the ceiling in a great gout that soaked into the sofa cushions and down into the rug. It found cracks in the wooden floor where more black branches were beginning to spread. It trickled down into the air vents. The sound of it was like being behind a waterfall and growing louder with each passing moment. The plastic garbage bag had fallen through, the hole in the ceiling now a gaping maw. It wouldn't be long now before the water was the only thing left, before the whole place crumbled to soggy bits around them.

I'm sorry, he told her. *I'm sorry. I'm sorry. I'm sorry.*

He stepped gingerly around Wilbur's body. It seemed so much smaller now that it was still and curled in on itself. The sores were all gone and the skin where they had once grown had become smooth like tanned leather. But for the hole in its head, it might have been sleeping. But for the stunted fingers that had erupted from its paws, it might still be a dog, maybe even the same dog he had once petted absently on the couch, in those times that felt so long ago. The rain had raised his sores but the rain had also taken them away. Scott wondered if, had it had more time to work, the rain might have brought the old Wilbur back to them as well.

He stared into the thing's eyes, still open, staring blindly, shining orbs clustered like tiny planets orbiting a dead star. He knew in his heart that the rain would never have let Wilbur go, that it would never let any of them go.

He carried Tallie to the kitchen, where the floor was still mostly dry. He tried to set her down on the counter but her arms were around his neck, clamped there like iron. She wouldn't let go, even though he could see in her eyes that she was still afraid of him. He told her that it would only be for a minute, that there was something they needed downstairs. The plastic sheet he'd left down there was torn, but it might be enough for the two of them, now that the two of them was all that was left. From where they were standing, they could see the front door hanging off its hinges, the house open to the outside air. It made him not want to let go either.

The sound of falling water behind the basement door was strong, but he opened it anyway. The sump pump had long-since died, and even in the dark he could see a shallow flood churning at the bottom of the stairs. When he pulled his phone from his pocket and shined its flashlight down—no sense in trying to conserve the battery anymore—he saw that it had risen almost to the first step. The plastic sheet floated on the surface and he thought that if he went down the steps that he might be able to reach it, but the creak the stairs gave out when he tested them made him change his mind.

A new sound rose up from the splashing water at the base of the stairs, a frantic squealing, a rhythmic splashing at odds with steady rush of falling water. He saw something float into the light that might have been a piece of insulation or some other bit of garbage but for the way it writhed. The mice were huddled together, pawing frantically at the water, seething with desperate energy as they bobbed on a raft made of their dead kin. They had grown large and horrid, gray and almost hairless but for a few wild tufts of fur. Their tails were twined together, caked with excrement and fused into a pulsing pink mass. When they saw him there at the top of the stairs their heads turned in unison and they let out a collective screech that sent a shiver through his already trembling limbs. He shielded Tallie's eyes and pushed the door shut, but not before he saw them turn and begin to paddle toward him.

Something fell with a crash on the second floor. A large piece of furniture. Maybe a chunk of the roof. At the sound of it, Tallie began to cry again, and Scott bounced her and patted her back with the good hand he had left and whispered into her ear.

I'm sorry. I'm sorry. I'm sorry.

He searched the already bare cabinets, tossing what was left of their contents on the floor like a ransacking thief, searching for something—anything—that might keep them dry. They clattered useless around his feet, and Tallie seemed to brighten a little at her father's sudden carelessness as if it were some new game they had only just discovered. But the game was over now, for he could find nothing to cover them for that long trek across the sodden yard, nothing that would save them from the rain.

Cool air drafted in through the open doorway. For an instant he could almost picture his mother standing there on the porch, her back to the door, her arms heavy with her suitcases. In that moment, the thought overwhelmed him that he could just leave too, just put Tallie down and walk outside into the dark and the rain. He tried to close his broken hand around the wound he had made in his palm, and somewhere in that roar of pain he was sure that the splinter was still in there, that it would be a part of him forever. Tallie must have felt his doubt, for she shifted and clung to him anew. Scott felt her warmth against him and knew then what he had always known. He could never abandon her, and they couldn't stay. The last choice—the only choice—was for the two of them to go out that door and face the rain together.

The boy had more guts than you, came that low, mean voice again. *The boy didn't flinch when he knew what needed to be done.* Only, the boy was dead now. Scott had killed him with his father's gun, and he could not bring himself to pick it up again.

He shuffled through the mess on the floor and his boot snagged a black garbage bag. It was the last one. He'd dismissed it out of hand before, but that was when he'd thought there was a chance that he might find another way. But there was no other way. He knew that now. It wasn't enough for both of them, but it might be enough for one.

33

"We're going to play a game," he told Tallie as he shook out the garbage bag, billowing it open like a balloon. She watched him doubtfully, her eyes still shining with tears. He tried to smile despite the pain in his hand, despite all the other pains that he wouldn't allow himself to feel because he was afraid that they would undo him. "It'll be like hide and seek, yeah?"

In emphasis, he slid the bag down over his own head and when he popped it back up again, Tallie was smiling. That was good. It meant he could make this work. It was the last bag, and it was only big enough to reach down to his belt. It wasn't big enough for the both of them, but it would be enough for her. It would be enough to protect the only thing left that mattered in this world.

He made to put it over her head, but stopped as she shrank away. He put it back over his own instead and held it there, drawing out the moment, leaning into the game. When he popped back out of the bag again, she let out a little giggle. He knew then that he could get her to go along with it. It wouldn't be for long, but he wouldn't need long. She'd go along with it, and it would be enough. It had to be enough.

From behind the basement door, he heard the scratching of tiny claws, no random pawing but the collective rhythm of a dozen tiny bodies working in tandem. He could hear the sharp teeth chewing at the wood, tearing great shreds of it loose.

Scott pushed the sound away and focused on his daughter sitting on the countertop in front of him, all reddened cheeks and wide, wet eyes. He tried the bag again and got it down over her chin before she reached up to push it away. He smiled at her, and wouldn't allow himself to do anything but smile.

He brought the bag down over his own head again and held it there. In the darkness that came with it, in that blackout world, there was only the sound of the driving rain. It was all around him, neither outside nor inside, but everywhere. He breathed and it was as if the sound of his very breath were being taken by the rain, until it was a part of him and he was a part of it. That would not be so bad, he thought. Not so high a price to pay, not after everything it had already cost him.

When he brought the bag away, Tallie was there. Tallie, who was smiling back at him now through the tears that ran tracks down her cheeks. Tallie, who was all that he had left in the world, whatever this world was becoming. The rain could fall as long as it wanted as long as he could keep her safe from it. His hand throbbed. The cruel voice in his head told him that he couldn't do it, but he *would* keep her safe no matter what.

He shook out the bag to fill it with air and brought it down over her head. When it was down to her hips he scooped her up from the counter and worked it down over her kicking feet. The chewing sound behind the door was louder now. He could hear it over his daughter's muffled screams as he cinched the drawstring tight. The plastic stretched as she struggled but he held her close to keep her still. More wood tore from the bottom of the basement door, but he was already moving. He barely paused to pick up the axe as he ran for the door.

He stumbled and nearly leapt from the deck as the rain hit him full in the face. It soaked through his clothes in an instant. It was warm, and the feel of it on his skin made him pause. He staggered, stopping to stare up into the roiling gray sky. The strange lightning played across the clouds, and as it flashed he could see strange shapes coiling and flexing within their depths. The afterimages they left on his eyes were like the lazy trails of fish cutting their way through a sunlit stream. He thought that he had never seen anything more beautiful.

Then the bundle squirmed in his arms, and he remembered. The garbage bag was slick, and the movement inside it almost sent the whole thing tumbling to the wet ground. Little fists punched and stretched at the plastic, but he pinned them down. He heard a little girl cry out—a muffled sound, almost not a sound at all—and he clutched onto her tighter, trying hard not to drop the bundle, trying hard not to drop the axe, too. He had to hold onto the axe. He would need it later, though he couldn't quite remember why.

Again the lightning played across the sky, and through the rain he saw the distant metal door set into the side of the low hill. Was that why he had come out here? Was that the reason he had carried the axe and the squirming bundle out into the rain? It was so close now, just a matter of a few dozen strides. And yet, it felt almost silly, the idea that something so small and so flimsy could keep them safe. It felt silly that there might be something that they needed to be kept safe from. The very thought seemed strange. More than strange, it seemed absurd. There was nothing out here but the rain, and the rain couldn't hurt anyone.

At once he was overcome with the feeling of being watched, and turned back around. There was only the house, standing in the spot where it had always stood. Its roof sagged. Its siding hung askew in places like loose teeth. He could see a faint glow of light through the broken door, and he knew that he ought to care about those things, but he was at a loss to remember why.

As he stood staring, a great section of the roof caved in with a crash. The light beyond the doorway flared. He ought to have cared about that too, but he was too intent on the feeling of eyes upon him. He could feel them watching from somewhere beyond the rusted pickup truck, from the shadows beneath the willow tree. He had a distant idea that he knew who those eyes belonged to, and the thought sent a tremble of excitement across his dampened skin.

The bundle wriggled against his chest. No, not just a bundle, he remembered, but a little girl. He could see her mouth moving against the plastic bag, drawing it tight against her lips. She was slipping from his arms. He wanted to let her, to pull the bag away and watch the rain fall on her face the way it had fallen onto his own and show her that there was nothing to be afraid of. Together they could play in the rain and stomp their feet in the puddles and he would hear her laughter and the laughter would make everything all right again.

But with that thought came another: a voice, once overwhelmingly loud, that now struggled to be heard. The voice was gruff; distant and faint, but gaining volume. It told him he was failing. It told him he was weak. But more than that, it told him that he had to keep the little bundle safe. It told him not to let the rain touch her because if it did it would mean that his failures would be complete, and all the distant events that had brought him here, everything that he was struggling so hard to remember, all of it would be for nothing.

The bundle thrashed, but he kept hold of it. He squeezed it tight to his chest with his free arm, with the broken hand that no longer felt any pain. There was something in his other hand. He held it up and watched the play of raindrops along the rusted metal head, the lovely trails they made down the length of polished wood, iridescent, like beetles crawling on a leaf.

The gruff voice inside him cried out, and he remembered. He remembered the woman who'd used the axe to save his life. He remembered the dog, its teeth snapping just inches from his face. He remembered a gunshot, and he remembered another. He remembered the boy—ah, the boy—gasping and bleeding, his life running out in his arms. He had not saved the boy. He had been too late, but he could still save the girl. He had forgotten from what, but he still knew that he could save her if only he could get her to that little door in the side of the hill.

He set off at a run. The bundle jostled and jounced, kicking him as he went, but he held it firm. He held it tight.

I'm sorry, came the distant voice. *I'm sorry. I'm sorry.*

Dark shapes swirled in the roiling sky. They darted across the gaps in the cloud cover that were only just beginning to open, slipping like eels among coral, bending back on themselves at boneless angles as they twisted and contracted. They made him want to stop and stare and wonder, but he forced himself not to look. He kept his eyes on the ground, on the rain falling onto the muddy grass, on the bundle in his arms, growing calmer now. The bundle was all that was important. The bundle was everything.

He hiked the bag up high on his shoulder as he came to the door. It was rusted and pitted—less a door now than just an odd piece of metal—but it was solid. There was a lock fastened above the handle and the lock still held it shut. That was good, the distant voice told him. The lock meant this place was still untouched by the rain and all the things that were gathering in the rain. The lock meant that this place was safe. The lock meant the voice had been right.

He brought the axe down on the lock. It didn't budge, and he knew that that was good too, because the voice was in his ears now, louder than ever before, louder even than the steady drum of the falling rain. He adjusted the bundle, now silent and still, and swung the axe again. The lock held, but this time the hasp tore away from the door with the screech of shearing metal.

Old hinges protested as he tugged at the door, but it swung open so easily that he almost lost his balance. He stared down at the stairs that led into that dry darkness in the side of the hill. He didn't want to go down them. They were rusted and they looked like they might not hold, and if he followed them they would take him out of the rain. The rain was warm, but the hole looked cold and he couldn't see far enough into it to know what might be inside. He almost turned back, but the voice was practically shouting now. He had come here with a job to do, and it would not let him stop until it was done.

The old metal steps rained down a shower of rust, and as his feet touched ground he could hear the crunch of gravel beneath them. Dry. How strange it was that dry should mean safety when all he wanted to do was to go back out into the rain. He could hear it falling through the open doorway, playing upon his senses like a song. Here, all was darkness and the air was thick and musty with age, but outside the sky was alive with the glow of the lightning, and the sound of the falling rain was like a chorus of voices singing only for him.

He stepped deeper inside, peering into the dark. Already his eyes were seeing more than they had ever seen, and despite the utter blackness of the place they had no trouble finding its contours. The cellar was small, barely bigger than a closet, its earthen walls shorn up with rough timbers. The air was close, and smelled of old rot, of dry earth and age. A nest of leaves and matted trash lay in the far corner, long since abandoned by whatever animal had created it. But the nest wasn't the only thing down there in the dark.

It lay heaped in the farthest corner, a long and delicate shape, grown brittle with the passing of years. Its limbs had long since gone to bone and one of its feet was missing. No doubt it had been carried off by that same animal, or maybe only relocated to the brushy depths of its nest. The shape wore a dress of pale flowers and there was a burlap bag cinched around its neck with a length of twisted wire. Standing beside it, almost like an afterthought, were two small suitcases.

The sight was like a distant bell ringing in the depths of his mind. He tried to chase it down, but the closer he got the farther away it seemed to be. The voice in his head was silent now and it would not guide him. All thought was lost beneath the steady patter of the falling rain.

He knelt beside the shape in the dust and listened to the rain as it dripped down through the doorway. He traced the flowers on the dress with his broken hand, and again he felt that strange chord being plucked, dissonant and faint, from his memories. He could almost picture a woman wearing that very dress, framed in the doorway, her back turned so he could not see her face. Or was it a dog with a gun pointed at its head? He could no longer remember. He touched the fabric. He held it between his fingers, and knew that he had felt it before. It had meant something once, but with the rain at his back, the steady music of it in his ears, he no longer knew what that could be.

He remembered the bundle, then

I'm sorry. I'm sorry.

and laid it down beside the woman in the flower dress. The plastic bag shined with beads of rain, even in the dark, and though it was no longer moving he knew there was something precious inside. Something the rain could not touch. Something he could not touch, not anymore, now that the rain had soaked into his clothes, into his skin. Something he knew he could never hold again, no matter how much he longed to.

The little girl was sleeping now. She was the only thing in this world he had left, though the thought of *this world* held less meaning than it ever had before. That thought had seemed so important once, what felt like forever ago. Now it was just an echo, lost beneath the sound of the falling rain. But he had brought the girl here. He had kept her safe. She was sleeping and he would let her sleep. The sound of the rain would be her lullaby. And if, when she woke, she chose to come and find him, he would welcome her, and hold her close, and they would be together once again.

Until then, the rain was calling to him.

34

He emerged from the storm cellar, naked and dripping. He'd left his clothes behind in a heap at the base of the steps. He no longer wanted them. The rain was slick and warm, and it was the only covering he needed. Already he could feel his skin beginning to thicken along his arms and shoulders, raising the first sores that oozed pale yellow when he pressed down on them. They hurt, but the pain was distant, like an old memory, and he barely noticed it. As long as he embraced the rain, as long as he let it wash over him and soothe away his pains, he would be all right. The sores would heal. He could feel new flesh knitting beneath them, and he thrilled at his own becoming.

He watched as the roof of the old house buckled with a crash and began to slide, sloughing away like an old snakeskin. He could see the new life that was growing inside it, filling the gaps in the walls, new tissue over old bones. In the distance, strange plants rose from the soybean fields, swaying in the windless air, their fronds grasping skyward like the mouths of baby birds. He breathed in their sulfur smell and watched the lithe shapes that swam above him through the clouds, moving almost lazily, as if in full confidence that they belonged to this place now, that it was being remade in their image.

Already, he was seeing deeper into this new world than he ever had into the old. Light pulsed through the trees, fresh growths on dead branches that surged with new life. It gathered itself deep beneath their bark and flowed down into the ground where it spread through unseen roots and along branching pathways like the veins along the back of a hand, like the cells of a giant brain. It pulsed up around his footsteps and hummed beneath his toes. And even as it pulsed it burned through the old matter of the old world, consuming it, making space for the new. It was blight. It was renewal. And it was beautiful.

Another crash, and a section of wall fell in a jumble onto the porch below. The overhang tore away, falling past the broken window, burying the body that lay there. He watched, feeling nothing but wonder as shingles and old boards heaped across what had once been a doorway. He watched as the things inside it, freed from constriction, unfurled and stretched skyward, fingers drifting like ocean kelp.

He had the dim sense that this should upset him, a faint tug that told him he was losing something. He could feel it there, but only barely, as if it were a distant voice calling out to him across a raging river. He felt the truth in that tug, and yet he also knew that the crumbling building held nothing else for him. It was a relic, a child's toy that he had only just outgrown.

And yet, that voice still called out to him. He knew down deep that he should listen to that voice, and yet he also knew that there was nothing left that the voice could tell him. He had finished the last thing he had left to do, the one last task that tied him to that old world. He had lost the boy, but the girl was safe. Safe beneath the earth where the rain would not touch her. All else was past, and the past seemed so distant that it might not have ever existed at all.

The clouds parted above his head, opening a circular aperture of roiling gray like the eye of a passing storm. For a moment the rain stopped, and he stared up into the column of clouds. Beyond it, he could see the first stars of evening shining against the blue-black sky. Somewhere, the sun was setting, and when it rose again, it would rise over a new world. He could almost feel the anticipation of those eel-like shapes as they darted and coiled, barely daring to emerge from the safety of their gray sanctuary where green lightning pulsed like the heartbeat of that new world. They would come, he knew, not now but soon, into this place that had been prepared for them, into this place that he too was being prepared for.

From the shadows beneath the willow tree came a pale creature, lithe and elegant, like a deer of the old world stepping gingerly toward him on two long and steady legs. Her hair was long and black as the night sky, and though her proportions were less familiar, her shape still lit the fire of recognition deep within him. She reached out and took him by the hand. His eyes played along her smooth and glistening skin and watched the bony ridges of her ribs expand and contract as she breathed in the air of this new world. He breathed it too, and knew that soon he would belong to this place as much as she belonged to it.

She watched him back, watched him with eyes newly opened, eyes that were wide with compassion and sympathy, even as the old ones blinked beneath them. She loved him still. He could see it in the multitudes that danced in those new eyes, in the subtle acceptance of her smile. Soon, he too would be able to see her the way that she saw him. Soon, he would have eyes to see everything.

The clouds gathered again, drawing closed as quickly as they'd parted. The rain came back, colder now, and as it fell upon their skin he stared at it, fascinated at the pathways it traced down their bodies on its way down into the earth. His skin tingled, warming to its touch, and to the touch of the woman who stood now beside him, silent and brimming with secrets. Hand in hand they watched as the last of the old house fell away, its ruins already partly obscured by branches the of new life that grew within it. He knew that, together, they would greet this new world. He knew at last that this was his home.

About the Author

Born and raised near the shores of Lake Michigan, Christopher Hawkins has been writing and telling stories for as long as he can remember. A dyed-in-the-wool geek, he is an avid collector of books, roleplaying games and curiosities. When he's not writing, he spends his time exploring old cemeteries, lurking in museums, and searching for a decent cup of tea.

Christopher is the former editor of the One Buck Horror anthology series. His works of short fiction have been published in numerous magazines and anthologies, including Read By Dawn vol 2, The Big Book of New Short Horror, Fusion Fragment, Underland Arcana and Cosmic Horror Monthly. He is a member of the Chicago Writers Association and co-chair of the Chicagoland chapter of the Horror Writers Association.

An expatriate Hoosier, Christopher currently lives in a suburb of Chicago with his wife and two sons.

Acknowledgements

Thank you to everyone who believed in me and gave this little book a chance. Thank you to Daniel Kraus, Clay McLeod Chapman, Lauren Bolger, and Alan Lastufka for lending their kind words of praise and support. Thanks to Fay Lane and Emily Kardamis for making me presentable. Thanks to everyone in the Chicagoland chapter of the Horror Writers Association for motivating me to keep going, even if it was only just to keep up.

To Ben, and Tim, and Kris, thank you for saving me from the rain.

Lastly, thank you to all the painters, plaster patchers, and roofers who helped to undo the water damage that plagued our home on no fewer than three occasions during the writing of this book. I won't go so far as to say this book was cursed–not out loud, anyway–but I know what I know.

- Christopher Hawkins, August 2023

Want to know more?

For the latest news about this book and a first look at news releases, join our newsletter at **downpourbook.com/free**. Just scan the QR Code below, or visit the website to get on the list and claim your **FREE** bonus ebook!

www.downpourbook.com/free

Made in the USA
Middletown, DE
14 May 2024